Praise for
The Lamoille Stories

"Bill Schubart's Vermont stories of a mostly-forgotten time and
place are fresh, authentic, funny in places and sad in others.
He knows his corner of the Green Mountains inside out and
writes with honesty and grace about its people."

—Howard Frank Mosher, author of *Disappearances*, *Mary Blythe*,
and *On Kingdom Mountain*

"Bill Schubart's stories are Vermont's answer to Chaucer's Canterbury
Tales: larger than life, triumphantly over-the-top, by turns erudite and
savagely, raucously funny. No good soul, no matter how low on the
social ladder, is beneath Schubart's fond notice; no lout, no matter how
highly placed, escapes his lacerating wit. People drink in these stories,
folks. They drink, and occasionally they damage their homes and cars
and boots and lifelong local reputations as a result. But in Schubart's
universe, such things happen, and such people remain loved. Laughed
at certainly, but loved just the same."

— Philip Baruth, Vermont Public Radio Commentator and
author of *The X President*

"These are fast becoming some of my favorite stories. Bill Schubart
captures something of Vermont that many of us barely remember, and
others may never experience. Each of *The Lamoille Stories* is a unique
experience—lovingly told, with insight, pathos, and especially humor.
You'll read them again and again."

— Joseph A. Citro, author of *Passing Strange* and
Cursed in New England

The Lamoille Stories

The Lamoille Stories

Uncle Benoit's Wake
and Other
Tales from Vermont

Bill Schubart

The Lamoille Stories : Uncle Benoit's Wake and Other Tales of Vermont
Bill Schubart

Copyright © 2008 by Bill Schubart

Originally Published December 2008 by White River Press
Republished August 2013 by Magic Hill Press

Front cover photograph
Loose Heifer by Richard Brown

ISBN 978-0-9897121-0-1

The previous edition published by White River Press of this book was
cataloged as follows:

Library of Congress Cataloging-in-Publication data
Schubart, Bill, 1945–
The Lamoille Stories : Uncle Benoit's Wake and Other Tales of Vermont /
Bill Schubart. p. cm.
ISBN 978-1-9897121-0-1 (pbk. : alk. paper)
1. Lamoille County (Vt.)—Fiction. 2. Vermont—Fiction. I. Title. PS3619.
C467L36 2008
813'.6--dc22
2008039370

Fat People (ISBN 978-0-615-39751-1) Magic Hill Press LLC – 2010
Panhead (ISBN 978-0-9834852-6-1) Magic Hill Press LLC – 2012
I Am Baybie (ISBN 978-0-9834852-9-2) Magic Hill Press LLC – 2013
Photographic Memory (ISBN 978-0-9834852-8-5) Magic Hill Press – 2014

Not only did I grow up in two cultures, I grew up with two family names *Couture* and *Schubart*. This book is dedicated to my primary family, whose name I bore until I was 14, especially to my half sister Claire Hancock and half brother Michael Couture, whose memories and love of story have greatly enriched this book. I would also like to thank my wife and often editor, Kate, as well as the editor for this book, Ruth Sylvester, who so often confirmed the good judgments of my wife. Thanks also to White River Press for making the original publication a joy.

~*Bill Schubart, October 2013*

The
Stories

Lyle's Dump 13
Lila's Bucket 17
Mr. Skiff's VW 24
Jeeter's Leaky Roof 30
Widowmaker 36
The Dairy Tax Shelter 42
Fanny Fancher and Crazy Chase 47
Jack Daulton's New Mailbox 58
Twist and Shout 64
Wyvis's Fence 70
Jack Daulton's New Camp 79
Jeeter Goes to New York 85
Uncle Benoit's Wake 95
The Morrisville Fourth of July Parade 106
Jack Daulton's New Woodstove 116
Emile's Beaver Pond 124
The Ferlands' Pet Pigs 134
Doc's Come-along 147
Duke's Mudwasps 160
Darcy and Father LeFarge 168
Edgar's Mother's Chimney 178
Anne's Biddies 190

Lamoille County, Vermont

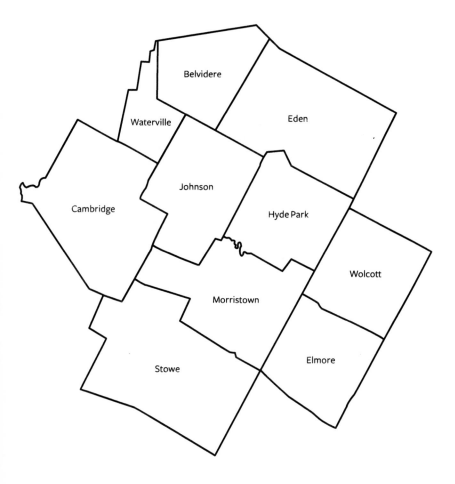

Lyle's Dump

~~~2~9~

THE DUMP'S FADING red embers were reflected above in the dusk settling over Morrisville. Sullen rats, emboldened by the quiet, scurried about amid the refuse searching for food scraps. Most townsfolk had completed their dump runs by lunchtime on Saturday except for a few stragglers. Late in the afternoon, a few boys on bikes with .22s or BB guns tied across their handlebars pumped up the long dirt hill that divided the Farr and Greaves farms to "pop a few rats" with Lyle's permission and then squat down near his shack to overhear the goings-on inside the dump shack where Lyle sorted and disassembled the day's haul, while the select few invited inside chatted and told stories.

As long as anyone could remember, Lyle Bohannon had ruled the dump. He took his work seriously, knowing there were those who coveted his office, not for its modest compensation, nor for the shabby hut from which he held court, but for the valuable franchise it conveyed.

Lyle's dump reign predated the language of today in which his dump would become a "sanitary landfill," death would become a "passing," animals would earn "rights," a C average would become an A average and the Overseer of the Poor would become the "Secretary of Human Services."

His dump lay off the southeast corner of Volney and Gladys Farr's dairy farm. Lyle arrived at the dump at 6 o'clock on Saturday mornings and stayed until well after dusk, depending on the day's harvest and who showed up with hooch.

The hut itself was about 12' by 24' and 8' high at the beam. Its framing ran more or less 24" on center with lumber scavenged after the war from countless drop-offs. The shack was held together largely by the 4' by 8' plywood panels nailed to the frame. These were donated in a magnanimous gesture by the Atlas Plywood Mill on the other side of town after the old hut collapsed in a major snowfall. Discarded linoleum sealed the interior walls from drafts and provided a disorienting interior decor. The only door was an exterior half-glass door that Lyle had painted a pale blue. It hung limply in its jamb and scraped an arc in the dirt floor when opened or closed. A floral design was etched into the rim of the glass portion of the door and greasy handprints covered the rest, making it impossible for curious kids trespassing in the dump's off-hours to ascertain what treasures were locked away inside. The door was secured by a rusty steel hasp that hung open on Saturdays.

Lyle was proprietary about his shack. No one entered without being invited in. The interior was lit only by two rusting railroad lanterns. A homemade sheetmetal woodstove sat in the far end. In another corner sat a small Mosler combination safe that Lyle had scrounged from the remains of Joslyn's Jewelry, a victim of the Portland Street fire of 1948. Although the paint had been badly blistered in the fire and the Bakelite combination knob and opening handles were molten lumps, the safe mechanism worked well enough. No one knew what was inside, as only Lyle had the combination. Speculation ran high on this subject. Some said it contained choice liquor from Canada. Pete Trepanier started the rumor that Lyle had acquired Wyvis's extensive collection of "scoot" pictures when Wyvis found God at the Calvary Band of God Bible Church in Eden Mills and somewhat reluctantly retired his renowned collection of dirty pictures. Still others whispered that it contained Lyle's most prized dump pickings, although few could imagine anyone discarding anything of enough value to keep in a safe.

Lyle's daughter, Donna, shared his modest trailer down by the Lamoille River. There she kept house for him, prepared meals, kept fires and, on her daily walks to school, gathered roadside butts with which to roll cigarettes for them both.

The dump opened at 7 a.m. on Saturdays and, in the summer, opened in the late afternoon for businesses. At least once during the summer, WDEV, the regional station from Waterbury, showed up for three hours with a specially outfitted delivery van to broadcast from the dump a show called "Music to Go to the Dump By." They served free coffee and donuts, and visitors were interviewed on a variety of subjects from prospects for deer season and the price of fluid milk to what goods and chattels they were discarding and why. These interviews were interspersed with bluegrass and old-timey music and recent hits from Don Fields and the Pony Boys. Senator Fred Westphal from Elmore was once heard to comment on air that when WDEV broadcast from the Stowe dump, the show was renamed "Music to Which One Discards One's Belongings." The Stowe dump was renowned for the higher value of its refuse.

WDEV also offered an alternative to the dump for items that might fetch a price. Listeners would describe an item on a 3" by 5" card "in 24 words or less" and mail it, along with fifty cents, to "The Trading Post" at WDEV. Everyone listened to the 6 a.m. broadcast with pencil and paper handy. The show was rife with descriptions like "little used," "good milker," "still some use in 'er," "well cared for," "barely wore," "house-trained," "some rust," "needs work." Lawn sales were decades away, as the notion of spreading one's personal wares on the front lawn and hawking them from a folding chair on a weekend had yet to occur to anyone.

Back at the dump, Lyle had clear and unquestioned rights to "first pick." He leaned on his three-pronged pitchfork, casually chatting with someone hurling trash out of the back of his pickup or station wagon. Lyle's casual banter belied his eagle eyes that tallied every item sailing toward the large crescent of refuse. As someone upended a galvanized trash can, Lyle was there by his side cataloguing the items falling to earth. There were no garbage bags to hide valuable salvage from Lyle's inventory.

A vehicle showing up with an appliance or a burned-out power tool simply left the item by Lyle's shed to save him the trouble of recovering it. Lyle stripped his findings, squirreling away parts in jars and cigar boxes for later use. The exterior of the shed was hung with hub caps, baby carriage and bicycle wheels. A randomly sized collection of smaller solid wheels hung from a loop of baling twine. To the left of the shed was a month's supply of discarded car, truck, and tractor batteries waiting for the metal monger to buy the copper plates inside. Elsewhere lay random heaps defined by their metal, one of copper piping and flashing, another of bent tin roofing and sheet metals flattened from filing cabinets, fenders, and panels from refrigerators. Farther back lay a hillock of cylinder blocks from small gas engines and compressors from dead refrigerators.

Lyle was a very private man and rarely gossiped or told stories, wholly content managing his burgeoning inventory. He assiduously catalogued parts and repaired broken tools, often making several broken items into one functioning one: lawn mowers, hand tools, baby carriages, wheelbarrows, starter motors, sump pumps and the like. Everything was for sale at modest prices, sometimes only a few cents. Lyle often gave parts to kids scrounging for various projects. His collection of wheels would be picked clean several months before the spring Soap Box Derby on the long hill at Peoples Academy. Early birds could count on having four matching wheels, while the "procrastorators," as Minister Pease used to call them, were lucky to get two matching diameters for their front and back axles.

As daylight gave way to the flickering light of the storm lanterns inside, Lyle, Wyvis, Bettis, Charlie, Duke, Pete, and sometimes Jeeter would settle in with hooch to tell and hear again many of the stories that follow.

Lila's Bucket

HARDWOOD FLATS DOES not appear on most local maps but is used by locals to describe an unmarked space between Elmore, Wolcott, and Worcester. It is a hardscrabble bog of isolated ponds, marshland, and mixed second-growth hardwoods and occasional stands of young evergreens. Walking in the woods one can always hear running water somewhere. Much of its terrain seems to float on an inland sea. Here and there, a few dirt roads, passable except in mud season, wind through the woods, feeding into corduroyed logging roads and then tapering off into hunting trails and deeryards. Occasional year-round dwellings nestle here and there on the passable roads. Hunters or hikers will occasionally run across abandoned farmhouses moldering in clearings marked only by their overgrown lilac bushes or unpruned apple trees. Farther in, they may encounter a tarpaper deer camp with sun-bleached antler racks over a padlocked door.

Lila and her husband, Theron, lived most of their lives in the Flats, coming out occasionally to the Elmore Store to "trade" for necessities. Lila was 91 and Theron, 93. Lila didn't get "the sugar" early like her girlfriend Flo, who suffers from terrible dropsy. Lila was diagnosed at 87. Except for a few skin cancers and a locked-up shoulder, Theron has kept his health. He grows cut flowers and root vegetables to sell at the Morrisville farmer's market or to aged hippies who sometimes come to their ramshackle house to buy them right out of Theron's stonelined root cellar where they are available year-round.

Rena LeClaire, the Morristown home health nurse, had been troubled for some time over Theron's steadfast rejection of her services. She took great pride in the home-based care she provided for the town's senior citizens. Last year, Rena was cited by the county for her "conscientious service" to seniors living at home.

It was suggested by some that she contributed to the economic demise of Copley Manor, the town home for dependent seniors.

Much to Rena's dismay, Theron rejected Rena's services outright. Theron told her he "din' wann 'er snoopin' roun' his house lookin' for vi-lations an' the loik." Rena was not accustomed to such out-and-out rejection. Occasionally, she encountered reticence on the part of a senior or family member that she attributed to modesty, Yankee independence, or pride, but she usually prevailed, patiently explaining that she is only there to help out and doing so only to the extent that her charge permitted. Most of the seniors on her route came to look forward to her ministrations and her company. She brought the mail, a clutch of local gossip, and light groceries if called in advance. While there, she changed bed linens, ran a load of wash if there was a machine, discarded old food, bathed those in her care, and with great authority checked their vitals. One of Rena's charges, who was hard of hearing and kept the hearing aid she brought him in the icebox "so the batt'ries doan run down," would hear "vittles" and insist that he had plenty to eat, then let her check his pulse and blood pressure.

Lila's sugar progressed quickly. She's a large woman, but not loosely fat like today's pale-fleshed girls. She'd always been heavy, but the weight that collected over the years like a retirement plan was evenly muscled by the steady routine of chores and helping Theron with his endless gardens and homemade greenhouses that sprung up here and there on their twelve acres. Last anyone heard, a diabetic stroke had left her incapable of speech and partially paralyzed.

This bit of news heightened considerably Rena's sense of urgency about Lila. She suspected things were not right in their home and that Theron had his reasons for denying her access to Lila.

She started up her rusty Subaru wagon and headed up Route 12 towards Elmore, turning off just north of the lake and bouncing along the Flats Road until the turnoff that led deep into the puckerbrush and finally to Theron and Lila's homestead. She pulled up into the dirt driveway, set the parking brake and waited a minute as she always did to give people a chance to gather themselves before she knocked on the door. Theron was just coming in from the woodpile with an armload of biscuit wood for the cook stove. A bright sun shone through the clouds. He spotted Rena and walked purposefully over to the car before she could get out, setting the firewood down hard on the hood of her car and peering into the closed car window. Unable to get out, she rolled down her window and began, "Now see here...."

"No need to git out, y'ain't stayin' and I ain' visitin'. We'se doin' foin w'outcha."

"Theron, I am not here to see you. I come here to see Lila. She's a sick woman and it's my job to take care of her and see to it that she gets medical care."

"She's been to th'ospiddle. They sen' her home and told me ta care for her and I do."

"You can't. You don't know how. She's diabetic. Lila needs special care."

"I give's her sugar med-cin and see's to her. Now git."

"Theron, I don't know what-cher hidin', but I am coming back with the sheriff."

"Bes' bring two, ya old bitch, now git."

Rena drove off down the dirt road, her chin high and her hands tight on the steering wheel, which seemed to have a mind of its own in the muddy ruts of the thawing road.

Something was not right in that household. The more Rena thought on it, the more her instincts told her Theron was hiding something to do with Lila. Folks often resisted the idea of someone from outside "doing for them." Even after seven years, Rena herself still spent a good hour tidying up her own modest home before Vi, her cleaning lady, came to redo the same. Rena did not want it bruited about the community that she kept an untidy home, and Vi was a gossip.

Theron's overt hostility clearly indicated to Rena that he was hiding something. She had seen enough in her lifetime of service to suspect men who were secretive and to fear that physical abuse might be the reason. Occasionally, the fatigue and resentment of caring for someone day-in-and-day-out could erupt into abuse. Rena remembered that some time back, Theron had had a run-in with the game warden for jacking deer on his own property. He claimed that he and Lila needed the meat. The confrontation escalated into a tussle after which the warden sported a black eye. No charges were ever brought and Theron was more discreet thereafter. But clearly Theron had it in him to strike out.

She drove straight to Willard Sanders's office. Willard ran the county social welfare office in Morristown. Before these services were consolidated in Montpelier, Willard had been the Overseer of the Poor, an office charged with caring for those unable to provide for themselves within the town. Willard was known as a fair man. One couldn't put one over on Mr. Sanders. He could easily distinguish sloth from need and was not afraid to do so. But he also understood the stress and indignity that poverty placed on families. It was in his nature to treat those in his care with great respect, and he made sure that Rena did as well. His father's sister had died young in the county poor farm.

Thursday afternoons at four, Rena reported to him on her service visits, noting any changes in health, family problems, or household issues. Sometimes folks ran out of wood before winter ran out of cold or well lines froze up leaving people without water. In time, their charges either died quietly at home or came to the hospital to die.

It took Willard several minutes to calm Rena down. By this time, Rena had worked up a pretty strong case that Lila was at risk. Theron's "rabid behavior" when Rena tried to see Lila made clear that something not right was happening in that household. Lila might be the victim of this crazy old goat, she exclaimed. Willard listened calmly to Rena, asked a few questions and promised to follow up with a visit of his own the following day. This did little to calm Rena and she urged that they return together immediately to rescue Lila.

"Theron and Lila have survived seventy years together. Another day is not going to make a difference," said Willard with calm finality.

Rena left shaking her head. After a reheated meatloaf supper, she checked her four-party line and, finding an interlude after a few tries, began dialing her network of chatty friends to try to garner support for her assessment of the danger Lila was in. "Willard's going up tomorrow. Won't take me, thinks it may be too dangerous," she told Gert, a nurse friend of hers who lived in Morristown Corners. "She may be blind now, God knows, stroke left her part paralyzed. The old fool probably doesn't even know she needs a special diet. Probably feeds her candy bars. Even if he don't 'buse her, he's probably killing her out of ignorance. It just troubles me. He won't let me near the house. He's hiding sumpin'. I just know it."

The next day the sun burned through the morning clouds by ten o'clock and the sky was radiant blue. The air was still crisp, but spring was definitely in the air. Sugarmakers were hard at it, driving their teams through the woods collecting sap in big, sledge-mounted, galvanized tanks.

Willard started up to the Flats in his Plymouth, trying to reconcile Rena's urgent report with the little he knew of Theron and Lila. The couple had never asked for help from his office and, as far as he knew, kept a modest household supported by the sale of Theron's root vegetables and cut flowers. Willard had not seen Lila for a good twenty years and, only then, once or twice a year when they came to Graves' Hardware or Gillen's Department Store.

Although determined to get to the bottom of Rena's report, Willard felt little apprehension as he followed the rutted roads deeper into Hardwood Flats. The sun was blazing down as the road wound into the endless stand of boggy alders and the rich smell of earth melting and water running again lifted his spirits. It had been a long winter.

Rena had written down the directions to Theron's farmstead, as there were no accurate maps of the area, divided as it was between the three towns. Willard remembered hunting here as a kid with his friend Eddy Kitonis and getting lost, finally finding their way to a large fire in a nearby logging camp at dusk, then having to spend the night there and following a new road out to Elmore the following morning.

Willard did not pull into Theron's yard, but drove farther down the road, parked, and walked back to Theron's. He climbed the uneven cinderblock steps to the steeply tilted porch and knocked on the screen door. He heard footsteps inside and Theron came to the door.

"'T'chwant?" asked Theron, "Veggies? Flowers won' be ready fer 'nother six weeks."

"My name is Willard Sanders and I came to inquire about how you and Lila are getting along," asked Willard, looking Theron square in the eye.

"Good enough," allowed Theron. "That nosey bitch Rena send ya?"

"No, I come on my own," said Willard gently. "It's been a long, cold winter and some folk is jus' havin' a hard time of it and I been checkin' on a few of 'em."

"You from that newfangled church what haunts people wi' their home preachin'?"

"No, I come from town and my job is just to see to folks. How you and Lila doin'? I know Lila suffers from the sugar."

Willard's calm tone of voice and willingness to look Theron in the eye seemed to allay somewhat his suspicion of the stranger and he asked Willard in off the porch. He pointed to a rocker next to the big Glenwood cookstove and slid the enameled coffeepot left so it was directly over the firebox. Willard settled in and was comfortable with the long silence.

"Jes' tell me what you wanna know and don't be 'round the bush," said Theron quietly, setting a mug of black coffee and a mayonnaise jar full of sugar in front of Willard on the cooler edge of the stove.

"I heard Lila suffered a stroke and it must be hard caring for her. Can she walk around? Did she lose her speech?"

"We make do well 'nuff. She can't walk, shuffles a bit, but I got's ta hole' her up. Sh' let's me know how she's feelin' by smilin' or frownin'. Tha's 'bout it since she suffered the sugar shock."

"When you tend your greenhouses and gardens, does she stay in the house alone?" Willard asked stirring some sugar into his coffee and looking up at Theron.

"I put 'er in the bucket," answered Theron, sipping his own coffee.

"The bucket?" asked Willard.

"The bucket," answered Theron. "I don't understand," said Willard.

"The bucket on my tractor. C'mere. I'll show ya."

Willard rose to follow Theron out the back door toward a ragtag array of greenhouses made out of scavenged windows and lumber. Near a cold frame was parked an old narrow-front end Allis-Chalmers with a bucket loader suspended by its hydraulics about four feet off the boggy ground. It was wrapped entirely in an old tarp and tied neatly with baling twine. Theron untied the tarp and pulled it away, folding it and putting it on the tractor seat. Carefully arranged in the bucket loader lay an old mattress on a thick bed of dry hay. There were a couple of old couch pillows at each end.

"I rigged this up for Lila 'cause she likes to be with me when I'se workin'. I lay's 'er down on the porch and roll 'er onta the mattress, then cover 'er up with her momma's quilt and some feather pilla's. I get's 'er comf-table and she smiles. I know she loikes it. I use these old straps to make sure she don' fall out when she shifts 'roun'. Then I liffs 'er up high and drive 'er to wherever I'se workin'. . .sometimes the garden, sometimes the green-house or the root cellar. She loikes being where I'se at."

Willard just stared at the contraption. "Looks mighty comfortable to me," he allowed.

"T'is. I tried it m'self. After awhile, Lila'll doze off in the sun and I wake's 'er wi' my special homemade tomata juice she loikes so much. Weather's nice like today, we have lunch where I'se workin'."

"I know you're a busy man, Theron, and spring's surely coming, so I'll be on my way. If you ever need anything, please call on me."

"No phone, but I can get them ol' hippies down the road to call. Thanks for comin'. Try ta keep that bitch Rena from comin'. She's alis lookin' fer trouble, e'en if there ain' none to be had."

"I will," promised Willard.

In August, Lila died. Doctor Phil was with her when she died and allowed to the nurse by his side that he'd never seen a diabetic patient with such clear and unbroken skin. In November, Denis Lefevre, a neighbor, reported that Theron "had took a corollary in the woods and doied."

Mr. Skiff's VW

IN 1952, MORRISVILLE's closest contact with the outside world was its neighbor Stowe, where tony people had begun to settle to enjoy the Nosedive, the National, the Perry Merrill, and the other trails hanging off the single chairlift. While Stowe was a smorgasbord of Austrians, Norwegians, and New Yorkers, Morrisville was a pale casserole of Catholics from French Canada and Protestants who thought they were there before trees.

Morrisville peopled the Mountain Company's trail-grooming snowshoe crews, liftline maintenance shifts, and hospitality services. It was also where the ambulances raced nervous flatlanders to have their broken bones set by Doctor Phil in the wood-frame Copley Hospital. Orthopedics was a growth industry in Morrisville in the fifties. Depression, known then as melancholia, had not even achieved medical status.

In faraway Manhattan, the emerging multinational Union Carbide and Carborundum Corporation, lashed by the fear of a nuclear attack on Manhattan, had just completed a study to find the two least likely places in the United States where such an attack might occur. The winners were Morrisville, Vermont, and some nameless erg in the Arizona desert. Morrisville was no doubt selected because of its proximity to Stowe's more urbane hospitality offerings and to the Montrealer that steamed its way north daily from Grand Central Station.

Morrisville had yet to hear of, much less form, such a thing as a Regional Development Authority, so it did little more than react with curiosity as the cinderblocks gradually took the shape of Union Carbide's supposedly bombproof vital records storage center.

Natives would, of course, be offered jobs, but it was understood that it would require the mental horsepower of a New Yorker to actually manage the place, so, perhaps because he had done something terribly wrong, one Mr. Skiff was chosen from the legions of Union Carbide employees in New York to manage the new facility in Morrisville. Father MacDonough's house next door with its matching wood-frame garage was acquired from the Holy Family Catholic church at New York prices and given to Mr. Skiff and his wife as a residence. The first four local employees were Charlie Bailey, Emile Couture, Stan Fitts, and Pete Trepanier.

Their jobs were all variants of receiving and putting away files in boxes on shelves and remembering where they were. Pete was the handyman/janitor. He immediately plowed up half the newly acquired building lot and planted the largest asparagus bed in Lamoille County. This required liberal, frequent, and heady applications of manure. Mr. Skiff allowed this unusual use of corporate assets for the time being in deference to Pete's ability to repair virtually anything, including Morrisville's first copier.

This novelty cost $3,600, the price of a home or a fleet of cars in those days, and was the size of a chest freezer. It had dozens of light bulbs and took eight minutes to produce one copy, a sort of daguerreotype printed on cardboard. Each copy cost $3 to produce. It was the envy of every business in town that relied on mimeograph machines to make copies that faded into oblivion often before they were read.

Mr. Skiff approached his exile with great good humor and natives took a cautious liking to this puckish executive from down country. His city ways were a source of endless discussion in Patch's Market, Peck's Pharmacy and Graves' Hardware.

Nothing, however, generated more rural chatter than his purchase from somewhere in Connecticut of a brand new black 1954 Volkswagen reputed to cost about $650. The car was designed by Hitler himself according to Peavine, who drove cab for Eugénie Delaire. The only available color was black. The price, had it not been reported in *The Saturday Evening Post*, would have been discreetly withheld by Mr. Skiff. After all, farms were still selling for $5,000. Though gas, at 11 cents a gallon, was hardly an issue, the VW claimed to go very far on very few gallons of it. There was not yet an EPA to authenticate VW's claims, but MPG meant little to Morrisville citizens, for whom gas mileage ratings were as alien as ski wax formulas.

The black bug, however, fascinated townsfolk the day it appeared, no one more than Pete Trepanier, a man with a strong affinity for internal combustion, external combustion (dynamite), fruited brandies, and moving objects. Pete was the adopted son of Clovis and Elise Couture and the informal stepbrother of his Union Carbide colleague Emile Couture.

Whenever he got the chance, Pete circled the odd-looking vehicle with its flat windshield, its gas tank in the front trunk where the motor should be and its curious little air-cooled, four-cylinder engine where the trunk should be. There was no dashboard other than a speedometer/odometer and an ashtray. When you ran out of gas, you flipped a lever on the floor and the gallon of gas held in the reserve tank got you to a gas station.

"Those krauts," Pete would mutter in a Québécois accent. Like many in the town, he was endlessly drawn to the curious car when Mr. Skiff parked on Portland Street to run an errand. The association with Hitler's Third Reich and the still painful experience of World War II kept a few in town at bay and intriguing quietly between lace curtains, while others stood on the sidewalk gawking.

Mr. Skiff took it all in stride and was quite proud of his car's status among the natives. He spoke politely with the curious, confessing his complete lack of understanding of things mechanical, but professing a deep affection for the appearance and fuel economy of his choice. He quoted to all who would listen the extraordinary mileage figures cited for the car. This meant nothing to his listeners, except for Pete, whom it annoyed.

Within the first few days of the car's arrival in Morrisville and a lengthy presentation to his workers by Mr. Skiff on the VW's design provenance and fuel economy, Pete was seized with a notion that he shared only with Emile and Charlie. A decision was taken to pool some funds so as to ensure that the gas mileage rating claimed by Mr. Skiff was exceeded. Pete secured a five-gallon gas can and job assignments were allotted. The proximity of the garage to the office was helpful. The proximity to the house was of concern.

That first evening Pete, the ringleader, snuck into the garage under cover of darkness and refilled the gaugeless gas tank without incident. Several days later, a much less comfortable Emile repeated the procedure and this simple process of reverse larceny repeated itself every few days into October.

It was several weeks before Mr. Skiff noted publicly that the vehicle he had bought had yet to use up its first ten gallons of gas in spite of the fact that he had put over 600 miles on the odometer. People outside the conspiracy began to take some notice. Mr. Skiff was proud but not cocky.

As November approached and the odometer crept up to 1,000 miles, Mr. Skiff became even more enthralled with his new car. He touted the heady figure of over 100 miles to the gallon, a rating that exceeded substantially the claims of the manufacturer. This he declaimed to all as he went about his errands.

Renewed interest developed in the "krautmobile," as some called it. Those for whom gas mileage meant little began to prick up their ears as Mr. Skiff, once an enthusiast, now an evangelist, carried on about his car's fuel economy. People even began to ask where exactly he had bought it, since there were as yet no dealers in Vermont.

The midnight refueling raids continued without being noticed and the mileage continued to rise. In early December, the odometer turned 2,000 miles and even those who had quit Peoples Academy in fifth grade could do the math. They were impressed.

Saturdays would find Mr. Skiff parked in front of the Morrisville town office earnestly reporting to Willard Sanders, the Overseer of the Poor and a former engineer by trade, the miraculous bug's fuel efficiency. Skeptical of the flatlander's encomium, Willard checked in with Ron Terrill at the Texaco and Armand Crevier at the Esso to determine if Mr. Skiff had been a customer yet. The answers were negative. The nearest other sources of gas would have been Stowe or Hardwick. Willard could not imagine Mr. Skiff venturing to Hardwick, a rough and tumble town in those days, and, a simple man in spite of his New York City roots, Mr. Skiff professed a dislike for the folly and pretense of Stowe. No one was selling him gas.

The now widely discussed mileage rating kept creeping up. Mr. Skiff astonished the patrons of Patch's Market one morning as he told them that his own skepticism had led him to drop a weighted cotton string into the gas tank to assess how much fuel remained. To his astonishment and that of his listeners, he found about half a tank remaining.

In early January, Mr. Skiff wrote the newly formed Volkswagen Corporation of America in Paramus, New Jersey, offering to bear witness in their advertising to the extraordinary mileage of their car, which at this point he calculated was between 350 and 400 miles to the gallon, depending on how one read the wet string. He did not receive a response.

Pete doggedly maintained the refueling deceit, though Emile and Charlie had dropped out, fearing for their job security.

Morrisville had ensured its good name among Lamoille County communities by voting each year to maintain its "dry" status. Thus Peavine, known only by his mother and the Department of Motor Vehicles as Alton, made weekly taxi runs to the "State Store" in Waterbury for the dry citizens of Morrisville drawn to alcoholic stimulants. Pete's passion for down-market, fruit-flavored brandies occasionally led to epic, bilingual ravings on Portland Street on whatever topic was most on his mind. His diatribe might concern the absurdity of using sweeping compound, the stupidity of changing rather than simply replenishing oil in a car, the use of dynamite in removing beaver colonies or in bass fishing, or the lactation equipment of one of the sisters who ran Mer-Lu's restaurant in Hardwick, noted by non-locals for its complete lack of a food menu or even a kitchen.

In time, his enthusiasm for blackberry brandy, or lacking that, a Nehi soda laced with grain alcohol from his shop, made the long-running deceit impossible to conceal, as the alcohol gradually gave Pete's mouth greater and greater sway over his judgment. One Saturday afternoon in the back room of Graves' Hardware, Pete loosed his secret to a thrilled audience of loggers gathered to admire a new Evinrude chainsaw.

Soon the whole town was privy to the prank, all but Mr. Skiff, who was still blissfully ignorant and enamored. Like Toad in *The Wind in the Willows*, Mr. Skiff never tired of sharing his calculations with anyone who would listen. His persistent calls to Volkswagen continued to elicit silence and may have delayed the opening of a dealership in Vermont.

As the first signs of spring approached, Mr. Skiff was obsessed with the marvel of his perpetual motion machine. On March 25th as Morrisville's French Catholics were celebrating the Annunciation, the mileage reached 500 miles to the gallon, a figure even Mr. Skiff had trouble embracing, but did.

His updates now elicited worried smiles. Emile had confessed his complicity in the prank to Father MacDonough, whose good Irish humor led to the imposition of only a few Hail Marys as penance. But Emile was still haunted by the thought that his promising career with Union Carbide might be threatened by the prank. He approached Pete about ending the deceit.

Pete would have none of it. So Emile and Charlie snuck into the garage late on a Sunday night and siphoned off all the gas, leaving only vapors and the reserve gallon.

The next morning Mr. Skiff reported sadly that his car had finally used up its fuel. He calculated and recalculated his final mileage to report it both to the manufacturer and to the Guinness *Book of Records* at 618 miles to the gallon. He told Emile and Stan that he would go to the Texaco at lunch and refuel his car for the second time in its life.

Word spread rapidly. At noon, the Atlas Plywood factory whistle blew and quite a crowd of folks gathered to witness the event. Mr. Skiff, running on his reserves, pulled up to loud applause. Chet opened the front hood, unscrewed the cap and refueled the small tank. Mr. Skiff got out, acknowledged the crowd, tendered Chet $2, from which he got change, and left.

The hoax ended after several more refuelings that occurred within weeks, rather than months of each other. Eventually, Emile, Pete, Charlie, and the innocent Stan got handwritten notes from Mr. Skiff that read, "Thanks for all the gas and the good fun. You sure had me going."

Jeeter's
Leaky Roof

JEETER'S WIFE, LOU, was feisty, not the type to "go broody" and hole up for a period with checkout counter magazines and palliative junk food like some of her girlfriends enduring beer-soaked marriages. She had no complaints about Jeeter personally, but rather about his projects and his "hulks," a '58 Olds and a '48 Chevy pickup. These "hulks" gave her countless opportunities to describe vehicle failures. To her best friend, Norma, she replayed her anxiety at setting out with a car that might fail anywhere in Lamoille County or mercifully before it even left the driveway where it would respond with eerie silence when she turned the ignition key.

Lou was undaunted by most of life's challenges, but standing tall next to Jeeter's highly recognizable wreck of a car clutching four bags of groceries while hitching a ride home from Brousseau's Market was, as Lou said, "...beyond the pole." She would confide her elaborate plans for revenge to Norma and to Cathy, the checkout lady at Brousseau's who had often let her use the manager's phone to call Jeeter when the Olds lay smoldering on Portland Street.

Jeeter's efforts to improve Lou's opinion of him as well as their social status in town focused mostly on shiny objects. If Lou's anger began to weigh heavily on him, Jeeter would bound off to Dagnon's Auto and come home with spiffy new seat covers, a car heater that plugged into the cigarette lighter (further taxing the exhausted battery), a new hood ornament, or some shiny accessory that would at best not compromise the car's motile function.

When the Vermont Legislature saw fit to liberalize vehicle-inspection laws, to accommodate a slumping economy and higher levels of auto body rot in deference to Vermonters on fixed incomes, Jeeter saw himself as off-the-hook with regard to the Olds' sheet metal. This led to several catastrophes for Lou that left Jeeter beholden and Lou suffering from what she often referred to as "postdramatic stress."

Like the time the 18-gallon gas tank fell out of the car on the way home from Norma's, yet again leaving Lou standing on the side of the road next to the Olds, its gas tank sitting several yards back in a large, darkening stain on the dusty Gap Road. Lou's fertile vocabulary surprised even Art Farnsworth, who picked her up and gave her a lift home in his pickup. Jeeter, oblivious to his wife's predicament and rage, was stacking wood and waiting for his bride to make a hot dinner. That night, Jeeter had Sugar Pops and slightly off milk.

Making his best effort yet to placate Lou, Jeeter took the bull by the horns. He rescued and remounted the gas tank with heavy wire and sheet-metal screws, then headed off to Dagnon's to buy a large bucket of Bondo, sandpaper, some fiberglass fabric, and a gallon of a discontinued Chrysler color—not unlike the avocado hue of Lou's gas range. With no patience for sheet-metal work and a weakened vehicle-inspection law, he slathered Bondo onto the fiberglass cloth that skirted the car and repainted the whole using an 89-cent brush that transferred all of the paint and most of the bristles to the Olds. He surveyed the lumpy result with pride. With little or no sheet metal for support, the newly painted fiberglass cloth and Bondo frill had a tendency to flounce a bit as the car rattled down Hardwood Flats Road.

Lou could neither muster nor fake any enthusiasm for the makeover, or for that matter, for Jeeter's glow of accomplishment. She knew what lurked under the hood. It wasn't paint and Bondo that would get her home.

This was the dawn of women's lib in Vermont. Few local women embraced it overtly, but they had their sympathies. Everyone tolerated and even enjoyed the more aggressive libbers in town—especially the "amazons" in the Fourth of July parade. Lou was not a "libber."

Every year on the Fourth, however, Lou walked in the parade wearing jumper cables as suspenders, a mini-spare tire on her back, a tow chain girding her waist, and a can of ether in her Carhartt jumpsuit. Counterfeit inspection stickers made on the new copier at the Eden town clerk's office protruded from the rim of her red-and-black-checked hunting cap. This always drew smiles and applause from those lining the street. Vehicle inspection was a distinct challenge for Vermonters in the '60s when oxidation began much earlier than it does today. There was a legendary model year for Rambler wherein one of its new Americans exhibited rust bubbles within a year of purchase and sported gaping holes in the second.

Lou carried no placard in the parade, just marched in cadence with the kids pumping streamered bikes, the prancing Western-style horses with their leatherfringed riders, the beaming, ruddy-cheeked farmers on their sputtering antique tractors, the self-consciously uniformed Little League team, the prom queen in the green '57 Chevy convertible driven by the Mayor, and a pair of local bloodred oxen yoked together. The annual parade with its patriotic and more recent, non-patriotic displays was really a few-questions-asked opportunity to strut one's stuff, whatever that might be—no permit needed.

Jeeter looked on with pride at his wife, poking a stranger when she strode by and saying, "That's my wife right there. She knows cars."

Jeeter's prowess at home maintenance was akin to his automotive skills. His efforts focused on innovation rather than simple repair. When the iron pipe from the springhouse on the hill behind the house oxidized into the earth and left them without water, Jeeter "innervated" ways to avoid excavating the whole 75odd yards to bury new PVC pipe. He settled on a plan to simply divert some of the ground water from the small brook of the spring's overflow that ran right by the house. If it was good enough to drink up there at the springhouse, it should be fine down here, if not better. After the arduous task of gathering and using large rocks to get 60 feet of coiled one-inch PVC flex pipe to lie flat on the ground between the deepest spot in the brook and the water inlet to the house, Jeeter beamed with pride at the ease with which his 'vention was executed. Lou was skeptical, though the black plastic pipe, bled of air and primed with a funnel and a bucket, had indeed delivered water into the kitchen spigot.

It also delivered an array of fauna that she saved in a jelly jar to show Jeeter that it wasn't working as well as he had hoped. But once an inventor, always an inventor, Jeeter tied a patch of cheesecloth over the taps in the kitchen and bath to filter out the critters drawn into the intake. He saved the filtered harvest of pink and waterlogged earthworms for his perch-fishing expeditions to the Green River Reservoir. On especially warm and sunny days, the long section of PVC pipe would reassert its original heliform shape and draw the intake out of the brook, compelling

Jeeter to reprime the whole operation. Baling twine and more large rocks swiftly ended this inconvenience. But all the engineering "innervation" ground to an abrupt halt with the first freeze in October. Jeeter was forced to call Darby's to come and dig a three-foot-deep trench from the spring to the house in which to bury the pipe. Lou was cheered, if briefly.

One of their more annoying household inconveniences was the persistent drip of dark water onto anyone relieving themselves in the second-floor bathroom when it was raining. There was a leak in the flashing around the toilet vent pipe through which water entered the house. It had built up over time, and the ominous, darkening bulge of distended sheetrock above the mother-of-pearl seat finally burst, releasing a gush of brown water. Fortunately, no one was there at the time. After the deluge of soggy sheetrock and brown water let loose, the steady drip over the toilet continued. Jeeter had relief options off the front porch and was somewhat less troubled by this than Lou.

To soften her insistence that the leak be repaired before snowfall, Lou prepared Jeeter's favorite dish, a glaucous concoction of Cheese Whiz, frozen broccoli florets, and Minute Rice. Jeeter took the bait and agreed to fix the leak the next day.

Jeeter was morbidly afraid of heights and had often tried to cajole Lou onto the roof to do his shouted bidding from below, usually with regard to a flaccid TV antenna. Lou, a woman of significant girth, was not easily persuaded.

Jeeter took the pickup to Graves' Hardware with a scribbled list of necessities: a gallon of roof patch, a square yard of flashing. He made a concerted effort at getting them to sell him two shingles instead of a whole pack. He was successful. They had a broken pack out of which Squeak—so named because of his involuntary neutering back when the state did those things—gave him two shingles. Jeeter returned home in the only vehicle currently running and set to work.

His fear of heights required extra safety precautions. In the collapsed barn next to the house was a cast-iron track dangling from rotted timbers. A large hayfork lay on the ground next to a coil of three-quarter-inch manila rope. Jeeter extracted the rope and secured it to the rear axle of the Chevy. The bumper had long since been detached while towing an enraged Lou in the disabled Olds, so Jeeter secured the rope to a nearby leaf spring.

From the truck's roof he made several attempts to hurl the heavy rope over the ridgeline of the house, as the vent pipe was on the far side of the house. After a half-dozen attempts, he succeeded, ran inside, and climbed to the attic where a gabled window opened onto the roof. Snagging the end of the rope with a mop handle with a bent nail in the end, he tied the heavy rope securely around his waist.

His pulse hammering in his temples, he stepped out onto the dreaded roof. He pulled the rope. It held. He edged his way over to the vent pipe and began to pull off the old shingles to determine where the water was entering. A section of flashing had rusted away near the vent pipe and the water was running down the outside of the pipe into the house. He pried open the tar bucket to dish out a generous dollop around the vent pipe flashing. As he layered it in and around the pipe, he realized he had forgotten roofing nails and would have to negotiate his way back along the roof and inside.

Just then the screen door on to the front porch opened and slammed shut. "Getting milk and bread at Brosseau's. Need anything?"

"Nope," Jeeter yelled down from the far side of the roof. He resumed slathering the tar on to the vent pipe with renewed confidence in his project.

Gratefully, he heard the motor turn over and fire. It was not, however, the familiar roar of the Olds, but rather of the more reliable Chevy which of late Lou had begun to use in a rather futile attempt at "learnin' shift cars."

Then the connection between the pickup's successful start and the manila rope looped tightly around his waist registered like a jolt of house current. Jeeter bolted upright and roared "Hold it." His shout coincided with Lou's habit of revving up the engine to test the oil-burner under the hood. A blue cloud rose gently into view as Jeeter clawed frantically at the knot around his waist and continued yelling.

Lou noisily ground the truck into gear and released the clutch. The truck lurched forward and the rope snapped taut as Lou headed off down the driveway. Jeeter, running perpendicular to the roof's incline, was drawn up and over the ridgeline down the front side of the roof still howling for Lou to stop.

Lou, tuned to her favorite country station and with a secure sense of forward motion, headed slowly toward the long dirt driveway.

Jeeter, yanked forward, bounced down the other side of the roof then over the gutter—to which he clung desperately until it detached from the eave—then clattered down onto the porch's roof. Swearing a blue streak, Jeeter was towed down onto the woodpile and across the lawn towards the gravel driveway.

Only the tarpaulin-like fabric of Jeeter's orange Carhartt coveralls protected him from the dog bones and hand tools strewn about the lawn. Meanwhile Lou, cocooned in the warm cab of a moving vehicle, hummed along to a Loretta Lynn tune that pretty well summed up her feelings about conjugal perseverance. Jeeter, now back on his feet, raced to keep up with her while clawing at his waist.

Still in the long dirt driveway, Lou was moving slowly enough for Jeeter to keep up. He gave up on loosening the knot, for each time he thought he was making headway, a tug from the Chevy tightened it back up. He now worked frantically to force the looped rope down and off his body. He gradually succeeded in getting the rope over his pelvis, part way down his thighs and onto his knees, alternating hopping on one foot and then the other as he tried to shed the rope.

Just then, Lou hit Elmore Road and gunned it. The acceleration hobbled Jeeter, who fell backward as the rope slid down his calves, snatched a green barn boot from his foot, and took it down the road in a trail of blue smoke. Lou, still humming, missed the drama behind her since the rearview mirror lay on the floor of the truck and a photocopied inspection sticker was scotch-taped to where it used to be.

Lou returned home about forty minutes later with a half gallon of milk, a king-size loaf of Bouyea's bread, and a half-pound of thick-sliced olive loaf, the long rope still in tow and the boot long gone. Relieved at having completed a round trip, she found Jeeter in the second-floor bathroom muttering as he hung a plastic bucket from the ceiling over the toilet.

Widowmaker

TOMMY CANNOT BREATHE. His 31 years of smoking Luckies have shortened his breath, infusing it with viscous phlegm that makes him cough and keeps Ann awake at night worrying that he will die as her father did, drowning with short panic-stricken breaths, unable to oxygenate the blood flowing to his terrified brain.

But Tommy is not Ann's father. Tommy is in the woods alone. He is dying, but not of emphysema. He cannot inhale. The crushing weight on his shattered ribs and seizing pain in his chest make it impossible to inhale the forest air.

In his close field of vision, the forest floor is a landscape of curled wood chips. Some are pale blond and others cinnabar, the mixed colors of black cherry. Farther off, pale green maidenhair fern fronds rise up like a preternatural tree, and in the distance he can see a mound of dark green moss covering a rock.

He can hear the gurgling of water flowing over rocks in Potash Brook a few yards away, and there is the sound of a phoebe trilling in the woods. Tommy is remembering where he is in the woods. He is far from Ann, far from their house, far from anyone. It is early April, and trout season two weeks away. The kids he often surprises fishing on his woodlot are still in school.

The fierce pain in his chest is increasingly anesthetized by the body's chemistry of shock. Instinct causes him to inhale, but pain overwhelms instinct and he relaxes, breathless.

His right temple is flat against the damp moss. He fell hard on his right side when his steel-toed boot caught in a loop of woody grapevine hidden among dead leaves. It happened fast. He tries to recall the sequence of events. The 60foot black cherry had pinched the bar on his saw as it began its fall. He let go of the saw and moved aside but his boot caught fast in the vine. He and the tree fell in the same arc.

He sees a wild turkey strutting hesitantly towards him, lifting each three-toed foot very carefully, setting it down gently before taking another step, always cautious, always guarded. Tommy is no threat, however. The turkey seems to know this, ambling ever closer, pausing at each step to scratch the groundcover and peck at worms and bugs beneath the bed of leaves. A few feet away, he stops, glances at Tommy but goes on with his feeding. As the bird moves closer, Tommy notices how the wary tom resembles the bronze meat birds his aunt raises each summer, lacking only the heavy chest and height. The coloring is the same.

Gradually, it struts away, all the while disturbing the earth and eating what it finds. It is the closest Tommy has ever been to a live wild turkey. He is used to seeing them in springtime, flocks of twenty or thirty foraging in the corn stubble in his lower field while the snow is still on the ground. The tom disappears over the knoll that forms the west bank of Potash Brook. Tommy can still hear him scrabbling among the dry leaves even over the sounds of the brook.

The pale blue two-cycle exhaust that hangs in the air when Tommy's chainsaw is whining has dissipated. The resinous smell of wounded wood is everywhere, mingled with the acrid odor of bar and chain oil. The hot saw lies sideways on the ground, stalled and quiet. Gas-oil mix leaks slowly from the carburetor. Tommy could never get it to idle properly without his hand on the throttle; something about the carburetor mixture he could never get right.

He is exhausted from the pain in his chest. Trying again to draw breath, a stab of pain from the rib that has pierced his lung overwhelms his effort. He stares at the fern fronds and listens to the water in the brook. In his mind, he sees the five and six-inch brookies under the banks undulating slowly to hold their place in the gentle current, an occasional flash of rose-colored light as one drifts into the midstream sun. He closes his eyes to rest and smells them in a black iron skillet sizzling in butter over the woodstove at home. Ann is breaking fresh eggs on the other side of the pan. The blue graniteware coffee pot sits on the far right of the woodstove, away from the intense heat of the fire box. His favorite breakfast.

His vision is blurring. He is dizzy but not yet confused. When he opens his eyes, the fern fronds now appear like an ancient tree; the moss, a bracken hill in the distance. Tommy himself is tiny. The wood chips are the size of cedar shakes and dominate his short field of vision.

Ann has always been there for him when he needed her, but this time she does not know he needs her, so she cannot help him.

He left early that morning. He arose quietly from their tousled bed, leaving Ann sleeping beneath a clump of quilts. They had made love the night before slowly, the way he and Ann both liked. Ann was shy about sex and had never gotten comfortable with the harsh anatomical lexicon of the act. Gradually they had adopted a language of flowers. Ann would whisper to Tommy, "Pollinate me," and their lovemaking would begin. The shared metaphor was their secret, adding pleasure. Ann got a book from the library and took a furtive sensual pleasure in her study of floral reproduction, introducing and explaining new words and their meaning to Tommy, often as part of their foreplay. They talked in an intimate code of petals, pistils, stamens, pollen, and efflorescence.

Before he left, he rebuilt the fire in the kitchen stove from last night's embers, first with biscuit wood, then with two splits of maple. The Glenwood cookstove with its rusty chrome that had been there when they bought the abandoned hill farm came slowly to life and began broadcasting heat in the kitchen and then up through a cast-iron register into their bedroom above.

It was his second marriage and Ann's first. Ann never asked Tommy about his first marriage as they had been friends through the sad and empty ritual of most of it. Like most of his friends, Tommy married while in high school. Some married as they were about to be fathers, others for what they thought was love. Tommy had liked her well enough, but might not have taken her for a wife were she not bearing his child.

With the help of Father MacDonough, Tommy convinced himself that he loved her. She, too, was Catholic, though French not Irish. This added pressure on both of them to legitimize their new child in marriage. As was often the case, she was visibly pregnant at the service.

The marriage lasted a little over two years. Tommy came to understand that he could never fill the billowing emptiness in her left by an alcoholic father and overly religious mother. After Jeanette was born, he gave up.

One Sunday after returning from Mass, she simply helped herself to his pickup in lieu of child payments and left with Jeanette for her father's home in Barton to care for him in his alcoholic twilight. Soon after, she landed a state job.

On the Friday after his wife and daughter decamped, he got a terse letter postmarked in Barton. He was to see Jeanette for a few weeks in the summer and at Easter, but he never did. After her father died of a grueling stomach cancer, his wife of two years remarried a man who did not drink and never got angry. Tommy felt the irony, for when his marriage ended so did his own drinking and anger. Twice he sent a brown envelope of cash to Barton, but both times it came back unopened, so he stopped.

He left for the woods, moving into his father's deer camp in Sterling Valley, and began logging in earnest. His father had been an avid hunter, taking Tommy into the woods with him when he was just five. Mahlon, too, had married for paternity, but his marriage to Tommy's mother survived the hardscrabble times and youthful drinking and grew into a durable friendship. Ella had a persistent and disruptive sense of humor. When things "went south" as his father used to say, Ella could always find something or someone to laugh at, including herself. This diverted many family crises from tears, anger, and harsh words to gales of laughter and eventual calm.

Mahlon died under a 1954 Ford Fairlane while removing the plug from the oil pan to drain and change the oil for his neighbor Hilda Hartigan. She lived in a trailer and a slurry of junk food and cheap sherry. She counted on neighbors to rescue her from various alcoholic misadventures. Mahlon would periodically help her out, thawing a frozen pipe or changing worn tires or oil. He was about to drain the oil under the jacked-up Ford when she leaned on the fender, pushing the car off the scissor jack. The full weight of the rusty Ford's drive train landed on Mahlon's chest, pinning him to the damp lawn under his back. Panicked, Hilda fumbled with the scissor jack lying on its side, all the while talking to Mahlon, who could not answer. Well after he stopped breathing, she told him to "wait a bit" while she went in "to get some more sherry and call a neighbor to help her lift the car off him." Ella never left the community and never remarried, seeing her son on Sundays for breakfast.

Tommy and Ann had always been casual friends in school. Not "seeing each other," but rather finding themselves together occasionally. After the breakup of his marriage, they ran into each other in the hospital where Tommy was visiting a friend badly mangled when his tractor tipped over on him. Ann was an LPN with plans to become a registered nurse. He had always been drawn to her winning smile and the way she lowered her eyes when he returned the smile.

He asked her to the Fourth of July fire station dance, she accepted, and they were married two months later in the town clerk's office in Derby Line. They honeymooned for a week in a damp motel room with swollen and water-stained Homosote walls across the border in Quebec, emerging only long enough to have breakfast and look around the small town of Stanstead.

With a loan from his mother Tommy had enough to make a down payment on a farm high up on the side of Sterling Mountain. The Lamoille Bank had foreclosed on it two years earlier. With a thousand-dollar down payment, a 25-year mortgage, and payments of $76 a month, Tommy and Ann had a home of their own. The bank was relieved of another failed hill farm and uninhabitable house.

Ann and Tommy loved the house, with its 5' by 3' flat slab of bluestone lying in front of the door. The outside bore no trace of its former paint, so Ann and Tommy set to work to seal the dried-out wood with creosote from Graves' Hardware. The house absorbed half again as much as Jack Graves had calculated it would. When they came back for more, he surmised that the raised grain of the badly weathered wood presented twice as much surface to seal. The place looked no different when they were finished, but they had slowed the long decay and deterioration.

On the inside, they did little other than to inhibit decay by pulling up the old linoleum, sanding and sealing the wide pumpkin pine floors, and patching and repainting plaster walls. The electrical wiring, a network of porcelain insulators with cotton-wrapped copper wire running from rotary porcelain switches to cracked porcelain sockets, had to be replaced. They agreed they only really needed electricity in the kitchen, to run the refrigerator, a GE toaster Ann had brought into the marriage, the white Maytag wringer-washer with its cast aluminum agitator and rubber drain-hoses, and a single bulb in a new white porcelain fixture in the middle of the kitchen ceiling. Tommy wired the kitchen while Ann painted. Tommy later added another outlet to plug in the red heat tapes he spiral-wrapped around the incoming water pipe to keep it from freezing as it cascaded into the cast-iron sink from the spring box on the hillside above.

They reveled together in how little they would do, agreeing to stabilize what was there, not to change or enhance it. They loved it as they found it and wanted only to preserve it.

Their woodlot covers 140 acres and abuts the old Languerand farm with its 800 acres of hardwoods. The Languerand widow lets Tommy work her woods as well in return for fifteen percent of the mill price. Tommy culls, cuts, and sells pulpwood in four-foot lengths, cordwood in 20 and 24-inch lengths, and lumber in mill lengths. He works alone, cutting and stacking wood in place and then retrieving it from the woods with his John Deere 510 and an old manure spreader into which he loads the wood. Tommy is almost always happy in the woods and looks forward to coming home to Ann.

Ann, too, is resourceful with wood. She can heft a running saw and cut birch and maple whips into biscuit wood for the stove, but has never managed to yank the starter cord hard enough to overcome the compression and get either of Tommy's cranky McCulloughs to fire. Ann likes to say she doesn't cut trees down, she cuts them up. Tommy always adds, ". . .and only if they are lying in a sawbuck." She prefers a sharp bucksaw.

He thinks of Ann now, but his brain, bereft of oxygen, produces only fleeting evanescent images and sensations from different times in his life: watching his mother, then younger than Ann, knead bread on a bird's-eye maple board with the rich smell of the yeasty dough permeating the kitchen; Ann using a baby teacup dipped in boiling water, hot to the point of pain, to draw wasp venom out of his forearm where he had been stung multiple times after a falling tree disturbed a nearby paper nest; helping his Uncle Norman split wood to heat the still in his ramshackle cedar oil mill; playing doctor with Annie Stewart in her stern father's hayloft and discovering the aching thrill and fear of passion; learning to drive Pete Trepanier's tractor at the age of eleven. The images and their sensations subside.

With great effort Tommy opens his eyes and sees only light. He hears the brook. His last thought is of Ann and how angry she will be to see him lying dead under a tree whose trunk is three times the size of his own. A small runnel of blood appears in his left nostril.

The Dairy
Tax Shelter

"I'SS HOW THE RICH gits richer," explained Eddie Purinton, blowing his left nostril onto the ground with his right index finger. "Some newfangle' plan where ya sell yer cows t'a rich person what's got taxes ta pay, but 'che git ta keep yer cows and he pays no taxes. Duke Sargeant in the 'stension service 'splained it ta me yesserday."

"I don' git it," answered his friend and neighbor Purvis Bettis.

"Ya sell 'em yer cows, they pays ya what they'se worth and maybe ya pay 'em sumpin' monthly for a lease. The rich peoples write the cows off 'n their taxes. Works fer me. I never made enough money ta pay no taxes anyhow," added Eddie.

"So they gives ya money, but 'che git ta keep yer cows? Where da I sign up?" said Purvis with a broad grin.

Morrisville residents only wore suits on Sunday, at funerals or at weddings. They were usually black, ill fitting, had some dried mud around the pant cuffs, and needed ironing. The man who accompanied Duke Sargeant on his farm visits in May wore a dark blue suit. Doug Peck of Peck's Pharmacy noted, "It looked as if it had been painted on him at the bank."

A number of farmers in Addison County had signed on for the "free money" in Anaconda Trust's Dairy Buy-Leaseback Program. The program wasn't for farmers per se, as they typically paid very little tax on their modest incomes, struggling instead to pay property taxes on their large farms. Rather it was for wealthy people looking to shelter large incomes by buying risky gas drilling rigs, oil wells, record and movie contracts, and now dairy and beef herds.

Lamoille County farmers approached the plan with more skepticism than those in Addison. After a presentation by the man in the blue suit, with vigorous nods from Duke Sargeant, seven Lamoille County farmers signed on to the persuasive, if incomprehensible, plan. Each farmer signed a clutch of unread legal documents in exchange for a lavish check and, as if the ink might disappear, Bub Rocheleau went out and bought a new tedder, Omer Ferland, a used bailer, and CC Tremblay a brand new Massey-Ferguson. Marcel Poulin braced and reroofed his slumping barn and added a silo. Thinking way ahead, Newt Estey bought a used trailer on a small lot in Hollywood, Florida.

Meanwhile, farmers went about their seasonal business of first and second cuts, corn planting and harvest, freshening heifers, and endless milking. Willis Hicks's auctions in Cady's Falls provided an opportunity every month to get together, discuss the weather and crops, sell some animals, and buy others. Life went on as before in Morrisville's small farming community and the threadbare farming economy of Lamoille County quickly absorbed the brief largesse from down country.

About a year later, storm clouds began to gather in the finance centers of New York and Boston as certain left-leaning congressmen began to ask tough questions about some of the more elaborate schemes for tax evasion. Since many regulators, lawyers, and politicians were themselves participants, rewriting the rules was unrealistic, but it became prudent to ensure that the rules for tax sheltering were followed correctly. So began a rash of audits.

Two suited gentlemen from Anaconda Trust and an IRS auditor flew into Burlington Airport and hired a Benway's taxi to take them to Morrisville, where they settled into two rooms in the newly built Sunset Motel on Route 100 just north of town. The first person they called was the last person they had talked to on their previous visit, county extension agent Duke Sargeant, who appeared somewhat nervous as he met them for breakfast the next morning.

Over coffee, eggs, and sausages, the three men explained the plan to Duke. It seemed simple enough and Duke pledged to help the men conduct the herd audits and get the information they needed to ensure the "boys in D.C." that everything was above-board in the program initiated by their firm. As outlined to Duke, it was a simple matter of verifying the herd counts on the seven farms to confirm that the distant owners' assets were consistent with what they were depreciating on their income tax filings.

"Ear tags," said Duke nervously. The three men looked puzzled. Duke explained that ear tags were how most farms kept track of their herds and that simply collecting the unique numbers on the ear tags was the easiest way to inventory the heifers. The three visitors looked at each other, nodded and seemed satisfied with Duke's solution. They agreed to begin work that afternoon, paid the bill, and left. Duke went back to his office and began dialing.

CC and Omer had all but forgotten about the deal.

"My girls a' turned o'er quite a bit. I just bought six heifers last week at Hicks's. Had one of ma girls die on me when she cast her withers and gave two ta ma son who's raisin' beefs," said Omer.

"With all due respect, Omer, shut up an' listen," Duke said out of breath, "Git 'em papers out the drawer. Find out how many animals you'se s'ppose' ta have. Make sure they's there when I get there at 1:30 with these guys or they'll be flying home with yer new silo. Make sure they'se all tagged too. If there ain' enough, borrow some heifers from Jimbo, but make sure ya got the right nummer."

In a notebook in his desk Duke found a list of how many milkers each farmer had sold to the tax program. With the help of Polly Limoges, the local phone operator, he reached everyone either at home or somewhere else in town. Both Bub and Newt had large cattle trailers that Duke pressed into service and everyone had ear tags and pliers. After talking with the seven farmers, Duke worked out a schedule of visits, doing two herds a day, one in the morning and one in the afternoon. The numbers weren't promising and the task would not be easy. A total of 386 milkers had been sold into the tax program, of which only 314 remained after the first year. This meant 72 would have to be accounted for by discreet transfers in the next four days. The trailers each held eight cows and no one farm had lost more than sixteen except Newt. So it was a matter of keeping at least sixteen heifers on the move for the next four days with an ear tagger hard at it.

That afternoon, when the four men pulled in to the muddy swale in front of Omer's barn, Omer stood outside at the ready, "looking ridiculous" according to Duke's later telling.

"They's in the stanchions," Omer allowed with a nervous grin. Duke later referred to it as a "tit in the wringer" grin.

"Let's get a count," said Duke nervously. "You had 38 head, right, Omer?"

"Yup."

The visitors looked uneasily at the mire between Duke's Oldsmobile and the entrance to the barn and stepped warily into it. The mud and manure mix was well over their shoes.

Once inside the badly lit barn, Duke scanned the row of stanchions and looked pale when he saw far down the row, six heifers with blood running out of their newly tagged left ears.

"You boys start at this end and I'll start at the other," said Duke, "Let's see if we get the same count. Note down the tag numbers as well."

Duke pulled out a handkerchief and whispered to Omer to get him an alum bar. "I ain' got one," Omer said, looking helpless. Dipping his handkerchief in a cast-iron drinking bowl, Duke cleaned up the bloody ears of the newly tagged cows and met the men halfway up the row where they compared notes. One of the men from the bank kept looking down ruefully at his mud-covered shoes and socks.

The IRS agent said, "You know we could finish this tomorrow afternoon at this rate."

"Won't work. Much easier to count 'em when they'se in the barn in early morning and late afternoon. Drive ya crazy trying to find 'em and count 'em when they'se pasturin'. We best stick to schedule," said Duke with uncharacteristic firmness.

The first stop the next morning looked even more suspicious, as the gap between what was sold 18 months earlier and what was left was even greater, meaning that a considerable number of cows had been transported during the night. Eddie left one of the cattle trailers right in front of the barn with the ramp down and the new arrivals were milling around loose in the paddock while his own cows were in oak stanchions inside. They did, however, all have ear tags. The men from the city did not notice that the cows in the paddock all had new ear tags and those in stanchions all had older ones. Duke noticed. The count was over in less than 40 minutes and the men were on their way.

As soon as Duke's Oldsmobile disappeared over the hill, Marcel bounded out of the kitchen and helped Eddie begin retagging and loading the herd for transport over to Bub's six miles away. The city men would not be there until 3:30 so that gave them several hours to make the switch. Bub was six cows down so they would only need one trailer.

The pace kept up through the last herd audit on Thursday. Only Newt's farm posed a real risk. He had sold 57 cows to someone in the plan, but had only 36 left, as he was winding down his dairy operation in anticipation of retirement.

Newt and Hilda had been farming for 38 years straight and in that time, had had only one vacation on the occasion of their 35th wedding anniversary. Their two grown children came home and moved in to manage the farm for ten days while Newt and Hilda drove across New York State to stay in a modest motel in Niagara Falls, enjoying the honeymoon they never had. Glenna Bumps, the Wolcott correspondent for *The News and Citizen*, reported on the anniversary party and the travel plans, finishing her chatty piece with her well-known signature line, "Fun was had by all."

Meanwhile, 21 cows had had to be moved between the morning and afternoon counts. Eight came from Omer's and 13 came from Marcel's in two back-to-back loads. The last cow was locked into a stanchion minutes before the men showed up in Duke's mud-spattered Olds. Much to everyone's surprise a few minutes into the count, the IRS auditor said, "I've seen this cow before." He looked up at the others and said, "This cow has a badly torn ear and there is a horn growing out on the right side. I know I've seen it in the last few days."

"Not surprising you'd think that, with all the cows we've counted," said Duke. "They begin to all look the same...happens all the time. Not to worry."

The IRS man stared at the cow and then much to Duke's relief, resumed his counting and noting down ear tag numbers.

With all their client assets accounted for, the two bankers and the auditor took Peavine's taxi back to Burlington. Duke slumped in his office and put his feet up on his desk. The phone rang. It was Bub.

"Well?"

"Think we're OK. You boys figured out the mess yet?"

"Workin' on it," said Bub.

"Well one good thing," offered Duke, "you boys know your girls by sight. Won't need no tags to get ever'body back where they belong, but it might take a few days. Sure hope 'em boys is satisfied."

Anaconda Trust never returned to Morrisville.

Fanny Fancher
and Crazy Chase

IT WAS HIS second day in first grade and his first time walking home from school. Maple Street was a half-mile long, one of several streets in Morrisville beautifully canopied with elms. There were twenty-three houses on the left side and nineteen on the right and, try as he might, he could not count both sides as he walked home from school. He would lose track as his eyes darted from left to right and the sums vanished.

Just below the hospital, Maple Street merged into Washington Highway, which led east out of town towards the hill farms in the shadow of Elmore Mountain. The street's lofty name belied its rutted gravel surface. His house lay just beyond the hospital yet still within the town limits, disqualifying him from riding on the school bus operated by his stepfather's parents.

The three-story, wood-frame Copley Hospital, girded with a rocker-filled white veranda and surrounded by tall white pines, dominated his sparse neighborhood. Just beyond lived Dr. Guthmann, the town dentist, and Adrian Morris, the president of the bank. Across from his house was the Collettes' house with its attached small-engine shop. Beyond lay Volney and Gladys Farr's farm, the Ned and Lyle Stewart farm, Mrs. Fisher's share-crop tenant house attached to the Stewart farm, the Morrisville dump, and, farther up, Greaves' Dairy.

In 1947, his stepfather had hired Oscar Churchill to build a home for his new family in the middle of Volney Farr's hayfield and then signed on as a carpenter to lower costs. Mr. Churchill's wife, Madge, taught seventh grade. Bill could not imagine being in seventh grade, and like other first-graders, lived in fear of kids in the higher grades.

His first-grade teacher, Mrs Fancher, was an avuncular person, if one can say that about a woman. The purplish wen growing on her lower left cheek was often the focus of her students' attention as she spoke to them. She was strict, but exuded a warm sympathy for her students' trials with their first efforts at learning. A generous bosom framed in a discreet décolletage and spindly legs with high heels made it often seem as if she might tip over. She was too heavy to genuflect next to the small desks in her classroom so she would lean over in order to assist a first-grader. Her generous décolletage would then dominate the first grader's entire view. His stepfather had had her as a teacher and confided in him that when they were little, it was referred to as a *balcon* in the French they spoke among themselves, "like the balcony in the Bijou downtown," he confided with a smile.

The tall, small-paned windows in the corner classroom flooded the square room with light. Silver-painted cast-iron radiators, noisy in winter, clung to the dark maple wainscot walls below the windows. The many applications of shellac on the worn maple floors were evident only in untraveled nooks and crannies and where the black cast-iron desk mounts were screwed to the floor, the aisles between desks subject to the endless scuff of small leather shoes and playground grit.

Five times daily the class marched single file to morning basement, morning recess, lunch recess, afternoon basement and final recess. Going to the bathroom was called "going to the basement" and was highly regimented. The school had no kitchen facilities so the basement was dedicated to boys' and girls' toilet facilities, janitorial services, and a massive asbestos-clad coal furnace visible only when the janitor's door was ajar. The entire basement was painted pale yellow. Students were admonished to hold the stair railings as they descended the flight of stairs and, on reaching the lowest level, girls diverted to the right and boys to the left.

Five minutes were allotted to basement duty and a vigorous hand washing with lye soap. Students then reassembled at the foot of the stairs for the single-file ascent back to class. Mrs. Fancher brooked no horseplay. She listened discreetly from outside the labyrinthine entrance to the boys' basement for the sounds of running water indicating proper ablutions. She oversaw this directly on the girls' side.

A plumbing innovation had been installed at some point to ensure proper toilet flushing in the boys' basement and, no doubt, in the girls' as well. The toilet seats were spring-loaded so that when one sat on them the flushing mechanism was activated. There were two problems, especially for first-graders. The toilets only flushed when sat on, rather than when left which meant they were often full on arrival. Second, only two people in the first-grade class where heavy enough to depress the flushing mechanism. So anyone needing a toilet on the boys' side, had to "do their duty" perched at a twenty degree angle to the floor, clinging to the tilted seat to maintain their balance.

Under the pressure of the five-minute rule, he hastily closed a gnarly metal zipper on his cotton pants and caught what was left of his tiny foreskin in the mechanism. The pain took his breath away and he cried out. Most of the other boys had left for reassembly at the foot of the stairs. He teared up suddenly from fear and pain and could not see. Any effort to move or even touch the zipper was excruciating so he just stood there crying.

The five minutes were up and Mrs. Fancher was tallying her brood. His absence was noted and she called in through the doorway, "Time is up. Boys reassemble." The two remaining boys left, noting Bill's predicament. They must have had trouble finding acceptable words to explain his predicament to Mrs. Fancher as her demands for Bill's exit became more adamant and then threatening. The bathroom segregation of boys and girls extended as well to adults and Mrs. Fancher enlisted Roland the janitor to extract him from the boys' room.

Roland was both kind and simple. He understood the problem immediately. A practical man, he also knew there was only one fix and it was not medical. He told Mrs. Fancher to go ahead up and that he would bring her student up shortly, explaining later. He told Bill to hold his breath and without preamble reopened the zipper quickly. Bill gasped in pain and then sobbed out loud.

Roland led Bill by the hand into his room next to the massive furnace that generated steam heat for the cranky radiators in all twelve classrooms, took a small brown vial of mercurochrome out of his desk drawer, and daubed a bit with a tissue onto Bill's torn glans. He assured him that the pain would subside and he led Bill by his hand back up to the classroom. There was no school nurse in those days. Roland spoke quietly with Mrs. Fancher, whose sudden intake of breath made clear to the class that he had revealed to her the full reason for Bill's tardiness. She said nothing, but gave him a maternal look of understanding and forgiveness.

Later that afternoon, Phyllis Ward wet herself. She often had a hard time "holding her water" as Mrs. Fancher would confide to her nervous mother. She sat in front and across from him and he first noticed the runnel of pale fluid running down her tan brown leg into her white socks. She cradled her head in her folded arms on her desk and sobbed silently. Bill could only imagine her terror.

Mrs. Fancher soon gathered from the snickers of the Forcier twins what had happened and, after roundly admonishing them with the threat of loss of recess privileges, ushered Phyllis into the cloakroom where she offered some gentle admonishment and told her to go to the basement and clean herself up as best she could.

Bill could not imagine coming back into the classroom in such ignominy. After some time had passed and Phyllis had not returned, Mrs. Fancher left the class "on honor" and went to find Phyllis, who was still in the cloakroom where she tried in vain to hide among the small coats next to her hook, crying and afraid to return. Mrs. Fancher comforted her and gradually brought her back to her desk while glaring furiously at the smirking Forcier boys.

The event elicited both fear and empathy in much of the class and deflected attention from his zipper incident in the boys' room. It also fueled the Forcier twins and the small clique of boys who endeavored to attract their attention and camaraderie. They safely withheld their taunts until recess and then made Phyllis's life miserable by broadcasting the event in an effort to curry favor and socialize with kids in higher grades.

When the lunch recess bell rang, boys and girls gathered the books and papers they were working on, stowed them in their lift-top desks, rose together, and filed to the adjacent cloakroom. The cloakroom was long and narrow, with a window at one end and numbered black cast-iron hooks screwed into the dark wainscoting about a yard above the floor to accommodate a six-year-old's height. From there, everyone filed downstairs and out the heavy front door held open by Mrs. Fancher onto the dirt playground with its swings, teeter-totter, and "go-round," all occupied and dominated by bigger kids in higher grades.

First-graders huddled together in defensive clumps in the event that they were approached by older kids. Eventually they began to swap sandwiches wrapped in wax paper and dig small pots with their heels against the building to play marbles with one another as the second-graders did.

At three in the afternoon a loud bell rang throughout the school signaling final recess. Children living within a mile of the school, in the village, or on the outskirts of town, walked home. Those who lived on the countless hill farms farther out rode the yellow buses lined up beside the playground.

On his first day of school, his mother had driven his stepfather to work, keeping the car borrowed from her new mother-in-law in order to pick Bill up. The second day Bill was expected to walk the mile home like other kids. At home, there was no talk of what had happened in the basement, as it did not warrant a written note home by Mrs. Fancher.

Classes were dismissed at five-minute intervals to allow for the orderly loading of buses. For those walking home, there were four crosswalks leaving the school playground, each managed by a sixth-grade patrol. They were vested with extraordinary power. Each wore a brass-buckled white patrol belt that encircled the waist and crossed the chest diagonally. A chrome-plated badge larger than Bill's hand was pinned to the white belt. As Bill stood on the curb waiting for the patrol to signal to him to cross, he watched in astonishment as the patrol walked out into the middle of Elmore Street, spread his arms wide, stopping the flow of traffic in both directions like Moses parting the Red Sea, and signaled to him to cross.

Once across, he ambled down Maple Street alone, as no other first or second-graders lived in that direction. Everything was still green, but fall was making itself felt in the cooler air. Bill tried to imagine what it would be like walking home in the winter and being narrowly confined to snow-bank-lined sidewalks. He stopped to look at play sets, peered discreetly into houses and kept his eyes peeled for others coming or going on the sidewalk The concrete squares that made up the ruptured sidewalk had heaved into odd angles either from frost or the force of elm roots underneath. This meant looking down as much as up in order not to trip. It also meant that the fourth-graders, who could ride their bikes to school, did so in the road instead of on the sidewalks.

During an up-glance he noticed a grownup striding towards him in the far distance and on the same side of the street. The purposeful gait and hunched shoulders indicated an older man. The black dangling purse indicated a woman. A pedestrian encounter meant he would be called upon by his upbringing to greet the person and perhaps even to carry on a polite conversation as his stepfather so often did. It seemed to him as though Emile knew everyone. He himself knew few people beyond the neighbors of his age group and their mothers. He dared not stop, but glanced down and kept walking towards the enigmatic person striding towards him.

Still a block away, he glanced up again to better see the hurrying figure. He thought the person saw him as well, but kept up his gait and the downward glance. Bill didn't know why he thought "he" as the person was wearing a light gray cotton dress with some white lace around the collar, large black women's shoes with a low heel and a nondescript pillbox hat perched precariously on a profusion of gray hair. He quickly glanced back at the pavement determined not to make eye contact as the person approached.

Still a house away, he dared another glance that unnerved him. He was convinced by the approaching figure's stature and stride that it was a man, but everything else indicated an elderly lady. The mass of gray hair was done up carelessly into a bun on which perched the dark brown pillbox hat held in place by bobby pins. The face was stubbled with hair even more extensively than Mrs. Rider's, whose facial hair was common topic among her fourth-graders. His left hand clutched a large black cotton purse with wooden clasp handles. But rather than carrying it high and close as a woman might, the person let it hang loose as if it were a plumber's tool bag.

Bill determined to walk the rest of the way home without looking up other than to ensure his left turn onto Washington Highway, the only direction he needed to follow to reach home.

Curiosity overwhelmed fear, however, and without moving his head he glanced sideways as the figure strode by on his left. The gender ambiguity was very evident in his calves, which bore the curved musculature and hair of a man, but were covered to below the knees in heavy textured nylon stockings rolled into a doughnut below his knobby knees. His gray dress covered the rest.

Bill knew that to be sure, he would have to see the person's chest. In a painful glance up without moving his head, he caught a glimpse of the chest. There were no breasts, nor a pretense of them. The limp darts of the dress underhung a hairy male décolletage decked with a large ivory-colored brooch.

Bill's glance went again to the safety of the sidewalk as he strode past, catching the wake of the man's scent. He wore no perfume, but had a slightly acrid, distinctly male smell edged with the faint scent of camphor or mothballs, the same smell Bill had noticed when he opened his father's valise to pack for his trip to his grandmother's or when he opened the old trunk in the attic.

He made no sound as he loped by, nor did Bill see the expression on his face. Bill imagined that he was angry and perhaps in a hurry to castigate someone for something they' done to him or had not done for him and he began to wonder what that might be.

He let three houses pass between himself and the passerby before looking back over his shoulder to ensure that the man's stride continued to distance them and that he had not changed his mind and turned around. A car passed heading toward town and Bill wondered if the young woman driving would see what he had seen and experience the same confusion.

As he turned left onto Washington Highway below the hospital, he saw in the distance that his mother was waiting for him in the front yard and he ran the last few yards home. Perhaps because she was anxious to hear about his second day at school and there was so much to tell, he didn't tell her about the man dressed like a woman he had just seen, but later that night lying in bed he detailed the encounter to his stepfather, whose smile he could see by the light of his nightlight.

"Sounds like you met Crazy Chase," he chuckled.

Bill did not press him on details. He fleetingly reviewed his experience in the basement and then fell into a deep sleep.

The next day at school was filled with new "learnings" as his grand-mother Elise called them. During recess, Bill won an aggie while playing marbles, which for him had the import that he imagined graduation or becoming a patrol might have.

On the walk home, he scanned the nooks and crannies of Maple Street and its few side streets, but saw no sign of Crazy Chase, though he looked everywhere. His stepfather's jovial tone indicated that he had little to fear and everything to be curious about.

The following Saturday, as the final days of summer waned and the cool nights of autumn began in earnest, townsfolk began preparations for the fall firehouse dance, an annual event that brought the eager and the disapproving together in a social truce. Local ladies busied themselves with the preparation of various casseroles and baked goods.

Pete and Lyle framed up a wood platform in front of the firehouse for the band and the primitive PA system, which included two public address horns borrowed from the steeple of the Puffer Methodists' electronic carillon system, a dented RCA broadcast mike borrowed from Ken Squier at WDEV in Waterbury, and a livid, static-emitting brace of vacuum tubes borrowed from Fred Westphal, the town's monophonic hi-fi enthusiast, shoe salesman, and arch-conservative who lionized the "Africa for Britons" policy of Cecil Rhodes to the few in town with any interest in the waning British Empire.

When Pete and Lyle finished the platform, it was turned over to the womenfolk of the Eastern Star Grange for decorating with bunting and other fall harvest flourishes. The dance raised money for the "pumper fund" and every year brought the town a bit closer to acquiring a refurbished LaFrance pumper truck for sale in Lyme, New Hampshire.

The afternoon of the dance saw Whitey, Pete, Clovis, and Lyle struggling to get the upright piano borrowed from the high school activity room up the steps to the new platform. Champ, later noted for his appearance on the *Ed Sullivan Show* as a member of the U.S. Navy Jazz Band, unpacked and set up his new chrome and mother-of-pearl drum set.

For the dance, the fire trucks were brought out and lined up on the street at the ready in case an inopportune barn fire broke out during the dance. Fall was noted for its spontaneous barn fires as a few farmers would invariably risk putting up wet hay when the weather did not cooperate with first or second cuttings. The hay would lie dormant and airless, heating up slowly to the ignition point, and burn the barn to the ground, endangering the livestock and occasionally the nearby farmhouse.

The emptied firehouse was lined with eight folding tables covered with pressed red-and-white-checked tablecloths also borrowed from the Puffer Methodist church basement. A number of donated, straight-back kitchen chairs brought in from various homes on pickups were set up for the elderly who came to watch and even to dance. The final touch was a tiara of clear light bulbs dangling from old cotton-insulated wire, bare in a few spots but still serviceable, that started at a socket in the firehouse and traced the perimeter of the macadam entrance to the firehouse that would shortly become a dance floor.

As the muted fall light began to fade in mid-afternoon and the air cooled in earnest, preparations for the dance continued. The black and chrome Prussian General inside the firehouse was stoked until its sheet metal glowed a faint red near the base and its heat radiated throughout the building.

The Ladies Firehouse Auxiliary arrived, aided by the Eastern Star and the ladies of the Uplift Club, all bearing baked goods. They vied for position on the tables, moving others' goods to the rear and placing their own out front where they would be admired and consumed. An empty pie tin or cake pan was the prize. Leftovers were an unintended slight and subjected one to gossip. "I knew there was too much salt in Gladys's apple turnovers, look how many are left!"

Marge Brown, the pianist, was also her own tuner. She fussed with her tuning wrench at the metal pegs in the cracked soundboard of the Kimball upright until she was satisfied that the tuning would complement her playing. Champ also had a drum key and tuned his drum set, alternately sticking the drum head and tightening or loosening the chrome pegs around the perimeter of the drums until he liked the sound.

It was pitch dark at 6:30. White ironstone dinner plates were washed, dried and put away throughout Lamoille County, cows were in their stanchions, biddies in their nests, and folks were gussied up and headed to town for the dance. Pickups, farm flatbeds, sedans, and even a tractor pulled up and parked along Elmore Street across from the firehouse. All vehicles were parked facing the firehouse, often to hide the concoction setups in the trunk or back of a vehicle. Drink included homebrew, hard cider, Canadian whiskey smuggled at no risk whatsoever, homemade beer, and "screech," which was made from various distillates. Discretion was required as the opprobrium of the religious ladies might linger and diminish one's prospects for marriage.

The readiness of womenfolk to engage someone of the opposite sex in conversation or dance or worse could usually be determined by their outfits. The flouncy, Western-fringed, full-skirted cowgirl look indicated a willingness to be entertained. The trussed-up, black and white floor-length outfit with flattened bosom and indeterminate waist conveyed a warranted distrust of men in general and an unwavering commitment to chastity and the pulpit. Girls too young to declare themselves wore plain cotton dresses and patent leather shoes and huddled in the corners giggling and pointing at the swains as they arrived.

It was not a school night and kids of all ages were welcome, even on the dance floor, but only the girls danced. The boys, unsure of their steps and confounded by puberty, disdained the dance floor and huddled together talking of the upcoming deer season, fall tractor pulls, or car engines they hoped to rebuild. Girls from French families step-danced side-by-side, often five or six at a time, while the Protestant girls sashayed one another like Western swing dancers, each imagining the other to be a handsome boy.

Bill arrived with his parents, but left immediately to seek the company of their long-time friend Ron Terrill, who owned the local Texaco station. Ron was watching the proceedings with amusement, and he kept up a running commentary for Bill about who was doing what to whom. Having no children of his own, Ron spoke to them as adults, so he was usually surrounded by a coterie of young people.

The piano began to play chords and Champ began to set a rhythm with his bass drum and snare. Across the dance floor, Crazy Chase, still an object of curiosity but no longer of fear to Bill, climbed the platform with a violin case and his purse. He set down the purse, opened the wooden case and took out a fiddle, which he tuned in about four strokes of his horsehair bow. He launched into a town favorite, "La Bastringue." The piano followed suit with pounding chords and Champ sought, rather than set, the rhythm taken by Crazy Chase. The dance floor filled within a minute and the dance was under way. Ron smiled and tapped his foot. He was not a dancer and seemed indifferent to female intimacy, although he had many women friends including Bill's mother.

Without looking down at him, Ron said, "Your dad tells me you met Crazy Chase."

Bill nodded. Ron asked him what he thought.

"Dunno," Bill replied. "Is he a man or a woman?"

"He is a man who dresses like a woman," Ron answered.

"Why?" Bill puzzled.

"Oh, I don't know, I suppose he just wants to. What do you think of that?"

"Dunno," Bill answered again.

"Hard to say," Ron said, still looking straight ahead, "One never knows about these things, but he has dressed that way ever since he came to town twenty years ago."

"Don't people tease and make fun of him?" Bill asked.

"The boys do sometimes, but a few whacks with his purse usually ends it," noted Ron, looking down and smiling at him.

The music ended, but the floor did not clear. The next tune was also a Canadian reel called "Le Reel du Pendu." His uncle Mendoza Couture undertook to impart to him and his nieces and nephews who spoke no French, bits of Québécois language and culture. He once explained to him at a family outing that the song was called the reel of the hanged man because the music evoked a vision of the twitching feet of a man just dropped from a gallows. Years later, he heard the true legend from Louis Beaudoin, one of the great Québécois *violoneux*. A criminal, sentenced to be hanged, asked for a violin and learned to play so well while in his cell that when he played his reel on the scaffold, the hangman and the crowd were so entranced he was spared the noose.

Bill left Ron's side and went to find his stepfather, who also was not a dancer but enjoyed the spirits and social aspects.

That evening Crazy Chase became a conductor, his bow a baton that brought the town to its feet. His fiddle kept them all moving with reels, jigs, hornpipes, two-steps, and waltzes. When he stopped, they stopped and looked anxiously around for him to start up again. His pillbox hat, faded cotton dress, and heavy rolled-up stockings no longer seemed out of place but curiously his own.

Jack, the dark-suited mortgage forecloser and Ned Fournier, the failing Hyde Park farmer, still smelling of fresh manure and falling further and further behind in his payments; Ray, the sad Rexall drugstore owner standing next to his daughter who shoplifted his cosmetics; Dora, the sixteen-year-old mother and her shy uncle and unwanted lover Alfred; Corinne, with no visible means of support other than the coterie of Brilliantined men orbiting her; Reverend Pease, the sober Methodist deacon and his wife who hid cooking sherry bottles in the parsonage—all danced to his music, noticing nothing except one another until the music ended.

Jack Daulton's New Mailbox
A Local Colloquy

I. Saturday morning on Flats Road

"Here's one that works."

"Looks like a mail-order job."

"Yes, why?"

"Graves don't sell that kind."

"What's wrong with it?"

"There's two kinds'a shovels. One has the boot lip curved back. Ya can't dig a hole with that kind, 'cause the lip keeps catchin' in the hardpan and hangin' up. Then there's this kind where the back of the shovel is smooth 'cause the boot lip curves to the front and don't hang the whole thing up. Use issun. It'll be a whole lot easier. Lean it on the tractor when ya's done."

"Thanks, my name's Daulton. I don't believe we've met. You live in the. . . er. . . cellar hole?"

"Ya mean the ranch-to-be."

"Yes."

"We bought this house in August. I moved up to teach at Johnson. My wife Martha is a food writer."

"What she write 'bout?"

"Oh, you know, cheese and bread-making, gardening and the like. What's your name?"

"Duke."

"Duke?"

"Duke. Jean and I live's up 'ere in the new house, still unner 'struction. Sometimes I works on the roads crew and sells wood."

"Well, my name's Jack Daulton and my wife is . . .well, you know, Martha."

"Please ta meet cha. Jes leave the shovel by the tractor. New mailbox?"

"Yes, we got a note from Elda Batty at the Post Office telling us to get a larger box because my wife gets a lot of packages and bulk mail so I got this one here. The old post was rotted out so I bought the whole set."

"Good luck. They loikes the shiny ones."

"I don't understand."

"Ya will."

II. Tuesday morning . . .a knock on Jean's door

"Hey, neighbor. Whass-up?" said Duke, holding a mug of coffee and squinting into morning sun.

"My new mailbox is smashed. You know anything about it?"

"Well, yes and no."

"What do you mean?"

"No, I din't do it and yes, I see'd it iss morning."

"Who would do such a thing? Yours isn't smashed."

"Mine ain't shiny."

"I don't understand."

"It's nothin' personal. They loikes the shiny ones. Kin'a like a bass eyein' a shiny new lure. They git a six-pack or two in 'em and they can't resist a stroike."

"I still don't get it. Who's they?"

"The boys."

"What boys?"

"Just the boys."

"You're telling me that boys drive around and bash in shiny mailboxes?"

"Not only shiny ones. Sometimes they git 'em all in a noight. They ain't picky. Them shiners stands out. Don' take it personal."

"Personal or not, I've got to spend eight bucks and another two hours to replace the mailbox."

"Shovel's inna shed, but I'd buy jess the box iss time. Yer post is all right."

"It was a set."

"Don' buy a set. Buy a box at Graves', a black one iss time, harder to see at noight. If it can wait 'til Sunday, I'll helps ya moun' it on th'old post."

"That'd be great. Thanks, Duke."

III. Sunday morning on the dirt road

"What ta hell is 'at?"

"Martha's parents sent it to us from Connecticut, a housewarming present. Handsome, isn't it? We thought it would go nicely here. It's the right size and the copper will dull down to a nice verdigris finish in a year or so. It will be even more beautiful. It's not something we would buy for ourselves, but they've always been very generous people. Between you and me, they can afford to be. Don't tell Martha I said that. Think we will have any problem mounting it on the post? Looks like the same size."

"I don' know what ta hell verty grease is, but I warrant cha iss copper shiner woon't have time to recover from the screw tightenin'. Bucky sees 'at—I mean the boys—they'd prob'ly get 'emselves one 'em new 'lum'num bats and some hightone brew jess fer th'ccasion. I woon't mount iss on the road if I was yer'in. Put it in your livin' room, your g'rarge, anywhere, but, as yer neighbor, I can't let'cha mount 'at thing on a town road. Cost too much."

"You mean to tell me that I can't mount this copper mailbox, a gift from my own wife's parents, without fear of it being bashed like the green one here?"

"You can. I woon't feel roight helpin' ya."

"Why?"

"Cause dump day ain't 'til Sat'day and the bashed copper'd look like hell 'tween now and then."

"You're telling me that this mailbox would be smashed before this Thursday?"

"I'll bet'cha Jean's biggest zucchini it woon't make it ta milkin' time tomorra."

"How would they even know we put it up if someone didn't tell them?"

"Word a' this 'ere trinket'd spread loike a forest fire. He'd know."

"Who is he?" "They'd know."

"You know who does this, don't you?"

"S' not alwa's the same guy. 'Pends whose car's runnin' and what brew's on sale."

"We really can't mount this mailbox then?" "Can, but I woon't feel roight helpin' ya." "What should I do?"

"Got a scissor jack in your Swedemobile?"

"I've never used it. I'll check the manual."

"Ferget 'e manual. I'll take a look-see. Open up 'e trunk."

"Why are you putting my car jack in the mailbox?"

"Hold yer horses. Now crank iss li'l crank. The jack'll push the dent out. OK, stop. No, not all 'e way. Have to leave it some dented or they gets ornery and bash it in agin. Iss good to leave some damage. See mine over 'ere, bashed but funct'nal. S'like he has to leave his mark on 'em."

"This is outrageous.'"

"Yep, but iss only a mailbox."

"When you've lived in the city and just have a wall of aluminum holes, a mailbox at the end of a road means something."

"Keeps yer mail from gettin' soggy."

"I don't get it. I mean this bashing thing. Don't they make an indestructible mailbox?"

"Spencer, the feller what built cher house tried one after 'bout five bash jobs. Poor guy was fixated on havin' a perfect mailbox as much as Bucky is with bashin' 'em."

"So you really do know who is doing this."

"Well, ever'body does 'ceptin' Off'cer Boright."

"Why don't they do anything, if we all know who's doing it?"

"Well, ya has ta ketch 'em in th'act and that makes fer stayin' up way past Boright's bedtime, ya know."

"This is nuts."

"Yep."

_____

IV. Several weeks later in Graves' Hardware

"Hey, Duke."

"Hi, Jack. Where'd'ya end up mountin' the shiner?"

"Once Martha got over not using it as our mailbox, she had me mount it next to the toilet. We keep magazines in it. Looks good there, a bit large, but safe from Bucky."

"Yer verty grease com'on a lot faster in 'ere I 'spect."

"I suppose. Say, that Spencer fellow, the guy that built our house, whatever happened to his mailbox?"

"Oh, he gave up 'n got a P.O. box safe 'n sound insoide 'e post office. No bashin' in 'ere, gob'ment prop'ty, fed'ral 'fense. Though, ya know, 'nough suds 'n Bucky moight try."

"What happened?"

"Well, Jean 'n I thinks Spencer frosted the outhouse, ya know, went a bit nuts. He woon't jes let it go 'n cave inta Bucky. His pride woo'nt let 'm. Firs' he bought one a' them indestructible mailboxes ya see in cat'logs fer 'bout 'e price of a rideon mower. 'At's loike spittin' in Bucky's eye. Chainsaw made short work 'a that."

"Didn't you and Jean hear the chainsaw?"

"Ya hears 'em alla time, nothin' strange."

"Then what?"

"Well, Spencer, bein' an engineerin' toipe, I seen him down 'ere on Sat'day mixin' concrete for his mail bunker—three foot deep footin', re-rod in the base, and quarter-inch plate steel box Fred Green made up special in 'is foundry. Had lag bolts hardened inta the concrete holdin' it all together—unb'lievable. Jean and me peeked out the winder admirin' Spencer's handiwork. Thought, this city slicker might a' beat Bucky fer a bit. Nothin' happened fer sev'ral weeks. Folks began ta wonder if 'n Bucky'd take up 'e challenge."

"Something must 'a happened. It's gone now."

"Somp'n did. I fig'red Bucky'd borrow a backhoe, but, bein' winter n' all, the ground was froze solid. 'Stead, Bucky called up 'is cousin Joe who's a dynamiter workin' freelance. No one know'd 'xactly 'ut happened, only when. Ya could hear it up ta Eden Mills. Spencer's bunker went up in one blast, leavin' jess a crater. I found some steel bits wi' ma mower. Off 'cer Boright asked me a few questions 'bout the 'splosion that I cou'nt hear so I din't answer 'em. He knew better'n t'ask me 'gain. Boright's a cousin on the bad side 'a the fambly. Spencer lef' the hole ta fill with water and rented a mailbox from Elda."

The postmistress winked at him when she took Spencer's first month's box rental, allowing, "Safer this way." Spencer took a job down country that fall.

Twist and Shout

BREAKING AND ENTERING, or "B 'n' E" as Officer Hubbell called it, was one thing, but B 'n' E in the white Methodist church of a small New England town was another, especially if the town was Stowe.

"Technically," Chris said defensively, "it was really just an E." Officer Boright had to agree: there was really no break-in. There was little reason to lock a church if the poor box was emptied nightly. There was nothing worth stealing in most small-town churches, just brass candlesticks, vases, worn hymnals, and pamphlets about the Lord and the church's various committees for dealing with church or spiritual upkeep. The church's only value lay in its simple elegance and its symbolic role in the community as a gathering place for the celebration of religious ritual.

Pastor Albright never locked the minister's entrance to the Stowe church, since it adjoined the rectory and he was usually back and forth enough to keep an eye on his own house as well as the Lord's. He did, however, begin locking it after the break-in. From the pulpit the Sunday following, Pastor Albright described the event as "an offense against God, the good people of Stowe, and the evening's peace. An irreligious incursion," he thundered. Some nodded seriously and others fought back smiles.

Chris, Jim, and Mike were not in the pews that Sunday, nor were they at 3 a.m. the Thursday before. They had entered the church quietly with a flashlight and a 7-inch square envelope just before 2:30 a.m., according to their easily obtained confessions and Officer Boright's handwritten report.

"Gaining entrance" through the unlocked rectory door, they avoided the nave altogether. It "made us feel uncomfortable," Chris later confessed. They went through the basement to the stairs that led up to the steeple and the electronic controls for the carillon. Mike had cased the location that afternoon and knew exactly where to go.

The three had formed a rock-and-roll band in their junior year and performed songs they wrote as well as hits of the prior decade by Carl Perkins,

Alan Freed, Chuck Berry, and Little Richard. There was little point in competing with current hits, they agreed, as these tended to sound better on current recordings. Chris was an "audio-nut," to the extent that his late-teen wallet would allow, and managed the recalcitrant collection of tube amps, lamp cord, and homemade plywood boxes with speakers inside that made up the band's PA system.

Stowe's night-blooming après-ski haunts offered the band a few winter venues, and the three annual Stowe High School dances occasioned additional opportunities for assembling and performing, but summer performances were always free in a large meadow up in Sterling Valley where a keg would be tapped and people would enjoy swimming, beer, and the highland meadow of an abandoned hill farm.

Electronic carillons were an expensive luxury brought about by the advent of hi-fi technology. They didn't replace traditional carillons, as no church community or parish in Vermont could ever afford the luxury of real cast bells mounted in a steeple.

The electronic carillon combined a Webcor 45-RPM record changer, a GE Telechron timer, four Bell Labs mono amplifiers, and four 36-inch Electrovoice PA trumpets aimed at the four compass points from high in the steeple. These components were familiar to Chris, who, as his band's soundman, had grappled with worse.

The technology could go unattended for a seven-day cycle. Seven 45-RPM "singles" containing Protestant hymns played on a real carillon were stacked on the changer Monday morning by the sexton, and the timer did the rest.

At 4:50 p.m., the timer turned on the system to warm up and at 5:00 p.m. sharp, the changer was engaged. A 45-RPM single dropped into position and played "A Mighty Fortress Is Our God" or "Onward, Christian Soldiers" for the spiritual edification of the residents of Stowe as well as those on the outskirts of town north and south on Route 100 and west up the Mountain Road to the ski lodges and base lodges on Mount Mansfield. The carillon's reach was a source of great pride to Pastor Albright and his Methodist flock, who had raised the money to install it. A large anonymous donation, believed to be from a notable in the Mount Mansfield Company, pushed the beleaguered fund drive over the top and secured the installation of the new carillon.

Chris's later confession indicated that the three entered the church about 2:15 a.m. The whole operation took a bit more time than they had expected because of the complexity of setting the tiny teeth on the GE Telechron timer. This electro-mechanical innovation combined the features of an alarm clock and a simple electric switch. To set it, however, one had to remove tiny little trigger fingers that rotated with the time and place them precisely on the diurnal arc where one wanted the switch to turn on. The hours were measured in military time, so vespers was set for 16:50. This flummoxed Chris until Jim helped him with the math and the placement of the little fingers for 04:00.

Carefully they removed the stack of devotional hymns and replaced them with an old, scratchy copy of the Isley Brothers' "Twist and Shout" from Mike's collection. Chris boosted the volume potentiometers on the four Bell amps from their regular setting of four on a scale of ten, to eight. They ran the flashlight beam over the whole and, convinced that they had properly set the timer, walked back to the entrance and across the dewy lawn to Jim's waiting '53 Ford.

From Stowe's postcard downtown, they drove up into Stowe Hollow high above the town to enjoy their prank with the two six-packs of now warm beer acquired on Mike's new ID at the store in Morrisville that sold beer to anyone able to both walk and flash a card with type on it. They drove past the Lang Farm up towards the old dirt track road that led to the high meadow on the hill overlooking town. It was a noted trysting spot for local teens as one could see cars coming from any direction and keep an eye on the village without being seen.

Mike opened three beers. The trio laughed, taking turns telling of their apprehensions during the operation. They speculated about all the things that might have gone wrong, but didn't and how officer Boright would react when he "got the call."

"My mother's gonna know." said Jim in a more serious tone. "She always knows."

"How could she?" said Mike. "There's 120 kids in this town could'a done it."

"She just knows," said Jim ruefully, "but she won't turn me in. . . I don't think."

"What time is it?"

Mike held his watch up to the moonlight and squinted at the Timex dial. "Quarter 'til."

They opened another round of beers and lay back on the grass to enjoy the warm summer night. There was no breeze and all town activity had long since ceased. An owl hooted far away towards the Worcester Range which loomed large in the moonlight behind them. West beyond the town with its white Methodist spire, Mt. Mansfield dominated the horizon. A faint light glittered intermittently from the Octagon at the top.

"Time is it?"

"Should be startin' now." said Chris.

The three sat upright and stared at the white spire. The peace continued.

"We screwed up," said Chris. "It's a quarter after."

"Maybe it's late," said Mike." It was hard to see them little teeth things."

"We must a' missed somethin'" said Jim. "Let's go home, I'm beat."

"Me, too," agreed Mike. "I have to work tomorrow."

"Probably just as well. Boright's still pissed about the bonfire." The three got up at half past the hour and began to walk slowly down the long hill to the Ford, whose blistered chrome glistened in the silvery moonlight.

As they approached the car and Jim was fishing for his keys, a sudden 60-cycle hum pervaded the night air, followed shortly by the very loud scratching sound of a steel needle touching down on the unrecorded opening grooves of a scratchy single. The quiet air crackled with hiss and over-amplified scratches.

"Crap, what did you turn that up to?" yelled Jim. His question was drowned out by the ascending bass and drum rhythm lead-in to the vocal that began, "Shake it up, baby, twist and shout."

"Holy shit! That is loud!" Chris yelled as they ran back to the top of the hill to catch the action and listen.

"C'mon, c'mon, c'mon, baby, twist and shout," roared into the crisp night air above Stowe.

The first verse was almost completed before a light went on in the rectory.

Mike opened the rest of the beers and the three stood in awe at the sheer volume emanating from the spire.

Lights flickered on helter-skelter in town as the steeple launched into the second verse. Mike pointed out excitedly the steady line of lights going on up and down Route 100 toward Morrisville and Waterbury respectively and west up the Mountain Road toward the protruding A-frames, kitschy Tyrolean cottages, and getaway mansions of the wealthy urban immigrants recently settled in Stowe, if only for the winter months.

A 45-RPM single was limited to about two and a half minutes, especially when the song enjoyed the dynamic range of "Twist and Shout." As the final verse roared through the valley and encountered the thunderous echo of an earlier measure bouncing back off Mt. Mansfield, their glee gave way to nervous fear. The fear amplified as the yellowish house lights and roving car headlights became interspersed with blue revolving lights converging on the church. The prank had now gotten the full attention of Officer Boright and "Tonto," as the kids called Deputy Hubell. "Twist and Shout," however, had enjoyed a full play on the Methodist carillon.

Still stunned by the terrestrial coverage of the concert, the three ran for Jim's car. Mike suggested they drive south through the Hollow and approach Stowe from the south. That way they could spend the night at Jim's house without passing through the thicket of cars and indignant town officials gathering downtown.

They parked quietly behind Jim's mother's Plymouth and snuck in through the kitchen door. The kitchen light was on and a strong smell of coffee was present. Alice padded in slowly in a bathrobe and slippers. "I know you did it," was all she said, sitting down at the kitchen table and stirring her coffee with a spoon. "You'd better get some rest before Boright comes for the three of you."

"Mom, what makes you so sure that he'll know it was us?" Jim said plaintively. "Who else would dream this up and who other than you, Chris, could jigger that bell ringer to do this? Think about it. It doesn't take a Sherlock Holmes to solve this case," she said, sipping her coffee.

The boys went down to the basement to some bunks that the family rented out to ski bums in peak season for $3 a night. They were too keyed up to sleep, however.

The knock came at about 7:30. There was little need for any complicated rights protocol. The boys were simply led away after Boright gulped down the coffee Alice poured for him.

"This won't go too hard on them, will it?" Alice inquired.

"Up to Judge Terrill," said Boright without fanfare. "We'll see how this rock 'n' roll stuff plays to his ear. It's the church part that won't go down well."

As often happens in Vermont towns, the town split down the middle on the issue of retribution. The buzz ran the gamut from outrage to chortles. For several weeks, people speculated about appropriate punishments for the prank. Some thought the whole matter harmless, worthy only of community service, while others were ready to haul the stocks out of the Stowe Historical Society.

Appropriately enough, Judge Terrill was somewhere in between, and wisely sensed the need to give a degree of satisfaction to both sides. For breaking and entering and malicious mischief, Chris, Jim, and Mike got three days in jail with credit for time served, and 90 days' worth of yard work for Pastor Albright. Satisfactory completion of this sentence would mean no blight on their record, good news for the offenders since all three aspired either to college or military service, neither of which looked kindly on a criminal record.

The Isley Brothers' "Twist and Shout" became a bestselling single in Stowe and the surrounding towns, as well as a hit on local jukeboxes, where it often drew applause in local watering spots and eateries.

Wyvis's Fence

WHEN WYVIS BUSHWAY bought the McKean place sometime after the War, farms cost less than a used car today. Those who knew Wyvis had no idea where the money came from, but it was gone within a month or two. Some said it was his GI Bill money; others opined that it was an inheritance from a New Hampshire uncle on his mother's side.

The McKean place was an ornery stretch of land, set right on Route 15 just north of Wolcott. In spring, the front meadow near the road was a boggy swale through which no one would drive a team of horses, much less a tractor. The price seemed right as Wyvis and he needed to begin an enterprise to generate income to feed the brood that Peaches began to bear shortly before their wedding in Morrisville at the Puffer Methodist.

Not sure what enterprise suited him, Wyvis threw himself into several. He bought a pig, two heifers, a pair of young Belgians recently retired from logging, a '43 Ford, and a 1936 John Deere H with a cast-iron flywheel bearing the John Deere logo. To start the cranky kerosene engine one had to spin the heavy capstan by hand. The H ran on kerosene, which was cheap, but it had to be started with gas, so there were two fuel tanks beneath the rusty green cowl. There was no rubber on the back axle, just four-foot cast-iron wheels with opposing diagonal ridges for traction in a dry meadow. These became anchors in a wet meadow. The power take-off on the rear had a belt-drive wheel for which Wyvis bought a rusty but sharp 42" steel saw mounted on an oak frame with a large fiber belt to connect it to the tractor. He then walked into Graves' Hardware on Portland Street and unceremoniously bought for cash one of every practical tool he could find. This last purchase depleted his reserves, leaving only enough for four bottles of a homemade liquor known as "screech" and a large fly-specked ham haunch curing in Patch's walk-in cooler.

Peaches was delighted with the last purchases and tucked into them both with glee. Often with child, she had the innate sense to drink only a couple of glasses of screech, but then again, a couple of glasses of screech usually left her snoring on the sofa with ham grease on her chin, which, after the birth of Godfrey, had sprouted a distinctive stubble.

Through good luck and hard work Wyvis' various enterprises grew. He borrowed a neighbor's bull, "freshened the girls," and began a small milking herd. Peaches's taste for ham led to an early demise for the new pig, but the sale of one salt-cured haunch led to the purchase of two piglet sows and a bristly young boar that lived happily in a new sty made from vertically arranged hardwood pallets scrounged from the grain dealer in Hardwick.

Wyvis' career options focused on "fixin' and innervatin'." Barter further propelled his enterprise. Few hill farmers had cash and most were perpetually behind in their credit at the "ag" dealer so they hauled their broken tractors, tedders, side rakes, disc harrows, hay lifts, plowshares, cutter bars, wagons, and flatbed trucks to Wyvis, who had recently mastered gas welding. Having traded a rebuilt manure spreader for a set of tanks and torches that Alphonse Fournier had bought but never mastered, Wyvis could now fix virtually anything, at least for another season.

Since Peaches had demolished his remaining credit in town through her steady grocery and dry goods charges, acquiring factory parts was a problem. He either fashioned them on the spot or extracted them from the various abandoned pieces of farm equipment that increasingly populated the adjacent meadow. Farmers would often bring him two broken pieces of equipment and ask him to fashion from them one working one, leaving the lesser of the two for payment and adding to Wyvis's cache of used parts.

In the '40s, farmers did not have the array of brands and annually changing models from which to choose when they sought new farm equipment. The dealers in Morrisville and Hardwick carried Deere, Ford, or McCormick. Models did not change annually unless there was enough innovation to warrant a new one. Respected models like the Deere H, B, and M or the Ford 8N and 9N were often seen on dealer lots for many years.

By the '50s, Wyvis had a thriving business in which he steadily reinvested what Peaches and the kids didn't consume. His own personal needs did not extend beyond three meals a day and a new blue-striped pair of coveralls when spilled battery acid claimed the old ones.

He had long ago converted the barn into a workshop and parts storage area. The random collection of livestock Peaches coddled into meals inhabited a leanto Wyvis had fashioned off the side of the barn with salvaged utility poles and 4' by 8' sheets of tin roofing. The enlarged sty now comprised a quarter acre and contained a noisy collection of "hams and chops" as Peaches fondly referred to her pigs. The bristle on her own chin and upper lip now rivaled that on her boar, Flanders, a name she had heard on WDEV out of Waterbury and had taken a shine to. When asked, she said he was a "pol'tician."

Of necessity, Wyvis had begun repairing cars as well. "The Bushway Estate" as it was known locally, rife with rusting farm equipment mostly stripped of critical parts, soon became dotted with pickup trucks and cars. Wyvis's ability to make things work a bit longer for a modest price was legend, and an endless stream of customers prevailed on him from all over Lamoille County and adjoining Caledonia and Franklin counties.

Transactions were simple and remarkably consistent. A customer would begin with a story, sometimes humorous to elicit laughter and goodwill, sometimes pitiful to elicit sympathy and a lower price. Wyvis always listened respectfully while he inspected the damage and would then announce a fixed price, factoring in the customer's story and the empathy he felt for him. Customers never challenged the price, although they often offered to barter if they had no money to pay. If their proposal had "equal value," Wyvis would nod and schedule the work.

Unlike tractors, car models changed annually. So Wyvis adapted his business to his customers' needs and became the garage where the less-well-heeled brought their ailing cars or trucks if they could not afford repair or replacement at the dealership, where negotiation was not an option.

In the fields on either side of his farmhouse and barn, cars and trucks soon outnumbered tractors and farm equipment. Wyvis and Peaches' eldest son, Godfrey, whom Peaches had named after her favorite radio host and crooner, Arthur Godfrey, was assigned the job of salvaging and cataloguing expensive parts like starter motors, generators, carburetors, brake pistons, voltage regulators, radiators, thermostats, water pumps, batteries that would still hold a charge, and the like. He was the best in the family at "book learnin'" and so became "parts manager" so Wyvis would not have to interrupt his repairs to go find and extract a needed part.

On the town deed, the Bushway Estate was fifteen acres "more or less" with boundaries determined by a "cedar post fence" that had long since succumbed to perpetual moisture, rotting away to mossy traces here and there along a now indeterminate property line. Wyvis plowed the remains of this man-made boundary under as he needed a bit more space than the deed allowed. The burgeoning array of junk cars, tractors and farm equipment now covered all of the "tillable" land, which meant any space not covered by trees or large rocks, and extended deep into René Quesnel's property next door. René seemed to notice that his estate was shrinking, but his fondness for Wyvis and the considerable debt he'd run up with him made a quibble over boundaries impractical. Besides, the Belgian horses, still alive, had wandered over one day to René's and never came home. René harnessed them up to haul pulp in their dotage and nothing more was said about it. Both neighbors seemed comfortable with the unrecorded land transaction.

Godfrey was further enlisted to condense the random arrangement of parts cars to make room for more. He responded by going to Hyde Park and enlisting in the Army, leaving Wolcott for good. The U.S. Army sent him to Korea and he never returned.

Alice, the youngest Bushway, was named after Ralph Cramden's long-suffering wife on *The Honeymooners*. Peaches first saw her daughter's namesake on her sister Louise's used Admiral TV set acquired from Henry Fogg in Morrisville. Henry kept the early TV models running for folks in Morrisville so those so inclined could squint and watch the one clear channel coming off Mount Mansfield or try to tune in the two "snowy" ones from Plattsburgh and Mount Washington.

The large black humming box with a greenish screen was coveted and often visited by Peaches. She pointed out to Wyvis that it had the added advantage of heating the room in which it sat. Wyvis was unimpressed with the novelty, but soon succumbed to Peaches' wishes.

Alice, now ten, followed firmly in her mother's footsteps, becoming a sturdy and regular consumer of both perishables and dry goods. The twins, still too young to function profitably in the family enterprise, enjoyed playing hide and seek and "doctor" with the neighbor girls in among the vehicle chassis.

Times were changing in Vermont in the late '50s. Locals in Stowe were selling out to skiers from down country at windfall prices, the proceeds of which would not cover three months' property tax today. Hippies were beginning to discover in Vermont what Thoreau had found at Walden Pond, at least until it snowed.

Vermont's citizen Legislature convened each winter in Montpelier. It had been made up almost entirely of farmers, who had less to do in winter, and tradesmen successful enough to leave their businesses for the few months needed to review and pass sparse legislation.

New Vermonters wanting more of an influence in their adopted state began showing up in the Legislature. Debate began to shift from the quotidian issues of agriculture, commerce, and caring for those in need to concerns in which farming, logging, and light manufacturing began to conflict with a new vision of Vermont as an idyllic place to retire amid nineteenth-century scenery, a vision captured gracefully in Ralph Nading Hill's *Vermont Life* magazine.

This impact was not felt as quickly in towns like Morrisville, Wolcott, and Hardwick as it was in the towns to which arrivistes flocked like Stowe, Woodstock, Dorset, and Craftsbury. In Wolcott, Wyvis' sprawling meadow of parts cars was a practical and comforting sight, ensuring the locals' ability to keep cars running well beyond their engineered lifetimes. Eric von Stroheim and Greta Garbo would have occasion to drive past the Bushway Estate in their James Young Rolls Royce touring car on their way to Garbo's friend's hideaway on nearby Caspian Lake, but the distraction of munching a caviar sandwich or soothing the two large Russian wolfhounds traveling with them in the back seat probably caused them to miss the Bushway Estate altogether. Other visitors, however, did not.

As time passed, the values of locals and newcomers came into increasing conflict, a conflict managed ably by Governor Deane Davis, whose mordant sense of humor and considerable diplomatic skills gave birth to Act 250, which durably enshrined values more or less acceptable to both camps. It was, however, an uneasy truce.

There were two pieces of legislation inching their way through the hybrid Legislature that affected the life and livelihood of Wyvis Bushway. One was a proposed law that, in essence, made the driving of unsightly vehicles illegal. The "New Vehicle Inspection Standards" law addressed, among things like brake wear and windshield cracks, the degree of visible body rot a car could have and still be legally roadworthy. The new unit of measure was "a hole the size of a dime." This created considerable hardship for folks financially unable to trade in their car every other model year. A dinner plate would have been a more appropriate standard of measurement.

Car bodies in those days were not galvanized before the finish coat of paint was applied and salt was spread as liberally on icy winter roads as it was on corned beef hash at the local fire department dinners. So sheet metal body work and the troweling-on of Bondo became a burgeoning business as legal application of the "dime standard" came under enforcement.

The other law, however, was considerably more ominous and, unbeknownst to Wyvis, was making remarkable progress through the increasingly arriviste Legislature. In effect, the law applied the *Vermont Life* standard to certain views, specifically views in which junk cars played a foreground role. Debate raged on both sides of the issue, and the bill that emerged was indeed a compromise, but one thought to considerably favor newcomers.

It required merchants and homeowners with more than five junk cars in their yard to erect a six-foot opaque fence around them. To many Vermonters a yard full of "parts cars" was an indicator of good automotive management, not an eyesore. Parts cars, however, were inconsistent with the pastoral photographs in *Vermont Life*, which might show one or two tractors working in a field, a wellkept pickup in a yard, or traditional horse-drawn implements that looked suspiciously as if they had been borrowed from the Shelburne Museum.

Apart from the scenic conflicts, many felt the new law breached the tradition of being left alone on one's own property. Local law enforcement officers puzzled over how they would impose the restriction on their neighbors or friends who often relied on parts cars to keep one running. Wyvis ignored the new law. Although the radio was always on in the shop, he never listened to the words, only to the music. His favorites were by Don Fields and the Pony Boys.

Peaches, however, was alert to the law. She had a habit of accompanying her substantial meals, libations, and snacks with media, either the bakelite Zenith radio blaring WDEV in the kitchen, a recent edition of Morrisville's *News and Citizen*, or the green glowing Emerson TV that stayed on throughout the day and some of the night in the living room across from the sagging, grease-stained couch.

She tried to warn Wyvis of the law and what it would mean to their enterprise.

"How ya gonna fence up a medder of junkers that covers close ta 18 acres?" she said, the question made more plaintive by a gulp of wine, to which Peaches had recently taken a shine. "Even the spruce stockade fencin's 'spensive and acquires a reglar splashin' a' creesote or it'll rot away faster 'n Reba Batty's teeth or Madge Kimbell's new Rambler."

Wyvis ignored the comment and the issue in general, focusing instead on the work at hand, in this case a rusty pale blue '54 Ford station wagon that needed a fan belt, a new gas tank, and a water pump.

The day of reckoning came slowly. The Bushway Estate was a comfortable fixture to those who lived in or passed through Wolcott and locals were hard-pressed to imagine it disappearing behind a six-foot fence.

The legislation, however, became law despite appeals and the sporadic, disorganized protests of locals. Those in contravention of the new law waited, curious to see what form enforcement might take.

The law had been on the books fourteen months when word came from Montpelier that the grace period was over and that town road budgets would be held hostage to local enforcement of the new statute.

"Easy for Montpelier to say," huffed René Dumas, pronounced "Rainy Doomus" by his friends, "they don't live here. Let them come over and wrangle with Wyvis. He might knock some sense into their pointy heads."

"Take it easy," soothed Jerry Kitonis. "Wyvis is one of us. Most likely he'll understand. We could help him build the fence."

"Je m'en doute," responded René, lapsing into his most familiar tongue.

Fred Westphal, the state senator from neighboring Elmore, happened to be visiting the town selectboard meeting that night in Wolcott. He lived on the road between Wolcott and Elmore and often attended meetings in both towns.

"I fought this bullshit law tooth and nail," asserted Fred, "but my horse's ass colleagues rammed it through anyway." Fred was noted for his direct language, both among friends, behind the counter in the basement of Gillen's Department Store in Morrisville where he sold shoes and classical LPs, and in the halls of the capital with his legislative colleagues.

"Yes, but what do we do about it now?" asked Dennis Demars, chair of the selectboard.

"I'll talk with Wyvis. He'll cooperate," volunteered Jerry Kitonis. "Wyvis and I go back to grammar school together."

"You do that," muttered Fred Westphal as he jammed his hat on his head and headed home to Elmore.

The discussion between Jerry and Wyvis meandered all over until Wyvis signaled his need to get back under Grace Tyndall's Dodge. The topic of the fencing in the lot never came up.

The selectboard decided to pay a visit as a whole to Wyvis and broach the dicey issue of the Bushway Estate's place in the scenic panorama of Wolcott. The discussion was friendly. Heads all around nodded in earnest assent, but nothing happened in the ensuing weeks to indicate construction of any kind except that Peaches expanded the sty with more pallets.

Summer was advancing. Gravel road regrading, roadside mowing, culvert replacement, tree limb removal, all the locally financed routine road maintenance was progressing apace. The single-lane bridge, however, to West Craftsbury, scheduled for replacement in spring and the repaving of a long section of Route 15 had not yet begun.

The state intervened. Wyvis was served with a "notice to comply" or face prosecution. Nothing happened. Wyvis was served again with a summons. Nothing happened.

Fred Westphal paid Wyvis a visit, but still nothing happened until several days later when a backhoe pulled up to the Bushways' and began to dig a massive trench around the front-facing property boundary. Folks in Wolcott were relieved that a standoff had been averted and that apparent construction of the fence had indeed begun. Two weeks later a truck-mounted crusher showed up to crush the parts-depleted hulks and haul them off for sale to a steel yard in Barre. This would reduce the perimeter of fencing required and the cost, so those who followed the drama assumed.

Folks in Wolcott awoke Thursday morning to a fully completed sixto eight-foot-high opaque fence around the Bushway Estate. The work had been done during the night. Wednesday evening the portable crusher had still been doing its noisy work and the backhoe was sitting idle, having finished the trench for the fence posts.

Word spread through the countryside of Wyvis' new fence and people drove from surrounding towns to see it. All agreed that it conformed precisely to the letter of the new law.

During the night, Wyvis, the backhoe operator and another unknown helper had used the backhoe and a large tractor with a bucket to arrange the crushed vehicles vertically in the trench, neatly placing them side by side with their flattened chrome radiator grills aimed skyward and their trunks buried in the backfilled trench. The collapsed roofs faced outwards toward the road and the undercarriages and drive trains faced inward towards the house and barn. The fence did not fully surround the now smaller meadow of car bodies, but fully blocked any view from the road as was required by law. Morning found Wyvis in his shop tearing apart a Massey-Ferguson whose hydraulics had failed.

A burgeoning number of cars were parked and double-parked outside the new fence, snaking several hundred feet to the north and south along Route 15, on which two lanes of traffic slowed to a crawl as passengers and drivers alike rubbernecked the glistening oddity. The bottleneck would eventually require traffic control, of which there was none in Wolcott.

Word of Wyvis's fence spread well beyond Lamoille County. City folks, journalists, picture snappers, and the curious came from miles around to see how Wyvis had conformed to the letter of the newcomers' law, while maintaining the Vermont tradition of practical utility and function.

Jack Daulton's New Camp

PETE LOVED TO FISH. His preferences were for bait casting and dynamite, although he had tried various schemes involving small makeshift dams on brooks with nets in spillways to catch brookies and browns. The topic Thursday morning in Hardwick, however, was his periodic attempts at trolling. Pete only trolled when he had been drinking heavily. He never trolled in his hometown, perhaps because at the time Morrisville was a dry town and Hardwick wasn't. In fact, no one could remember Pete trolling anywhere except in Mer-Lu's restaurant, noted for the bottles without labels on the bar and the lack of a printed menu.

As Lou—the "Lu" in "Mer-Lu's"—told it, Pete had been drinking alone since mid-afternoon. The bar filled up around 6:30, becoming unusually rowdy for a Wednesday night. All the booths were filled with customers and there were only two open seats at the bar. A crew of loggers stood around the juke box sipping beer from glass pitchers each held in his gnarled hands. The juke box alternated between Patsy Cline and Hank Williams most of the evening, with a repetitive favorite being Hank Williams' Cajun classic "Jambalaya."

Pete was sitting in a booth by himself nursing a small Mason jar of hooch that he brought with him. He couldn't imagine paying for liquor when he made so much himself, so he usually ordered one drink from the bar and replenished it from his own stock. In the course of the evening, friends would drop into the bench across from him for a visit but sensing "a mood comin' on" would eventually leave in search of better weather.

"Jambalie, crawfish pie, filé gumbo. . ." infiltrated the loud conversations around the bar. Having gotten an urgent call from Lou that the place was "hoppin'" and she needed help, Mercedes came in about 8:30. Lou had set a plate full of bologna sandwiches and jars of mustard and mayonnaise on the bar to dissuade hungry patrons from ordering anything from the kitchen. The mound of drying and curling sandwiches made clear to all that the kitchen was closed.

According to Lou's telling, Pete started trolling around 9:15 and left a few minutes later with Rena Fournier, the cook at one of the nearby logging camps in Worcester. Pete fired back a shot glass, emerged from the cramped booth and went into an empty corner where he proceeded to unbutton the fly on his green and black Johnson Woolen Mill pants and remove what Lou later referred to as his "trouser trout." Then with a broad grin, he slowly tiptoed backwards from booth to booth eliciting hoots of laughter and salacious remarks. "Cute minnow, but I ain't boitin'," muttered Betty Aseltine, looking up from her pitcher half full of beer with a shot glass lying in the bottom. The men at the table roared with laughter as Pete proceeded slowly backwards to the next booth where a huge mound of a woman named Tiny Leriche lifted her greasy glasses up on her forehead, stared for a minute and said simply, "Dace." Relieved at the rejection, Pete continued stepping backwards slowly and deliberately. At this point the place was packed and, according to Mercedes, she saw Pete and Rena leave a few minutes later.

By Saturday, the gossip had died down and Pete was drop-fishing alone at his camp with a coffee can full of nightcrawlers. His rowboat floated just off the reedy shore on Little Hosmer Pond in Craftsbury. Occasionally, he would pull in a "punkinseed" or perch, but the smallmouth bass he sought were simply not biting, and he drifted into a hangover nap.

The sound of a large truck pulling up on the nearby shore interrupted his reverie. Pete opened an eye warily, his sight adjusting slowly to the bright sunshine. Not fifty yards from his house, the parked truck was unloading framing lumber into a clearing near the shore. Little Hosmer Pond was not a magnet for summer homes. There were deer camps in and around the hills surrounding the shallow pond and a dozen primitive fishing camps dotting the two and a half miles of shoreline. The pond was too shallow and reedy for motor boats. It supported a healthy population of wood ducks, mallards, rock bass, perch, a few pickerel, an occasional heron, and vast expanses of cattails. A robust population of snapping turtles, water snakes, leeches, mosquitoes, and a silty bottom discouraged normal camp recreation.

Pete had bought his lot from Wyvis Bushway for $600. Wyvis inherited the land from his father, who had farmed nearby but saw no reason to live near a "swamp." The deed described the parcel as "60 acres more or less" clearly marked by ax blazes on perimeter trees that Pete had long since cleared for firewood. There were no surviving markers of the original property lines so Pete simply claimed what he saw or needed as his own.

The growing pile of lumber not more than 80 feet from his camp alarmed him enough to reel in his empty hook, drop the oars into their oarlocks, and make for shore.

He pulled the flat-bottom boat up into the small area cleared of reeds, set the oars in the bottom of the boat, and made straight for the truck. The truck driver stopped unloading long enough to look up.

"Ta hell's iss?" inquired Pete.

"Dunno, jess 'liverin' the lummer," responded the driver, resuming his work.

"Who fer?

"Lummer yard."

"Ya, but who bought it?"

"Feller named Daulton on the invoice."

"Flatlander eedjit, wassa he doin' wi' dis lummer?"

"Dunno, buildin' I 'spect."

"Buildin' what?" "Dunno."

"Dunno much, do ya?"

"No, but I ain' askin'."

Pete spun on his heels and went back to his camp. He rooted around in the cabinet over his tool bench and found the deed and the yellowed plat map. Nothing on the map looked anything like the land on which he had been summering for thirteen years. Early Monday morning, he was in the Craftsbury town clerk's office asking Mabel who bought the adjacent land and if there was a map. Mabel confirmed that the property had been bought by a Jack Daulton and that he had allowed that he was going to build an A-frame camp, but was unwilling to pay to have the co-op run electrical lines to it.

"Ya mean like 'em tings in Stowe, 'em peaky roof jobs?" asked Pete.

"An A-frame is all it says on the sheet," answered Mabel.

Pete stared at the map, but could make little sense of its lines and contours.

At work the next day, he used the Carbide phone to try and call Daulton directly and ask him what he was up to, building on land he didn't own. There was no answer. Polly Limoges, the local operator, told Pete the next day that Daulton was in New Jersey selling his elderly mother's house as she had just moved into a small house next to his and that he wouldn't be back for three or four weeks, according to what he had told her.

Pete watched the A-frame take shape on what he thought of as his property, although he couldn't be sure. In either case, it was too close for comfort. The 12' by 18' camp sat on six cinderblock pylons. The framing and sheathing were done in three days. The shingles went on the fourth day and the interior was left bare with no electricity and plumbing.

Whitey showed up the last day the carpenters were there and installed a metal chimney and enough stove pipe inside to connect to the small woodstove. The Aframe was completed within two weeks. Pete looked with disgust at the structure. He went inside and looked around. There was only one usable space in the middle. The areas near the roof-walls were useless, since no one could stand up there. He went back outdoors and looked back at his camp less than a stone's throw away. He had no interest in having a neighbor this close. Twice he went back to the town clerk's to study the map Mabel unrolled for him, but he could not connect the map's topographic markings with the features on his property.

The following Saturday, Pete set off early in his pickup for Fred Greene's foundry, where he borrowed a 36-foot log chain and two eight-foot iron pry bars. From there, he drove north to Jeeter and Lou's to enlist Jeeter's help. Jeeter was out of favor with Lou since neither of his vehicles was running, so he greeted Pete's invitation to help eagerly, knowing it would come with an offer of screech.

Back at the camp, Pete and Jeeter reconnoitered farther down the shore and found a clearing about 100 yards north of the A-frame through a low stand of prickly ash and alders. The clearing was well out of sight of his camp, a point they verified from both locations.

Pete had a pile of round cedar logs he had harvested on Cletus Dempster's land farther south along the shoreline. Cletus hadn't walked on his property since the day he bought it and would never miss the young cedars, or find the large pile of slash left in his woods. Pete planned to use the logs for high fencing to keep deer out of his garden.

Pete and Jeeter took a deep quaff of screech from a Mason jar and began work. The two men used the pry bars to boost the A-frame sill on one side up off the cinder blocks so they could maneuver the two heaviest cedar logs underneath to further pry the structure up on one side. This enabled them to knock out the cinder blocks on the other side and have the structure slide down three four-inch greased maple planks onto eight cedar logs laid out in parallel. Twice the A-frame came close to tipping over, but finally slid down, slightly askew, onto the evenly spaced logs.

Pete fired up his "N" tractor and fastened two log chains between the structure's sills and the drag bar on the rear of the tractor. He edged the tractor forward in low gear while Jeeter scrambled to grab logs from behind the structure and place them in front so that the whole might ride along on the logs underneath. Pete managed to maintain a steady two miles an hour in first gear and Jeeter, occasionally refueling from the jar of screech, kept up, moving logs from back to front. When the tractor entered the stand of prickly ash, Jeeter, now numb from drink, got quite badly cut up by the endless thorns that bounced back into place after being flattened by the slow-moving structure.

By 11:00 that night, using two come-a-longs, two log chains, and Pete's pickup, the men had the A-frame up on its pylons. Pete surveyed their work and tidied up the site with a garden rake. Jeeter was seated near some cattails singing a *Sons of the Pioneers* song at the top of his lungs. Realizing Jeeter's condition, Pete drove the tractor back to camp and then came back to get Jeeter, who seemed to be trying to yodel. He drove Jeeter back to Eden, arriving long after midnight. Lou was sleeping soundly on the sofa next to an empty box of Cocoa Puffs.

Several weeks later, Pete saw smoke coming from down the lake and walked over to see what was up. Jack Daulton was sitting there on the front of the stoop. Smoke was pouring out of his new chimney.

"Too cold fer ya?" asked Pete. "Noon sun, it'll hit 80 degrees. Dat still be cold in Jersey, eh?"

"No, I was trying out the new woodstove I got from Whitey," answered Jack.

"You got it from Whitey, it ain' new, iss stolen," allowed Pete.

"Someone else said that, too. Does he really steal all those stoves?"

"He don' think so," answered Pete. "When did you build your camp?"

"I had it built while I was in Jersey selling Ma's house. You like it? It's a new A-frame model. Only cost me $1,200 bucks. Neat, huh?"

"I like it," said Pete. "It looks good here."

"Only one problem," continued Jack, "It's not level, It seems to slope quite a bit towards the lake."

"Makes it a lot easier ta clean," observed Pete, leaving abruptly.

That evening saw him at Mer-Lu's with Rena in tow. Mercedes hovered over their booth to ask how the fishing was. Pete nodded. Rena ordered a soda for Pete to doctor.

"Hear you have a new neighbor," continued Mercedes.

"Not anymore," answered Pete, pouring hooch from his jar into Rena's soda pop.

Jeeter Goes to New York

JEETER WENT TO New York once and, whenever his friend Whitey teased him in front of "the boys" about never having been out of Lamoille County, he could stand tall and proclaim, "I been to New York once," letting the ambiguous allusion to New York City stand unless called to further account by Whitey.

"Oh, yeah, where in New York?"

To which Jeeter, curling up his lip, would respond "Upstate," hoping to put an end to interrogations assailing his urbanity.

"What town?" Whitey would persist, trying to humiliate his friend.

Jeeter would be reduced to confessing, "I dunno, a small town on t'other side of the lake."

Whitey would then lead a chorus of hearty laughs at Jeeter's expense.

Whitey visited New York City each year to replenish his supply of "scoot pictures" as he called them. Since the King Reid Shows stopped touring the county seats of Vermont, the live girlie shows that filled the largest tent had disappeared as well, leaving him only with his modest collection of *National Geographic* magazines pilfered from the Hyde Park Library showing unclad ladies from the Masai and Pygmy tribes in Africa and a few indigenous ladies from Polynesia. They were about it for scoot in the Northeast Kingdom after King Reid rerouted its shows to larger venues in the Northeast. Gypsies also made the rounds in Vermont in those days and could sometimes be counted on for scoot photos but, like many Vermonters, Whitey didn't like "tradin' with eye-tinerants."

Jeeter envied Whitey's sophistication in these matters. He went to the big city, drank store-bought liquor, and knew the ways of the world. Jeeter himself had never even seen a scoot show, having been dragged unceremoniously by his wife Lou out of the tent by the scruff of his shirt, and that after he'd bought and paid for his ticket. Having heard from Whitey and his friends about the enticing and almost unbelievable things that went on inside the scoot tent, Jeeter had always tried to find a way in, but Lou kept a close eye on him when "carnie" was in town and never let him out of her sight.

He would shoot distractedly at ducks, trying to win a stuffed animal for Lou, but the sensual images painted on the scoot tent kept catching his eye, and he would as likely shoot a teddy bear or the swarthy proprietor as the bobbing target ducks floating along a rusty section of roofing gutter in a forced stream of fetid water.

Jeeter's one trip out of state coincided with his ardent determination to take up ice fishing. He could never determine from his buddies who annually towed their homemade shanties on skids out into Missisquoi Bay whether the fun was in the shanty construction, the whisky consumed therein, the flashy tip-ups and tackle, or the fish caught and pan-fried with butter and washed down with a case of Labatt Cinquante at home. He just knew ice fishing was for him.

Late in January, Jeeter got an ultimatum from Lou with regard to their rooster that was hell-bent on moving into the house. Quite capable of flying short distances, the rooster was not content to hang out, service and discipline his hens, but sought a better life by the fire inside Jeeter and Lou's house, where the unswept floor, especially under the table, offered a salubrious array of meal fallout. Besides, a red fox had scratched a route into the henhouse and had been methodically reducing the size of his harem. The rooster had no intent of sharing this dark fate.

Like Lou, the rooster was feisty and did not cotton easily to strangers. Unlike Lou, however, it would attack ferociously if confronted or occasioned upon, using its spurs and raising its lurid hackle feathers. It had drawn blood from several befuddled dogs that had wandered into its path, as well as from Lou's aunt Hilda. Lou was terrified of the bird. She fled the house if she was between the rooster and the door or locked herself in the bedroom if the rooster blocked the front door. Lou would shout until Jeeter came running with a long-handled fishing net and gunny sack to remove it.

In the latest confrontation, Lou had walked into the kitchen and found the rooster on the kitchen counter thrashing a piece of cooked bacon from side to side in an effort to reduce it to edible crumbles. She was terrified and cautiously edged her way around the periphery of the kitchen to the door. The rooster eyed her suspiciously, dropped the bacon, and flew at her. Lou yelled and bolted for the door with the rooster on her back pecking furiously at her flannel shirt. She batted at it over her shoulder with the broom until it relented and flew back to the counter to finish the bacon strip. Lou slammed the door and launched a volley of curses at the rooster while simultaneously bleating for Jeeter who, rightly sensing her urgency, promptly came running from the nearby woods with a still idling chainsaw.

Lou made a hysterical and enraged case for the immediate execution of the rooster, to which Jeeter acquiesced reluctantly. The alternative was the possible loss of the only person in his life who knew how to combine Minute Rice, frozen broccoli florets, and Cheez Whiz into his favorite meal. Still trembling, Lou left for town, telling Jeeter to call her at Hilda's when the job was done.

Jeeter fetched his capture tools and went cautiously inside to find the rooster standing tall on the back of his sagging Barcalounger with a dangle of bacon in its beak and a fresh white turd on the antimacassar. In a hectic chase that knocked over the wicker étagère with Lou's treasured collection of ceramic salt and pepper shakers in the shapes of animals, cute children, and loving married couples, he managed to net the enraged rooster and get it into the gunnysack flapping furiously and crowing demonically.

He marched outside onto the lawn, took a round-head shovel and dispatched the rooster unceremoniously inside the gunny sack. He emptied the gunnysack out of sight over a hillock just outside the kitchen sink window.

Disappointed at losing his favorite cockerel, Jeeter determined to find a new one that was less combative, and to follow his friend Dudley's instructions to pull out its few flight feathers each spring.

Although Jeeter harbored deep fears about ice and what lay beneath it, he turned his attention to ice fishing. But his modest cordwood receipts did not afford him the option of acquiring building materials to construct the type of shanty his companions had. Some looked sturdy and plain; others looked like miniature Dutch cottages with Metalbestos chimneys. Jeeter also knew that the scaling leaf springs in his '48 Chevy pickup's failing suspension would not carry the weight of a full-fledged shanty. Also the motor, like Lou, suffered from below-freezing temperatures especially in a stiff wind. This meant making the shanty of lighter materials. He began by fabricating a two-runner skid out of two abandoned pallets. The former owner of the pallets didn't know he had abandoned the pallets, but Jeeter assured himself of that fact, noting their weathered look.

The ice fishing shanty took the shape of a lath frame over which Jeeter stapled the dried out remains of a neighbor's new refrigerator box. Its total cost was the sum of one box of insulation staples and two rolls of duct tape. The scratched Plexiglass windows were salvaged from the Wolcott dump, along with the bent iron pipes serving as runners on which the shanty could easily be hauled across the ice. Of necessity, Jeeter denied himself the small kerosene burner that warmed the more sophisticated shanties of his friends, instead relying on a bottle of screech from his pal Whitey.

His arrival in Pilcher's cove near where the Lamoille River empties into Lake Champlain was met with cheerful greetings from his friends, who refrained from noting the parlous state of the cardboard shanty perched in the back of his truck.

Whitey, of course, showed no such restraint. He noted the large Frigidaire logo on the shanty and entertained his colleagues by asking, "Not cold enough for ya, Jeeter, or is it for all the fish y'er gonna catch?" Jeeter muttered to himself while Hubie Grimes helped him lift the shanty to the ground.

As he stood there on the ice with his new shanty, his fears returned. As a boy he had lived for a time with his Uncle Buttrick in a house on Ticklenaked Pond in Glover and, at night in the spring, he would lie in bed and listen to the eight-inch-thick ice on the pond moaning and whistling eerily as it cracked and the layer of air between the water and the ice was forced out through tiny fissures.

His Uncle Buttrick's former neighbor Purvis Shanley, demented from drink, had long since lost his home and moved in with Jeeter's uncle, promising to help him split the wood he cut for a living in the winter and sold for firewood to the cityfolk on Caspian Lake in the spring. Purvis, however, quickly settled into the stained upholstery and resumed his drinking rather than being any sort of help. Uncle Buttrick didn't have the heart to abandon him to the Poor Farm in Hardwick.

Purvis told young Jeeter one night that the moaning sound of the ice was in fact a *wendigo*, which to Purvis in his macerated condition had somehow morphed from a subject of Native American lore into a twisted vision of his own violent mother who, he warned, swallowed men whole who taunted or sassed her. Young Jeeter absorbed just enough of this slurred tale to steer clear of ice and angry women. He certainly was not going to drive his one functioning vehicle onto it.

With some frayed manila rope tied to the front of the bent pipe runners, Jeeter nervously ventured onto the bay on foot, pulling his featherweight shanty. His friends' shanties had been in place for some time, forming a cozy community since Whitey had drilled a hole ten inches deep on New Year's Day and declared the lake safe for vehicles and shanties. Jeeter positioned his shanty on the outer edge of the small cluster of shanties figuring erroneously that the ice would be stronger in the middle of the lake.

He waved to his pals, opened the cardboard door with its duct tape hinges, went inside, and tried to decipher the array of paraphernalia that Ben Slocum had lent him to get started. He quickly drilled a hole through the ice with a borrowed augur, spent a few minutes fussing with the complicated tip-ups, then set them aside to fish the way he had on brilliant summer mornings on the pond in Glover.

He rolled a slice of Bouyea's bread and some lard into several small dough balls, placed one on a hook and lowered it through the ice, simply holding the varnished cotton line with his hands and waiting for a gentle tug.

There were nibbles that often necessitated rebaiting his hook, but Jeeter waited patiently for the big one, signaling that a fish had taken his hook. He rubbed his hands together and patted his arms to try to counteract the cold seeping in through the slats in his pallet floor. Envying the shanties from which pale white smoke billowed, he uncorked his bottle of homemade screech and took a generous nip to warm his chilling body. The wind whistled in above the runners and even the flannel shirt, long johns, coveralls and Lou's XXL Johnston Woolen Mill jacket couldn't keep out the icy cold that crept into his shanty from below and began to chill his thin frame. He noticed ruefully that the wind had picked up considerably during the late morning.

Jeeter's nose began to run steadily and freeze on his chapped lips. The cuffs of Lou's red-and-black-checked wool jacket were now varnished with his efforts to stem this flow.

Finally, there was a solid tug and Jeeter hauled in the first of a steady run of 6-inch smelt hitting his doughballs. His uncle's ash creel began to fill with shiny smelt and Jeeter celebrated his success as an ice fisherman with another long pull of screech. The perception of warmth coursed through his body and his pride bloomed. He'd show Whitey when he opened the creel. There'd be enough smelt for him and four others for supper.

Excavating a nostril with his right index finger, he pulled hard again on the screech with his free hand. The wind was picking up again. He set down his line for a second and peered out his cardboard door to see how his neighbors were faring. The wisps of white smoke were horizontal in the stiff wind and it was hard to wrestle the light door shut again, but everyone seemed to be enjoying the same run of smelt as no one had emerged onto the ice as they so often did when the fish were not biting.

Nervous about its eventual depletion, Jeeter began to nurse his unlabelled bottle more gently. Suddenly, a hard gust of afternoon wind lifted one runner of his shanty a foot off the ice and set it back down gently. Jeeter moved more to the center of the front pallet to better balance his weight on the floor and anchor his shelter against the wind.

The smelt began hitting hard again. Jeeter could barely keep up with the baiting, harvesting and rebaiting as the creel filled to overflowing, and he began stuffing the small shiners into the pockets of Lou's coat.

This run of smelt was punctuated by a low moaning sound that raised in Jeeter the unpleasant specter of Purvis' dreaded mother. It was short-lived, however, as the sound of the wind went from a moan to a gale-strength roar.

Jeeter's shanty lifted again up on one side, but this time passed the tipping point and slammed down on the door side, pitching Jeeter against the windowless wall of his shanty. The impact put undue stress on the structure and the pallet floor and runners ripped free of the cardboard housing and fell back to the ice. Jeeter was now exposed to the full force of the wind and looked up nervously at the lowering sky. He stuffed the bottle of screech into a large front pocket already filled with smelt and tried to collect his fishing gear and creel, but the wind beat him to it, scattering his borrowed gear on the ice.

The shanty, now free of the anchoring weight of the pallets and the modest traction of the runners, lay on its smooth side and became a spinnaker in the accelerating wind. Jeeter howled in vain for Whitey, but the gale force wind bore away the sound of his voice before it even approached the insulated shanties close by. Clasping his creel, Jeeter rolled himself into a corner of the cardboard box. He cowered inside as he steadily picked up speed on the smooth ice, propelled by a fierce easterly wind. He rooted in his pocket for the bottle and gulped another mouthful of screech as the shanty careened across the ice at breakneck speed toward the middle of the lake.

The Plattsburgh ferry farther south had closed for the winter since the lake had frozen all the way to the New York side. Jeeter did not know this. With only the view of the receding Vermont shoreline and its huddle of warm shanties, Jeeter gave himself up to the certainty of freezing to death in the waters of Lake Champlain.

Screech had earned its name in Acadia among sailors and fisherman who noticed that people who drank this unique rum-like mixture to excess often screeched at the top of their lungs. Some did so as a prelude to blindness if the distiller was not experienced—and many weren't, given the general lack of employment at the time in Nova Scotia.

As the shanty accelerated in the brisk wind, Jeeter let out a powerful "wheeeee. . . haw." This was succeeded by several "who. . . eeeeeeees." There was no one to hear these howls, nor could anyone hearing them have made out whether they were expressions of terror or excitement from someone hurtling fifteen miles an hour towards New York in a Frigidaire box with a pocket full of smelt and a belly full of screech.

After quite some time of high-speed travel, a tremendous impact on the roof brought him to an abrupt and painful stop. The impact almost knocked him out. He lurched forward on all fours and crawled outside to look around. He had hit a tree, the stump of which appeared to be on land and the trunk of which seemed to disappear into the iced-over shoreline. He had lost all sense of direction, had little grounding in local geography, and assumed, since he had never deliberately left, that he was still in Vermont.

A cluster of shanties was evident in the next bay and dark smoke coiled out of one of them. Jeeter struggled to his unsteady feet. The screech had not affected his vision, but it played havoc with his sense of direction and balance. He pulled the empty bottle out of his pocket and tossed it into the tattered remains of his shanty. The ice was windblown here and snow-drifts were few and far between. Jeeter tried to focus on the shanty in the distance and trudged off in its direction.

It seemed like forever to Jeeter. He would look down at his cracked rubber galoshes to steady himself then look up occasionally to regain his bearings, but the shanty never seemed to get any closer.

After what seemed like an endless trudge in the blustery wind, Jeeter noticed a red Jimmy truck headed towards him at full speed across the ice. It was Whitey's, and he could make out Whitey and Ben Slocum in the front seats.

He dreaded the confrontation. Better to have been picked up by Purvis's mother if she were alive, Jeeter thought to himself.

The Jimmy pulled up next to him. Whitey rolled the window down. He could barely contain his glee. "Fishin' better here in New York than in Vermont? That's one helluva fast shanty ya got, cherself, Jeeter. How 'bout a ride back? Ya look a bit shaky from the roide. I'll help ya fold up yer shanty."

"I got ta git ma creel. I gotta lotta smelts," pouted Jeeter.

"Ya mean yer box kite," Whitey roared.

Usually put off by Whitey's sarcasm, Ben erupted in uncontrollable laughter.

Jeeter, defeated, clambered in behind Ben. Whitey had long since removed the rear seats and was using them for deck furniture in his new Flanders pre-built Wonder Home. Jeeter guided Whitey to the tattered box in the fallen tree several hundred yards down the shore. He gathered up his creel full of smelt and left the remains of the shanty and the empty screech bottle to float away in the spring melt.

He felt better on the way back after he had vomited generously into Whitey's tackle box. Whitey, still warm from his cozy shanty, had the window open and was oblivious to Jeeter's abdominal malaise as he kept up a patter of abuse that Jeeter worried would endure into the next decade.

On reaching the Vermont shore, Jeeter fled the vehicle and his friends, taking refuge in the warmth of his oxidizing pickup and the long solitary drive back to Hyde Park.

Back home, he found the radio on, the house empty and very cold. The fire in the stove was out and both aluminum doors were swinging in the still significant wind. Some snow had drifted onto the welcome mat. There was no note. Lou had clearly left in a hurry.

Jeeter shrugged and hung up Lou's jacket, forgetting the fresh smelt in the various pockets. He rang up Hilda and asked if she knew where Lou was. Hilda, no stranger to screech herself, sounded hostile, but allowed that Lou was with her, but "weren't coming home in the nearby future." Jeeter, confused, sensed disaster.

"Could ya put Lou on?" Jeeter asked tentatively.

He could hear muffled traces of conversation with Hilda's hand covering the receiver. Lou was getting lots of advice from Hilda. Finally, after a hiatus, Jeeter heard Lou's unsteady voice.

"You didn't kill that rooster!" she said accusingly.

"Course I did," returned Jeeter.

"You think so. Well, I was uncloggin' the kitchen sink again when over that bank where you throw'd his carcass, come that rooster with vengeance flashin' in his one eye. T'other eye was hangin' from its socket. He was peerin' straight at me through the window like he thought I done it 'stead o' you, draggin' one wing and pulling hisself by his claw over the ground towards me. He knew I din't like 'im."

He was hell-bent on killin' me. I din't hang around, jes' lit out for Hilda's. I ain't comin' home till that demon rooster's buried deep in the frozen groun' and I read about his funeral in the *News and Citizen*." The phone went dead.

Jeeter dropped the receiver, grabbed Lou's jacket and a badly rusted 12-gauge that his Uncle Buttrick had warned him about when he left it to him. It had a Damascus steel barrel that had not yet blown itself or its owner to ribbons. With modern shot loads, these antiques often blew their spiral-formed barrels into a floral design. Jeeter accepted it with trepidation and simply added it to his legacy of terrors.

Feeling somewhat steadier, he walked deliberately to the coop where, sure enough, the battered rooster was again holding court among his diminishing clutch of biddies.

The rooster spied Jeeter and charged, flapping one wing furiously in an effort to take flight. Jeeter waited until he was far enough from the hens, leveled the 12gauge and pulled the trigger. The blast flattened the rooster and left a shallow canyon in the floor of the henhouse. The barrel stayed together. The hens scattered. Jeeter hurled them a handful of smelt and they recovered quickly. He took the carcass and a shovel and buried the rooster in a snowbank on the edge of the property knowing that a fox would smell the blood before nightfall, find the carcass, and haul it off as soon as it was dark.

On the phone, Lou grilled him suspiciously as to where the burial site was and how he had managed to dig a hole with the ground frozen solid. Jeeter concocted a complex lie that seemed to convince Lou, who said she'd be home when she "got 'round to it and make supper."

At dusk, Jeeter heard the Olds pull up. Lou entered the trailer looking around suspiciously. Jeeter regaled her with his ice fishing exploits, leaving the New York trip out entirely.

Lou who disliked fish except for canned tuna mixed with Campbells' mushroom soup and Minute Rice, looked balefully at the creel full of stiff shiners that Jeeter proudly displayed. Next day, she discovered the overflow in her coat pockets.

To Jeeter's satisfaction, Whitey's Jimmy broke through the ice in late March and had to be salvaged from 28 feet of icy water. Its V-8 engine had to be rebuilt from scratch as it was running when it sank.

When Jeeter was asked about the extent of his travels, he would look around cautiously for Whitey and then brag that he had been to New York.

Uncle Benoit's Wake

WHEN I WAS TEN, just after my mother had buried my grandfather, Uncle Benoit died in a spectacular late-night car wreck. Uncle Ben, as he was called by us kids or "Mon Onc'" as he was called by his own generation, was my father's uncle on his father's side. My father's mother Eugénie had married Gaston Delaire, acquiring Benoit as a Ðbeau-frère." Gaston had died several years earlier of pneumonia. Another brother, Arnaud, took holy orders and became an Edmundite missionary in South America among the rainforest people.

Uncle Ben and his wife, Colette, had a pristine farm off Route 100 in North Hyde Park. A hundred and fifty acres and as many Holsteins and Guernseys produced thousands of pounds of milk each day and a good living for their growing family. Uncle Benoit won countless "Green Pastures" awards from the Ag Department for his exemplary farm. Just behind the house sat a 120-foot dairy barn and farm equipment shed, and a smaller barn to the south sheltered poultry.

The "viewing" was to be a two-day affair at the farm to accommodate the many relatives already making their way from the logging camps of northern Maine, the convents of Quebec, and the trailer parks of western Florida. White's Funeral Home could neither dedicate two days to the event nor feed and house the stream of relatives already en route to Hyde Park.

Benoit's surviving brother, Père Arnaud, had been notified by telegraph and native runner and was already aboard the first of three flights from Cartagena to Burlington.

News of Uncle Ben's death spread quickly through the community by word of mouth, overheard party-line conversations, a notice in the *News and Citizen*, and remembrances from the pulpits of Lamoille County.

The Delaire Family were known and respected for their industry. Gaston and Eugénie ran a transportation service. At its heart was the jitney between the train station in Waterbury where, daily, they greeted New York Central passengers on the northbound Montrealer and the southbound Washingtonian and took them to the inns and ski slopes of Stowe. They also owned the Peoples Academy school bus contract, chauffered the Trapp Family Singers on their North American singing tours in a "stretched" passenger car specially built for the tour, and provided ordinary taxi service for those needing transport.

For the wake, my father wore one of his two grey wool suits. I wore my scratchy church clothes, and my nine-year-old brother, Paul, twisted uncomfortably in woolen pants, a starched white shirt, and one of Dad's ties knotted to allow the right length in front but a large amount of unused tie in the back, which he then stuffed inside Paul's shirt, leaving an unruly bulge. My six-year-old sister, Ann, looked like a fleur-de-lys in her First Communion dress.

Dad knocked firmly on the front door of the farmhouse, an indication that this was to be a solemn affair. Only out-of-town salesmen or "state boys" approached the front door of a farmhouse. Comings and goings were through back or side doors leading into kitchens, usually through a wood storage area with a rusting second refrigerator or chest freezer. Living rooms were used only for large gatherings or formal occasions, when their prized furniture and additional space were needed to accommodate and impress guests. Winter saw farm families gathered in their kitchens near the woodstove or sleeping in chilly bedrooms under heavy blankets and patchworks quilts.

The door was opened by Bruno and Yves who looked both solemn and pleased to see us. After a brief expression of sympathy by my father in French, we were waved in and immediately to our left I saw Uncle Ben laid out in a shiny wooden casket with two large brass handles. He seemed very much alive as he lay there in what had been an anteroom, now cleared of denim coats and barn boots. A faint odor of manure persisted underneath the strong smell of lilies cascading from vases behind the casket. A prie-dieu borrowed from Holy Family Catholic Church in Morrisville was centered in front of the casket. I kept waiting for Uncle Ben to sit upright as he lay in the profusion of white silk, smile broadly, and greet us loudly, as he often did when we came on him during his nap after the large noonday meal prepared by Aunt Colette for all the boys and hired hands. My father nudged us towards the display. We followed his example, kneeling down on either side of him on the padded kneeler, and bowed our heads while keeping a curious eye on Uncle Ben. We had never seen a dead person before except in the movies.

Uncle Ben had been a source of wonder to all of us kids. The only family elder who seemed to enjoy children more than adults, he would often erupt in laughter at our antics. He took us in turn on his knee and taught us to count to ten or recite the Lord's Prayer in French, his breath smelling faintly of whiskey or his own homebrew.

Kneeling there I heard my father under his breath begin, "Notre Père, qui est aux cieux, que votre nom soit béni." I tried earnestly to remember what Uncle Ben had taught me. I could recite most of it, but always tangled with the "Donnez-nous notre pain quotidien." It rattled around in my small mouth like a dozen marbles and whatever came out elicited gales of laughter from Uncle Ben and the others in the small audience of family or hired hands.

Seeing my father close his eyes, I followed his example, anxious to do the right thing in this solemn moment.

Drifting somewhat, I remembered myself sitting far back on the bench seat in the cab of a snowplow. It was dark out and Uncle Ben was at the wheel of his sister-in-law's dump truck with its two rusty yellow plows on the right front, a curved scarifier plow that lifted the snow from the ground and then a deflector blade higher up that sent the snow aloft in a continuous white stream to the side of the road, burying the pasture fence.

The cab of the truck was filled with the smell of coffee. Two white porcelain cups and a brown paper bag permeated with the grease sweating from hot doughnuts sat on the seat between us. A plaid thermos was nestled in his wadded-up, red and black-checked wool coat on the floor between the larger of the two stick shifts and the truck's torn bench seat. I was too short to see out the window, but my eyes were fixed on the endless stream of airborne snow lit by the high-mounted headlights.

Uncle Ben hummed to himself whenever he wasn't talking, jigs and reels I faintly recalled from the firehouse dances where they were played by Crazy Chase and other local fiddlers.

"Tabernak, look at dat snow, can' see nuthin' dere. Climb up 'ere and look at dis."

I scrambled to my knees and, kneeling on the truck seat, I leaned onto the warm dashboard and peered out the windshield ahead. A faint morning light was dawning over Elmore Mountain, enough to see the landscape taking shape ahead. We were careening down through a field with two feet of fresh snow, bluish in the predawn light, guided only by the fence posts lining either side of what had been a road before the night's heavy snowfall.

"Weren't for dem posts, I'd no idee where dis road be," roared Uncle Ben over the engine noise. He glanced over at me, perched like a collie against the dash.

"Pour some café when we hit de pavemins," he roared over the engine noise and the sound of the plow grating against gravel.

I sat back down and uncorked the thermos, carefully pouring out the muddy coffee, rich with fresh unpasteurized cream and sugar into the two mugs until they were half full as he had taught me.

"Don' be stingy," laughed Uncle Ben. "A little spill in dis truck only brighten it up," he roared again with laughter at his own humor. I poured a little extra into both cups and handed him the fuller one.

"Beignet," he shouted, slurping the hot coffee. "You dip in your café, mighty good."

One at a time, I pulled two warm dark brown doughnuts from the bag and handed one to him. He broke it in two, dipped a half into his coffee and bit deep into it, never looking away from the expanse of white ahead. I did the same, but in smaller bites as pieces of soggy doughnut fell back into my cup.

"Good to have my assistan' wid me," he said smiling. "Your Aunt Colette don' like bein' up in da middle of da night 'cept for hanky's panky. I take my eyes off da road or whoosh, we be on our side in da ditch and Eugénie gets all h'angered."

Benoit was helping out Eugénie, who managed the family business after his brother Gaston's death. Eugénie would call after a big storm and ask her brother-in-law to help with the plowing. In winter, there was little for him to do other than to oversee the milking by his sons and the hired hands well before the school bus arrived. Dropping bales down from the hayloft, graining chickens and pigs, mucking out cow stalls and gutters, and spreading manure when his tractor could get into the fields made for most of the winter chores, so Ben looked forward to helping his sister-in-law after a storm. After Gaston succumbed to pneumonia, Eugénie bid to retain the portion of the town snow-removal contract covering Route 100 north of town and the back roads that fed down onto it from the surrounding hills.

Dad got up, crossed himself again. Awakened from my reverie, I followed suit, keeping an eye on Uncle Ben as we left the anteroom. In the rarely used sitting room, a swarm of people had come to pay their respects to the family and to say goodbye to Benoit.

Aunt Colette held court from an overstuffed chair with needlework doilies in the corner. Her daughters, Nicole and Yvette, stood on either side, occasionally sitting down on the expansive arms. As visitors approached to express their condolences, Aunt Colette clutched her embroidered white handkerchief, bringing it to her mouth and sobbing, nodding all the while, accepting the expressions of grief and loss like a priest hearing the confessions of his parishioners. Between these receptions of sympathy, Aunt Colette would revert to her role as hostess, smiling orders and requests to her children and the legion of women who had come bearing casseroles, pies, baked goods, and sandwich platters to help feed the several hundred people who would come to pay their respects over the next two days. Friends and relatives progressed into the dining room where mountains of egg and ham salad sandwiches lay arranged on white ironstone platters and glass pitchers of homebrew were constantly replenished from the milkshed.

The front door opened again and two large men wearing dark green woolen pants with leather suspenders and flannel shirts burst in waving a loud "Bonjour" to Ben in the anteroom, but not pausing as was expected. They were followed by a very small woman in a black nun's habit with a white wimple and shawl.

I had heard of Sister Ste. Alphonse but had never met her. She trailed behind her brothers, Rémy and René, loggers in the forests of northern Maine. They had driven their pickup truck to Trois Rivières, Quebec, to pick up their sister and bring her to the wake and funeral of their second cousin Benoit. I tried to imagine this tiny woman wedged between these two giant men for the five-hour drive.

Our grandmother Eugénie, "Me-mère" to us, had told us about Sister Ste. Alphonse. When she was a young girl, both her parents died in a flu epidemic for which there were no antibiotics locally. Sylvie, her given name, had nursed them as long as she could at the age of eight, and sat with them as they died without palliatives. Mercifully, they died within two days of each other. Sylvie's older brothers, Rémy and René, were at a logging camp 60 miles away and did not learn of their parents' deaths until the spring log run ended in May, and they returned home to rest with their meager savings. A Mi'kmaq neighbor who had helped young Sylvie bury her parents took her in in exchange for help with her own chores. When the brothers returned and found the house empty, they set out for the nearest house, found their sister working as a domestic and learned of their parents' deaths. They sought the advice of the local priest, who suggested that the boys give their sister over to the care of the nuns across the border, as they often took in orphaned girls.

Sylvie was surrendered to the Carmelite nuns in Trois Rivières by her brother René in a farewell without tears. Later that spring, the boys, now men, returned to the logging camp near Presque Isle to support themselves and to send a modest stipend to the convent for caring for their sister.

Sylvie thrived under the strict but benevolent Carmelite sisters. She assumed the name of the saint that the abbess chose for her, St Alphonsus Mary de Ligouri, and took vows of poverty, chastity, and silence at the age of 15. The latter vow had very little impact on her daily life as she had said very little as a child, except when required to recite at the one-room schoolhouse she attended in Quisibis until her parents died.

Sister Ste. Alphonse went straight into the anteroom. She crossed herself with the hand holding her wooden rosary, kissed its cross, knelt down on the prie-dieu, and bowed her head in prayer, pausing only occasionally to look up at her cousin and the wooden crucifix hanging amid the lilies above the casket.

Rémy and René made their way through the crowd nodding and greeting relatives in Québécois. Aunt Colette could not suppress her own smile at seeing them approach her with their broad smiles and loud greetings. She rose from her chair and received their hugs, which lifted her well off the floor. Rémy swung her around and set her back down.

In the dining room, where Paul and I were chewing on egg salad sandwich halves, Henri Landry unpacked his fiddle from its wooden case. A violoneux and distant cousin from Asbestos, Quebec, Henri lived alone in a very small house on the Nicolet River and had worked all his life in the Jeffrey Mine, the largest openpit asbestos mine in the world. Unlike his father, he had suffered no ill effects from his work and in his retirement had become a celebrated fiddler, known for his ability to play for many hours without ever repeating a jig or reel. We watched as he took out the dark sprucewood fiddle from its red velvet-lined case, rosined his bow, fit the luminous instrument between his chin and left shoulder and began to play. Just as the music began, I bit down hard on a piece of eggshell, then tried to extract the humid mass of chewed egg and bread from my mouth without notice.

"La valse fâchée," roared someone in the crowd, and the music began. Toes tapped everywhere and somber faces lit up as Henri played from his perch on a red vinyl and chrome chair, part of the matching dinette set that had been dispersed to provide seating for the guests.

The table disappeared like an altar under the steady stream of eucharistic offerings from ladies in stained white aprons carrying heaping plates with pale sandwiches, sliced carrot cakes, casseroles, and plates containing every sort of pie.

A French-Canadian pie crust can be home to any kind of filling. There were sugar pies, confected of various forms of molasses, maple, or penuche melted and blended together with Karo syrup into a gelatinous filling that spilled out of the crust when sliced and served. Sugar pies always got a wistful look from the heavier ladies who suffered from "the sugar," a lay term for diabetes. Meat pies were offered in several variations, some with pork fillings and others with minced venison. The pitchers full of homebrew emptied quickly and were replenished just as quickly by the ladies ferrying food and drink from the large farm kitchen.

The front door opened again and Father Arnaud arrived looking pale and weary from his long trip from Colombia to Hyde Park. He nodded to the guests who noticed his arrival and then joined Sister Ste. Alphonse on the prie-dieu, staring intently at his dead brother. The resemblance between Arnaud and his brother was remarkable: crested shocks of black hair, deep-set eyes, short thick noses, and prominent, furrowed foreheads. Arnaud wore glasses. Uncle Ben in repose did not.

Dad was lost in conversation with his cousin Yvette, the oldest of Ben's children. Yvette had the round face and warm skin tones of the graphic renderings of the Blessed Virgin Mary in my missal. The faint smile on her pale brown features betrayed a lambent sadness, sadness not brought about by the crucifixion of a son, but rather, according to Dad, by the suicide of an admiring boyfriend.

Dad had told us the rudiments of the story when it happened, and we had heard it later on the playground in greater detail. It had shocked the community and changed Yvette forever. She had just turned nineteen, graduating from high school near the top of her class. Her choices were marriage, holy orders— marriage of another sort—or finding a job as a teacher or librarian, both of which required additional education. There were also the jobs that led nowhere, such as cook, counter person, or secretary, but Hyde Park and nearby Morrisville had precious few of even those jobs.

Yvette had often talked to Dad of how, as a young girl, she had dreamt about the course her life would take. They were not that far apart in age and an early friendship had developed between the two cousins. She told him that in her dreams she did things that men did, like farming, opening a store, sitting behind a desk and managing something of significance. Her father had called on her when she was twelve to drive the red International tractor as he wrestled the large square hay bales extruded from the baler up onto a trailing flatbed truck driven by Bruno, only ten himself but taller than Yvette.

As Dad later told the story, Rosaire was a sallow boy with thin hair, a narrow face, aquiline features, and an Ichabod-like frame. Hopelessly in love with Yvette since ninth grade, he was shy at first but had declared his love the previous summer. Yvette indulged his affection with occasional dates, demure occasions where both talked uncomfortably of events and people and then later, with somewhat more intimacy, of their aspirations. This was fatal. Rosaire's aspirations were to be the mechanic who kept the single chairlift's engine running. Yvette's aspirations were higher.

Yvette borrowed her father's Oldsmobile 98. She resolved in this meeting to tell her persistent friend that she did not intend to accept his proposal of marriage, that she liked him well enough, but did not love him.

Yvette later told her father and the state policeman that they had driven the back roads deep into Sterling Valley. After crossing the covered bridge over Sterling Brook, the road paralleled the brook, meandering past Blodgett Falls and up towards the old Lapine Farm. At a pull-off, Yvette parked the car and the two ambled down to a favorite trysting spot, a naturally formed basin in the brook where local people came to swim on hot summer days.

Dad often took us there and my own memory of the place was of a gentle fall of water cascading down over moss-covered rocks and spilling into a natural basin. Brookies swiveted just under the falls, agile shadows venturing occasionally out from the darker recesses into the sunlit parts of the basin, flashing their pale neon colors amidst the sparkle of quartz crystals embedded in the surrounding rock.

Yvette sat down on a boulder and stared into the water. She knew what was coming as Rosaire cleared his throat. She turned and gently smiled at Rosaire. She made clear in a few plain words that, although she liked him, she would never marry him. To help ease the pain, she declared that she would never marry anyone. Rosaire stared into the dark woods beyond the water as she spoke slowly and gently to him.

When she was done he got up and walked back to the car alone. Yvette waited for his return, heard the gunshot, and began to sob violently. She left the car and Rosaire's body in the turn-off and walked to the Levesque Farm two miles back down the road. They had no phone, but drove her home where her father called the police and told them in somber tones what had happened.

Yvette was marked forever by this event. She considered again, as she had many times, joining one of the three orders of nuns in Burlington. A marriage to Christ would forever be a monologue without the dark complexity of requited love. She could not speak of this with her mother, Colette, whose persistent joviality did not brook sadness. She talked with her father who consoled her and told her that he loved her with all his heart. She refused all social invitations and worked hard on the farm. The only nun in the family, Sister Ste. Alphonse, spoke to no one but God and could not talk with Yvette about her idea of taking holy orders. Yvette was alone and felt that way.

In the living room, Yvette and Dad continued talking together in hushed tones.

I went again into the kitchen where muscular ladies of girth wrestled with heavy platters. It was warm from the wood oven and redolent of the meat pies warming inside.

Father Arnaud and Sister Ste. Alphonse had left Uncle Ben to make room for the local parish priest, Father Dufault. Sister Ste. Alphonse smiled broadly as she nibbled around the edges of a ham salad sandwich. Paul and I talked in hushed tones about how it would be to go through life without ever being able to say a word to anyone.

"How would you ask someone for help if you were in the bathroom making number two and found there was no toilet paper?" giggled Paul. I laughed but stifled it for fear we would be overheard laughing at a funeral.

Suddenly, from the kitchen, the fiddle began again. It was a much-loved reel we had often heard at town dances and kitchen tonks, "Le Reel du Pendu" or "Hangman's Reel" as the misnomer went. It was, in fact, "The Hanged Man's Reel," but had over time simply elided into the "Hangman's Reel." The sound of the fiddle seemed to galvanize the room. Conversation faded as people began to tap their feet and nod their heads in time to the rhythm.

Nicole stepped forward, lifted the front of her black dress, and began a lively step dance as everyone turned to watch. She was soon joined by three younger girls ranging in age from six to about ten, dancing slowly into a straight line. Uncle Alcide grabbed a pair of spoons from the table and began to play them with his right hand and knee and René Dumas pulled up a chair, sat down backwards and began mouthing the traditional yet incomprehensible musique à bouche.

"Deedideleedelumdeedideeumdedidelumde do"

Then to the surprise of everyone in the room, including Aunt Colette, Sister Ste. Alphonse stepped forward beaming from ear to ear, gently lifted the front of her black habit high above her ankles exposing her dark heavy stockings and high black lace-up shoes and began to step dance with a fluidity and grace that none could have imagined. Although there was not a sound coming from her other than the hard click of her leather heels, we could see her lips moving silently as she followed the music and presumably mimed her own ecstatic form of mouth music. The girls and Thérèse opened a gap in their line for her and she moved swiftly into the center keeping perfect time to the music.

Paul and I watched from the safety of the dining room as Sister Ste. Alphonse moved up and down in rhythm with the other four girls. Nicole's well-developed breasts rose and fell inside her black high-collared dress in rhythm to the music, inviting the attention of the men clapping their hands and nodding their heads to one another in louche appreciation. The enthusiasm was so great that each time the reel sped to a close, it began again, but at a slightly faster pace. Hands, feet, and heads rose again to the occasion, chasing the newly accelerated rhythm.

Finally, after a very fast-paced finale with lots of pizzicato and percussive bowing that called to mind the twitching feet of the dying man dancing in the air below the gallows, Henri Landry brought the reel to a climactic close and the room was silent for the first time since we arrived. A burst of applause followed. Conversations resumed in French and in smaller enclaves of English as more and more people from town dropped in to pay their respects, eat, and sample Uncle Ben's renowned homebrew.

It was getting dark as Dad signaled to us that it was time to say goodbye and head home. Paul and I said goodbye to anyone we knew and waited for Dad by the door, peering occasionally into the anteroom to catch our last glimpse of a dead person.

Driving home, we were quiet. As we drove up towards our house, I ventured a question.

"Why didn't mom come with us?" I asked.

"She is still sad about your Pappy's death. I suspect she was not ready for another just yet."

I tried to remember my own maternal grandfather sitting on the twin bed next to mine telling me one of his made-up stories. I could hear the story, but I could no longer see his face.

The Morrisville Fourth of July Parade

～♪♪

PUD AND GINGER LELAND bought the lot next to Union Carbide and built a modern prefab ranch house, the first of its kind in Morrisville. Later, the most popular model came to be known as the Flanders Wonder Home. One could erect it on a lot in a matter of a few days and it came complete with interiors and appliances. The formal front door with its shiny brass finish hardware hung in the street-facing façade three feet above the ground and next to the "pitcher winda" as Pud called it. The door was largely decorative, as Pud and Ginger didn't pay extra for the precast concrete steps with filigree wrought-iron rail that led up to it. Fifty feet of perfectly manicured lawn separated the house from the LaPorte Road leading south to Stowe.

The newly erected home was modest, yet fulfilled all Pud and Ginger's residential dreams in one compact package. Ginger herself painted it a pale blue to match the interior of the half-buried upright bathtub that would eventually enshrine the Virgin Mary they planned to buy at the church supply store on their next trip to Burlington. Under the "pitcher winda" lay two halves of a former kerosene tank that Pud cut in half lengthwise with a welding torch and painted silver. This innovative planter was to hold a profusion of purple and white petunias that Ginger had started from seed in trays on the rear sundeck.

Pud was neat. He liked order. The purview of his job as town constable had expanded by his own initiative to include "keepin' the taown lookin' smart." His civic drive, however, was not always matched by his aesthetic sense and his beautification projects sometimes set tongues wagging. In the dead of winter, he planted in Morrisville's early-eighteenth-century horse-watering trough, cut from Vermont granite, a large array of badly faded silk flowers he'd salvaged from Lyle's dump. Pud's cheery intent looked bleak to some and to others like a dismal prank.

The town constable's job was generally to help out wherever he could, resolve domestic or neighbor disputes, remove roadkill, help with traffic control during the town dances at the firehouse, train the school safety patrols, organize the Fourth of July parade, and assist with other miscellaneous tasks to maintain order. Much to Pud's disappointment, however, the town steadfastly failed to provide him with a uniform. He had made the point a couple of times in town meeting only to elicit hoots of laughter.

"Get Pud a uniform and nex' ting ya know, Lyle'll be wannin' a dumpkeeper's uniform, the firesmen be wannin' ep'lettes," railed his nemesis, Whitey, who took it as his job to heckle earnest petitioners at town meeting.

Pud gave up, but with considerable resentment, resolving not to let the lack of a proper uniform compromise his performance.

One day early in spring, Ginger, in a halter, pedal pushers, and green boots, was bent over positioning the new Virgin Mary within the upright bathtub. Pud had just finished removing the tub's clawfoot legs with a crescent wrench when they were both startled by a loud wolf whistle followed by the nearby roar of Pete firing up his Gravely mower.

Pete was the handyman and groundskeeper at the Union Carbide Records Storage Facility next door. The manager, Mr. Skiff, had given Pete permission to trench and backfill a two hundred-foot strip of Union Carbide's lot adjoining the Leland property with several hundred asparagus plugs and a large amount of ripe manure he'd hauled from Mendoza's farm just down the road. Pete had a tiller attachment on the Gravely. He was tilling the top few inches of the still-dormant asparagus patch, guiding the unruly machine by its handlebars. When he reached Pud's lawn, Pud waved frantically to attract his attention, but Pete pretended not to notice or hear over the din of the unmuffled engine.

On his next pass, Pud was waiting in the patch and as Pete approached, Pud deftly reached down and flipped the shorting switch on the cylinder head to kill the motor so he might reason with Pete about the proximity of the new bed to his lawn. A burst of high voltage shot through Pud like a lightning bolt and knocked him to the ground. The Gravely began to misfire, dieseled a bit and finally died. Pete roared with laughter and let out a loud "Sacré bleu!" The ancient magneto ignition on the Gravely gener-ated so much current that the moment Pud touched the metal switch, the current found the shortest route to ground, knocking Pud onto his lawn. Pud picked himself up muttering, "Shit and go bang bang, wha's da hell in dat machine?"

"Show ya keep yer han's ta yerself. She doan' like ta be touch'," said Pete grinning from ear to ear and staring at Ginger.

On his feet again but still feeling the pins and needles in his arm, Pud appealed to Pete to move the fragrant bed farther back on the Carbide property so it didn't border his lawn. But Pud could not tell if Pete was lis-tening as he watched Pete wrap the dowel-handled manila rope carefully around the starter reel in the front of the Gravely, give a light tug to set the flywheel against the compression, and flip the kill switch open again. Pete yanked on the rope and the Gravely roared to life. He slammed in the clutchless gear with a loud clank and the tiller resumed its slow crawl forward.

By this time, Ginger had joined Pud and the two of them looked at each other in dismay. Neither could hear the other over the din. They went inside for a lemonade.

Having gotten nowhere with Pete, Pud resolved to raise the mat-ter with his friend Emile, who worked at the facility. If that produced no results, he would talk with Mr. Skiff, the manager, who had moved to town from New York City. He lived in the white house with blue shutters on the other side of the Union Carbide lot and seemed like a nice enough fellow. He had, after all, been quite gracious about the long-running prank played on him by Pete when he bought his Volkswagen.

Neither Emile nor Mr. Skiff offered Pud much help, since they respected Pete's fierce independent streak; besides, he had sought permission for the asparagus patch before Pud and Ginger had bought the adjacent lot and built their home there. The only recourse left to Pud was to tell the tale of injustice to everyone he met.

Pud also had a thing about dandelions, or for that matter any invasive plants that disturbed the golf-green beauty of his lawn. He and Ginger picked over the lawn daily, removing alien seedlings or occasional litter from passing cars. Ironically it was an old asparagus cutter with which he would, at the first sight of a yellow blossom, dig the plant out by its roots using the V-shaped blade at the end to remove the deep root and toss it in his trash. The tool was perfect for dandelions and he determined to try it out some night on the vegetable for which it was intended, though neither he nor Ginger liked green vegetables. Together, they kept their lawn free of "the yeller menace" as he called them. Pete, preferring the French name *pissenlits*, made no similar effort next door on the three acres of lawn surrounding the gray cinderblock building. The lawn was in fact more yellow than green by the end of June, and Pud became increasingly anxious at the thought of a dehiscence of airborne dandelion seed being carried aloft in the summer breeze and taking root on their own pristine lawn.

One Saturday, Pete was riding along on the dolly behind the Gravely, cutting a 36-inch swath through the diaphanous silver balls that had once been bright yellow dandelions and releasing into the breeze a gossamer cloud of dandelion seed. Pud had set up two black rotating fans on the edge of his property in an effort to divert the airborne plague, but to little avail. After Pete's third pass near the Leland property, Pud's lawn was blanketed.

Ginger came out with an Electrolux and began to vacuum furiously, but the bag clogged quickly so Pud and Ginger retired again for some heavily sugared iced tea.

Pete finished his mowing, shut down the mower gingerly with a long dowel he kept on the handlebars, and pushed the machine inside through the garage door on the side of the facility—the same door through which trucks periodically came and went depositing a steady stream of vital records from New York City to be stored in the nuclear-insignificant town of Morrisville.

Relations between Pete and the Lelands became increasingly strained over the next few months.

Pud's pride and joy was the Fourth of July Parade. It had become for Lamoille County a one-day economic boon as folks poured in from as far away as Greensboro, Worcester, Johnson, and even Stowe where the well-heeled arrivistes amused themselves observing the simple pleasures of Lamoille natives.

Pud had enlisted the usual line-up of participants: Mendoza would walk behind his matched team of blood-red oxen. Mendoza's brother Clovis and his wife Elise, who had raised Pete, would don the Sunday go-to-meeting togs of their grandparents from Abitibi, Quebec, and ride atop Morrisville's earliest stagecoach. The cramped coach was drawn by a team of Belgians in period tack and sported its original paint and badly faded interior upholstery. It was kept in the carriage barn adjacent to their house even though it now belonged to the nascent Morrisville Historical Society. The wooden coach preceded by 35 years the jitney bus they now operated daily between Morrisville, Stowe, and the train station in Waterbury.

The westerns playing at Blanche's Bijou Theater enticed many town-folk into adopting cowboy-style riding gear. Pud invited them each year to "'zibit" on their surly Appaloosas and roans with their ornate western saddles, large wooden stirrups, Stetson hats, pearl-button shirts, fringed chaps, and shiny spurs.

The revered fire department would appear in force with their 1927 LaFrance ladder truck and 1947 Dodge Power Wagon pumper. Firemen would toss hard candies wrapped in wax paper to the children running alongside the newly buffed red vehicles.

The Fourth of July was a welcome respite from the endless rigors of logging, haying, milking, mining asbestos or talc, gluing plywood, splitting firewood, or otherwise pursuing the endless exigencies of rural life. Country people lay down their travails and came to town, first for the parade, then for the town barbecue that was sponsored by the Farm Bureau and served up by the members of the Grange and the Future Farmers of America, and finally for the dance at the firehouse catered by the ladies of the Eastern Star.

The parade began at 10:30 and lasted until noon. It wound from its starting point at Smalley's Motors on Brooklyn Street down Bridge Street and then up Portland Street through the middle of town. It then proceeded across the intersection to Congress Street by the Randall Hotel down East High and came up the middle of town again, ending at the elementary school on Elmore Mountain Road across from the firehouse, where the barbecue infused the air with the smell of cooking chicken and panpipe racks of beef ribs.

Pete owned a 1922 Model N John Deere, formerly called a "Waterloo Boy" that he had bought still running from Wilfred Leriche and restored. Pete scoured the countryside for parts and machined what he could not find at Fred Greene's foundry. The two-cylinder, 15-horsepower tractor burned kerosene and weighed over 6,000 pounds. It had two forward speeds, two and three miles per hour.

The first tractors had no rubber tires. The "N" had cast-iron wheels in the front and large iron wheels with cast traction cleats in the rear. Pete replaced these with conventional rims and used tires so he could drive the rig on paved roads. He used the machine to work the woods at his camp on Little Hosmer Pond, but mostly enjoyed tinkering with its primitive engine and the envy it induced in his mechanic friends.

Old machines were an endless source of fascination to the town's menfolk. "One-lungers" as they were called were an exotic treat in the parade. Mounted on haywagons with large hand-painted signs declaring their model and provenance, they took their place in the parade, towed behind a tractor or pickup. Wyvis Bushway's 1927 McCormick Deering "thumper" always drew a crowd at the "'zibit 'sembly" in the schoolyard after the parade where floats were arrayed during the barbecue for closer examination and banter with the proud "'zibitor."

Pud had tried unsuccessfully for three years to convince Pete to drive his "N" in the parade, especially now that he had fitted the rear wheels with rubber and the rig would not tear up the new pavement on Bridge and Portland Streets. Pete would have no part of it, however, preferring to pass the day in his fishing boat at camp with a pint of blackberry brandy, a raw onion, and a clutch of raw franks. Now that relations were deeply strained between the two, Pud's entreaties were even more futile, so he enlisted Willard Sanders, a respected member of the town, someone to whom Pete might listen.

Willard, in his dual capacity as Light and Power Commissioner and Overseer of the Poor, knew how to deal with people. Every person was different and Willard understood that to convey something to a person required a conversational prelude in which topics of interest to that person needed to be broached prior to any serious discussion. It might be a question about a spouse's health, the capacity of a new barn, the market price of milk or whether Atlas Plywood would be giving raises this year. Willard knew intuitively that to express interest in the affairs of another and to listen thoughtfully to that person established a bond that would prove useful later in the conversation when a thorny question or favor was asked.

The "haphazard" conversation with Pete followed this course. Having read what he could find in the Morrisville Library about how the Waterloo Boy Engine Company had become the John Deere Tractor Company, Willard expressed his secret interest to Pete in antique tractors and his intention to restore an old "B" that was rusting in the back pasture of Volney Farr's farm.

Pete circled the bait warily. But Willard persisted, asking Pete about his knowledge of the "B." Sensing an odd job to his liking, Pete took the bait, the line went taut and an agreement ensued to walk out to the pasture together and assess the feasibility of a restoration.

"Oh, by the way Pete, I expect to see that 'N' in the parade this year or I'm goin' to be mighty disappointed," added Willard over his shoulder as he walked away.

"May do dat," responded Pete, on his way to Graves' Hardware.

Willard had what he wanted and Pete thought he had what he wanted. Few people outfoxed Pete.

"Tink he'll 'zibit?" Pud asked Willard the following Saturday at the dump.

"'Spect so," answered Willard.

Hostilities between Pud and Pete only escalated, however. Pud and Ginger spent a weekend planting a row of variously sized cedars between them and the asparagus patch hoping to wall out the smell and the effusion of windborne dandelion seed. Pete simmered, knowing all too well that the asparagus would suffer from the shade of the cedars and their tendency to acidify the soil around them. Late that evening, he salt-circled and watered the trees and within two weeks they yellowed out and died, leaving a rust-colored hedge that further compromised Pud and Ginger's "wonder home." Pud was furious, knowing full well that the death of his trees was Pete's fault but unable to prove it.

Pud distracted himself by putting all his energy into the parade. Pete had confirmed to Willard that he would drive the "N" in the parade as long as he could come last. Willard agreed to this on Pud's behalf, even though the tail end of the parade was by tradition a fleet of kids on their streamer-decorated bikes.

Boys and girls alike bought red, white, and blue bunting and sparklers at Gillen's Dry Goods and Lucien Renaud's drugstore and spent the day before the parade hidden in garages decorating their bikes, weaving thin strips of bunting through the spokes of their wheels and wrapping it around handlebars and crossbars, and taping flags on the handlebars and sparklers to be lit en route.

The Fourth of July came. The *News and Citizen* published an article with the headline, "To be Safe on the Fourth, Don't Have a Fifth on the Third."

Pud's "nervasthenia" as Ginger called it, recalling Dr. Goddard's diagnosis some years back, had escalated into panic. He was at the assembly point at Smalley's Motors at 9 a.m. yelling at people pulling in with their floats and flailing his arms to little notice. The parade was the parade. It proceeded along the lines it always had and the marching order was posted on the side of the showroom window for all to see.

Pud's only accomplishment was to see to it that the green-and-gold-uniformed Peoples Academy Band began the "street beat" precisely at 10:30. The large band could be heard throughout the town and this was a signal to all those lined up in folding chairs on lawns and sidewalks, those sitting high up in kitchen chairs in the backs of pickups, kids on car roofs, and elderly folks leaning out of second-story windows on Portland Street that the parade was underway.

The band began to wend its way toward town with only the percussion beating out a march cadence to set the pace. The Sousa marches would strike up at certain predetermined points on the route where the largest crowds were assembled. The signal to start would be given by the scantily clad drum majorette with a sharp whistle and the sudden drop of her baton.

Behind the band came a blue and white 1954 Chevy convertible donated by CC Tremblay to carry the Cakewalk King and Queen. The couple were formally dressed as antebellum plantation owners and were chosen by their senior class peers to adjudge the skill and presentation of the rest of the class who paired up to "walk fo' de cake," an annual tradition in many Vermont towns.

Cakewalk occurred in late May before graduation and was as popular in town as the parade itself. Pairs teamed up and began practicing for the event in February. The "cakewalk" had historically been a humiliating artifact of slavery wherein Negro slaves competed for the prize of a cake offered by the plantation owner and his wife to the pair who could perform the most proficiently extravagant high-stepping walk. In Vermont in the 1950s, it was seen as a vaudevillian affair in which aspirants kept their arms low behind the back and high-kicked towards the reviewing stand to Sousa's *King Cotton* march.

The slow-moving convertible sported the elegantly dressed plantation owner and his belle in the rear seat and the winning pair of cakewalkers in black face, baggy pants, and oversize shoes in the front all waving to the crowd. There was a naiveté and insouciance to the display that lasted until the advent of a national consciousness about racism, civil rights, and discrimination rightly soured the event forever.

The Morrisville Volunteer Fire Department followed with their two large trucks. These men were all heroes to townsfolk as many had a chance to benefit from their services, extinguishing a barn fire started by damp hay, a chimney fire started by a cracked flue or, worse, a full-fledged conflagration in which cows or family members were lost.

The town fathers came next, riding in a red 1924 Chrysler touring car owned by the Reverend Pease and inherited from his mother down country. It had elegant side doors with flaking chrome handles and a fabric roof that was folded down for the occasion.

This was followed by the twenty-two Women of the Eastern Star marching in close rank, then the Masons, the Future Farmers of America, and the American Legion with three surviving veterans from the Great War all in uniform with shouldered carbines marching behind the flagbearer.

Then came the town band, a ragtag collection of eighteen men and women who had played in the far more disciplined school band when they were young and were not ready to give up their avocation. They did not have uniforms, so simply dressed in the blues familiar to janitors. The alto and baritone horns and a sousaphone, all too badly dented to use in the high school band, devolved to the town band. They tooted out a march that no one could name, but that everyone recognized.

A succession of agricultural exhibits followed, led by Mendoza's oxen and an entourage of antique tractors and one-lungers. Jeeter's wife Lou marched as usual with her starter cables and various automotive survival gear. Those who knew Jeeter understood the humorous import of her participation. The rest either had no idea or were content to assume that she symbolized the intrepid farm wife.

Next came antique cars, followed by men and women in western gear on horseback astride prancing horses displeased with the loud noises and the slow pace of the parade. Elda Batty was always a hit, managing at each crowd to get her horse Jasper to rear up, whereon she would wave her wide-brimmed hat and smile they way they did in the oaters she so loved.

The parade was beginning to wind down and the kids on patriotically decorated bikes came into view, pumping frantically and managing the occasional wheelie. In the distance one could hear one more very loud internal combustion engine. This was an obvious breach in parade protocol, so onlookers were curious to see who was bringing up the rear. Around the corner near Fred Greene's foundry came Pete astride his freshly painted "N." To everyone's evident surprise, however, the "N" was pulling a large manure spreader filled to the brim with fresh manure, liberally distributing its cargo behind it and enough to the side so that parade watchers had to step back considerably to avoid being pelted. Pete was waving at no one in particular with his right hand and taking large swigs from a pint of blackberry brandy in his left. Although no one could hear above the roar of the unmuffled Waterloo, it was evident that Pete was singing at the top of his lungs one of the many French-Canadian ditties that came easily to his lips with drink.

The parade progressed faster than word of Pete's float so townsfolk moved back only when they realized what was bringing up the rear. The rapidly spinning tines in the rear of the "honey wagon" were very effective at covering the parade route and much of the sidewalk. As Pete approached the reviewing stand at the intersection of Portland and Main, Pud rose to his feet to see what the hubbub was about. Although Willard had intended Pete's participation to be a surprise to Pud and to the community, Pete's decision to include the honey wagon was a clear surprise to Willard, who could not suppress a smile. Pud flailed frantically, believing his patriotic efforts reduced to ridicule. Much of the laughter however was good-humored. The sight of Pete bringing up the rear of the parade with a manure spreader in tow was a source of vast amusement to many in the crowd. The story was told for decades in the small town of Morrisville.

Jack Daulton's
New Woodstove

"GERT JUST TOLD me about someone named Bettis who sells woodstoves, but she couldn't tell me where his shop was. Do you know, Art?"

Art smiled, "Have to ask Bettis. It moves around."

Jack looked puzzled, but many local answers puzzled him since his move to Mud City. There really was no town as he had imagined one. The nearest thing to a town was Morristown Corners and that was merely an intersection with a gas and beverage store. The nearest real town was Morrisville, with Gillen's Department Store, Patch's Market, Graves' Hardware, Copley Hospital, the Bijou Theater, a Carnegie library, Tippy Bailey's Drive-in, and the Morrisville Drive-in Theater.

Jack stopped by the town clerk's office to see if the building permit for his recently completed garage had been approved. He took advantage of the opportunity to ask Martha where Bettis's Stove Shop was. She smiled and said, "If you find it, let Officer Boright know. He's been looking for it for three years."

Jack was flummoxed. As he left the town clerk's office, Martha whispered loudly, "Give Whitey a call at 4494 and ask him. He'll know." Jack jotted the number down on the notepad in his Volvo and headed home.

"Whitey, you wouldn't know me. My name is Jack Daulton and I'm new in town, but I'm looking for Bettis's Stove Shop. No one seems to know where it is. Can you tell me? Everyone I ask either says it's moved or just looks funny at me."

There were several moments of silence in the earpiece and then he heard a voice, "Who'se iss again?"

"Jack Daulton."

"Wha' choo want a stove fer?" "To heat my camp."

"Oh, ya know Bettis personal, do ya?"

"Never met him. Where does he live?"

"Roun'"

Silence.

"Wha's yer nummer?"

"3299."

"I'll tell 'im ta call ya."

Click and then a dial tone....

Puzzled by the truncated conversation, Jack continued with his errands. Next day after lunch, the phone rang.

"Daulton?"

"Yes, Jack Daulton. Can I help you?"

"'Pends iffen ya still wanna stove."

"I do," answered Jack eagerly. "Is this Bettis? Where's your shop?"

"Ya know where Mud City Loop road is? Go up 'ere and turn right on Star Road. Drive 'til the end 'n' I'll meet you by the fell-down elum. Can't miss it. Twenty minutes, bring cash. 'Tcha drivin'?"

"Green '62 Volvo wagon"

"Should'a know'd."

Click and then a dial tone....

Jack looked at his watch and hustled out of his new but as yet unrestored farmhouse to his new garage. The house sat on fourteen acres once part of a 240 acre farm in the shadow of Sterling. Its widowed owner, Bennie Jackman, farmed until the end, but to no financial avail. His fondness for his bovine "girls" prevailed over the advice of two farm Extension agents, and the lots just kept going up for sale until there was nothing left but the old L-shaped house and the last fourteen acres. Bennie now lived on Social Security in a trailer that he shared with his sister in a park in Morrisville. The park didn't allow animals though, so on weekdays he helped Lyle Stewart with evening milking and chores for a few extra dollars.

Thanks to new town road signs, Jack found Star Road and started up the narrow gravel track. Even at the outset, the woods encroached on the road, but as he made his way farther up the windy track, it darkened as the canopy of overhanging trees closed out more and more daylight. Soon, he noticed with some concern that there was no room for an oncoming car to pass and he would have to retreat in reverse to the last driveway to let an oncoming car by. About four miles up, the road ended abruptly at a turnaround. There had been no houses or inhabited cellar holes for the last mile and a half, nothing, in fact, but hardwoods and beds of high ferns. It occurred to Jack that even for Mud City, this hardly looked like a retail section of town.

Parked in the turnaround was a faded blue and white Bronco. The rocker panels, tailgate, and wheel wells had long since oxidized. A rack of spikehorn antlers hung askew from the pitted chrome radiator grille held fast by lamp cord. Jack noticed that none of the four tires were of the same brand or tread type. One rear window was covered with floral contact paper and the windshield was cracked end-to-end. On walking around the car, he noticed that the front and back license plates bore different numbers and dates. The car appeared empty. Jack approached and peered in through the opaque plastic. There were holes in the dashboard where the instruments and a radio had been. A ferocious deepthroated barking from the back seat caused Jack to jump backwards and fall against his own car. From the woods, Jack heard a hearty laugh. "Bear don' like folks much," said a deep baritone voice. "Shuddup, Bear," roared the voice, still unseen. "He's got wicked displeasure in his rear hips, and it pains him some when he sits."

A barrel of a man emerged from the woods, about Jack's height, but heavily muscled. He was solid, not fat. A full gray beard and long hair framed a craggy weather-beaten face with a knotted purple scar on the left cheek that extended up to a half-closed rheumy eye. A rectangular red lumber-marking pencil nestled horizontally in his thick beard. He wore a light-brown Carhartt worksuit deeply stained with oil and no shirt underneath. Massive hairy arms hung at his sides. His two hands shared seven fingers.

"Kinna stove y'interested in? Un'a "em antique Prussian Generals like most slickers want or a new fancy one?"

"I was thinking of one of the Scandinavian models, enameled cast iron with some of those nice country scenes cast into the metal."

"Like a Yodel-type? They're real pop'lar now."

"Yes, that would be nice. Where's your shop exactly?"

"Git in."

"Your car?"

"Yeh."

"There's no passenger seat. Does the dog bite?"

"Only when he's angered. Won' chase ya, tho'. Hips is wore out, displeasure, they call it. I have to lift him in and out from the back seat to his chair in m'trailer. Hasn' walked for two years. Kinna drags hisself, tho. Here, ya kin sit on this."

Bettis handed Jack a brown "Greaves Dairy" plastic milk crate from the back.

"Never mind the bottles."

Bettis nestled the upside-down milk crate in among a clutter of Carlings Black Label beer bottles. The crippled German shepherd shared the back seat with a yellow Poulan chainsaw perspiring bar and chain oil into the upholstery. A Remington 30.06 was racked in the rear window.

Jack gingerly settled onto the milk crate and slammed the rusting door. The window glass promptly dropped out of sight into the door.

"Shit," muttered Bettis.

"Sorry," said Jack.

"Not'cher fault, does it all the time. Jumps right off the goldarned track. Bronco's a piece a shit. Use to have a Dodge Powerwagon, but the power train seized up from haulin' pulp logs. Hang on, 't'sa bit rocky, this road."

"Road?" gasped Jack. "There is no road."

Bettis veered the rattling Bronco off the road into a lush bed of ferns and began bushwhacking onto an abandoned logging road.

"Don' see much traffic on this highway no more," offered Bettis with a wry smile. "I stopped loggin' up here couple years after that peckerhead from Stowe bought it and posted it. Don' b'lieve he's ever been on it though."

The Bronco pitched and rolled as Bettis' scarred hands rolled the cracked steering wheel back and forth like the wheel of a boat.

"'T's kin a' rocky. Come spring this 'ere's a streambed and runoff washes everthin' away but the big stones, so'ss a bit rocky. This 'ere Bronco has tough springs, the shocks is shot, tho."

The violent pitch and roll had Jack clutching the sharp-edged dashboard hole where the radio had been with his left hand and the window post between the open side vent and the passenger side window that had disappeared into the door. The milk crate had no link to the heaving vehicle other than the weight applied by Jack's trim frame, so it pitched and rolled among the noisy bottles on the floor as Jack strained to maintain balance.

After fifteen minutes climbing the streambed, the way leveled off into a high meadow and disappeared. Bettis deftly slammed the car into second gear without using the clutch. Jack relaxed his grip while Bettis rummaged between Bear and the chainsaw for a Carling.

"Wet cher whistle?" offered Bettis.

"No thanks," answered Jack as Bettis accelerated through the high-grown hay. A red-tailed hawk gyred overhead searching for small prey.

"Where exactly are we going?" asked Jack, trying to subdue his uneasiness.

"Said ye wan'ed a stove, di'ncha?"

"I do. I just don't know where we're going."

"Where I keep 'em."

"So there's not an actual store?"

"Never was, have to move 'em around some."

The meadow ended again and Bettis aimed the Bronco toward what looked like a solid wall of hardwoods. As they approached the trees, Jack made out a tumbledown stone wall just inside the tree line with a narrow break in it. Slowing down somewhat, Bettis eased the Bronco through the break and onto what looked like a cow path. Jack clung to the dashboard. They entered the dark woods and bounced along more slowly as Bettis tucked into the beer in his left hand. The cow path wound through ferns and maples. A whitetail doe and two fawns paused farther ahead, stared for a few seconds at the oncoming alien and bounded off into the darkness.

"Venisons," Bettis pointed out. "Sandwich deer, 'em little ones, tender as all git out."

Jack nodded appreciatively as he tried to maintain his perch on the milk crate.

After another five minutes of slow and precipitous climb, they emerged again into a clearing, smaller than the lower meadow but closer to the elevation of the mountains in the horizon. Bettis maneuvered the Bronco over towards a large cluster of faded lilac bushes and killed the engine.

Jack noticed large patches of blue here and there in the meadow too consistent to be flowers. He tried vainly to open the door, but the few remaining chrome objects just hung loosely from their mounts and did not seem to be mechanically linked to anything that might free him from the Bronco. Bettis reached out through the torn plastic on his side and opened his own door from the outside, lumbered out, strode around the front and opened Jack's door from the exterior. Jack, stiff from trying to maintain his seat, emerged from the Bronco and stretched.

"Sorry 'bout the seat," Bettis offered.

Jack nodded, still stretching.

"'Chout fer cellar holes," Bettis cautioned. "There's two or three up 'ere. Use to be Uncle Cletus's farm, milked 28 Jerseys 'en he lived up 'ere. He was on my mother's side the fambly."

Jack nodded again. "About the stoves...."

"All around ya. Take a look. Kine ja wan' agin?"

"I don't understand."

Bettis strode over to a large sun-faded blue tarp that was beginning to shred into small rectangular strips that scattered as he whipped the large tarp from a cluster of huddled stoves.

"These 'ere is Yodels."

Bettis walked around the clearing whipping blue tarps from clusters of castiron stoves ranging in age from late models to ancient six-burner Glenwood cookstoves with pitted chrome and riddled with surface rust.

"Nev'r mine the rust, comes off with some double-ought steel wool and stoveblack. Good as new in minutes. Chrome's another matter. Mi' have to be rechromed, but Freddie Green'll do it for a song and the other 'alf yer life savin's. Which'n ya wan?"

Jack was stunned. The clearing contained an array of woodstoves from small Norwegian Jotuls to massive antique coal-burning kitchen stoves with two ovens, a dough-rising shelf, eight burners, and a copper hot-water reservoir.

One blue tarp concealed Bettis's prize offering, a battalion of oak-leafed Prussian Generals. Some had had their finery rechromed and interior sheet metal replaced; others still needed that work done.

One tarp concealed a crimson red Aga range. "Got that up ta Stowe. Had to drag it up here on a stone boat, fell off twice, used ma 4-ton come-along to get it back on the rig. Couple chips in the enamel, but still works good. Only fine 'em in Stowe. Be the lasta them bastards I ever recycle."

"These stoves are recycled?"

"Yup. Ever' one runs their mouth 'bout it," Bettis pronounced.

Jack nodded and opened the iron door of a green-enameled Jotul 118.

"You guarantee these stoves?" asked Jack nervously.

"'Gainst what?" asked Bettis, "Chipmunks, smokin', or goin' out? Stove's a stove. Wha's ta guarantee?"

"I guess you're right," replied Jack, "I'll take this one."

"That there'd be hunerd-fitty cash."

"OK," said Jack without dickering. He had brought considerably more. Jack walked around the high meadow, looking at what must have approached a hundred stoves clustered over an eight-acre clearing. Bettis replaced the blue tarps over the stoves and weighed them down with stones. The field was blueflecked with the sun-wrecked pixels of tarp and looked from a distance like a mountain meadow laced with bluets.

Jack's reverie was interrupted by a shout from Bettis.

"Need a hand 'ere."

Jack turned and saw Bettis holding the dollar-a-pound stove up against the back of the Bronco and realized he needed help securing it. Jack loped over.

"Jes' wrap the horse blanket 'round the stove and grab me that loggin' chain while I steady 'er."

Jack fumbled with the blanket and Bettis, applying his weight to the stove, which hung against the back of the Bronco, secured it with two log chains to a tow hitch and the rear seat.

"Don' wanna scratch yer pretty pitchers," said Bettis smiling.

Bettis made one more pass around the field to close up shop. And Jack remounted the milk crate, pausing to adjust the bottles to level it for the ride down.

Bettis checked the security of the stove, tightened the chain a bit, tucked the horse blanket in, and swung his large frame into the cab.

The trip down was slower than the trip up and they emerged onto the turnaround just as the sun began to set.

Bettis held the stove while Jack undid the log chain and horse blanket and the two of them turned the stove sideways and laid it on the back floor of the Volvo wagon. Bettis offered Jack the shredded horse blanket, but Jack declined and said that the stove would be fine there. Bettis muttered that some folks preferred to cover their purchases. Jack again looked puzzled.

Bettis extended his hand, now red with rust from the log chain. Jack reciprocated and the two shook on the deal. Bettis looked at Jack, but Jack, still somewhat anxious about his purchase, looked away towards his car.

Bettis volunteered to "hook 'er up fer nothin'," but Jack said it would be some time before he could hook it up in his A-frame so he would just keep it in the garage for now.

"Yer choice," replied Bettis.

"Say, Bettis, where do all the stoves you recycle come from?" asked Jack with a new sense of camaraderie.

"Folks like you," said Bettis with a grin half-hidden by his crayon-bearing beard.

Emile's Beaver Pond

ONE COULD BUY dynamite sticks and caps from Graves' Hardware if one's intent was known to be constructive. There were no written rules to be followed or credentials required for its purchase. A child could not walk or crawl in and buy dynamite. A highly intoxicated individual raving about a perceived slight or betrayal would probably not walk out with dynamite. A farmer whose wife had just left him for the hired hand might have to wait a week or two to acquire dynamite, especially if the new couple hung around. Good judgment was the rule.

Pete Trepanier was the largest single consumer of dynamite in Lamoille County. To Pete, dynamite was a handy tool that could be applied to almost any task, not unlike a hammer or screwdriver. From rock and stump removal to bass fishing, dynamite was a staple in Pete's arsenal of tools.

Not a registered "triple A" dynamite man, Pete nevertheless knew from years of experience and acquired wisdom its many practical applications. He kept a large wooden crate of sticks and caps handy for any task and had his own handmade plunger, twisted-pair wire, and lantern battery for detonation.

Pete boarded at Elise Couture's. As a troubled youth, he had been adopted by Elise and Clovis. The home balance sheet in those days did not count children as a liability, but rather as an asset, not something to pay for, but something to help pay. A good number of children, one's own or another's needing family, assured that crops were harvested, animals were fed and mucked out, snow was shoveled, wood was cut, split, and stacked, and the countless tasks required for survival got done.

Pete grew into a self-sufficient man, had a brief try at married life, sired a son, and then returned to board with Elise after Clovis met his end in a slow and agonizing death from stomach cancer. Elise continued to feed

Pete two meals a day and wash his clothes until his own death of cancer at the age of 68.

The only exception to this routine was the time Pete spent alone at his modest summer camp on Little Hosmer Pond in North Wolcott. Little Hosmer was a reedy, bass-filled pond where a few local folks had deer or fishing camps or a just a getaway. Pete's summer place had largely been cleared with dynamite, a log chain and his '48 Ford truck. Recalcitrant boulders were blasted either to smithereens or off the property depending on the extent of the charges he laid. Tree stumps were likewise blown into a fine shower of kindling, and in no time flat, the two-acre parcel looked like a finely landscaped estate with a majestic lawn extending down to the water's cattailed shore. In the middle, Pete erected a disproportionately small, one-bedroom fishing shanty with white painted Homosote interior walls, an unfinished board and batten exterior, and a roof of motley tin panels scoured from abandoned barns.

The camp was Pete's refuge. There he never suffered the opprobrium of townfolk or of Elise, whose life-long enemy had been whiskey drunk to excess by males in her family. For Pete, the mixture of alcohol and dynamite was a comfortable one and, on occasion, led to the setting of charges for sheer fun. Occasionally, exploded debris rained down onto a neighbor's property. Pete would then dutifully clear it away.

Pete's black '48 Ford pickup was maintained like a museum piece. Those who cared about such things in town agreed that Pete was a master mechanic and any machine he owned was perfectly maintained, functioned at its peak, and was a joy to behold. He routinely machined parts for his various machines and was even known to fashion his own tools, which he declared far superior to "storeboughts." Pete's only mechanical eccentricity was that he did not believe in discarding used motor oil. He was convinced that motor oil did not deteriorate with use. He routinely drained it, filtering the dirt and metal bits out of it with a dairy filter and then reused it endlessly, replacing only that which was consumed in an aging engine. This fueled regular debates with Chet, another master mechanic in town, about the durability of oil in an internal combustion engine or a pumping device. The debate was never settled, but Pete's various vehicles, tractors, mowers, and pumps outlasted everyone else's.

At camp Pete would drop-fish for hours, sitting comfortably in his homemade flat-bottom plywood rowboat with an ancient Evinrude three-horsepower outboard he had salvaged and restored from the dump where it had been discarded after its prior owner had failed to mix oil with the gasoline, causing it to seize up.

He would float quietly among the reeds and lily pads with their white lotuslike blooms, waiting for a bass, pickerel, or even perch to tug at his bait, all the while nursing a pint of Canadian whiskey acquired from "Peavine" Graves, the taxi driver who shuttled spirits from wet to dry towns. If the fish did not respond to the buffet of earthworms, cut worms, tent caterpillars, tadpoles, large beetles, or rolled bread balls that Pete offered up on a sharply filed hook, and if Pete was counting on a nice supper of fried bass in cornmeal batter or a large, bony pickerel poached in cream, and if his patience ran thin as the Cadillac Club pint in his tackle box ran out, Pete might well resort to the single stick of fused dynamite that always lay carefully wrapped in wax paper at the bottom of his tackle box.

This more industrial method of angling was illegal even then, and required great discretion. The pond and the few camps on shore would have to be vacant. Even though there was little noise and the charge was the lightest available, the sudden upward rise of water was quite visible from the shore and the corona of floating bass, perch, pickerel, suckers, pumpkinseeds, the odd pike, countless frogs and even an occasional stunned river otter was evident for some time and betrayed the novel technique. After the depth charge had done its work, Pete would paddle around as if he were moving through a seafood shop. He selected the choicer species and sizes, hauled them into his floating shopping cart and headed quickly for home. The destruction was never as thorough as the floating carnage might indicate. Many fish and frogs would float for a few minutes appearing dead, then suddenly return to their senses and swim back to the bottom to a full recovery. Others would float around until appreciative birds of prey gyring above the smorgasbord carried them off for a private feast.

Needless to say, Pete's cornucopia would exceed his appetite. He would haul ten or fifteen pounds of choice catch to shore, carefully clean them and wrap them in wax paper, stow what he wanted short-term in his condenser-topped General Electric "ice box" and then drive off to deliver the balance to friends and neighbors who needed or enjoyed fresh fish. The remaining parcels he would take to the space in the Morrisville Community Freezer Locker that he and his hunting friend Lyle Bohannon rented together. The two had an understanding that either might remove items at will for his own use. So meat and fish were never bought at Patch's Market, but simply selected from the rich array of venison, pork, bear, brown and lake trout, Northern pike, bass, rabbit, partridge, wild turkey, and even beef, as Lyle had been known on bibulous occasions to "miss" a shot and hit a Jersey bull—which he would claim looked like a whitetail deer. The proprietor of the Community Freezer Locker, Charlie Bailey, would notice the "terrific catch" and signal his knowledge of the caper to Pete with a wry wink.

After two hours, Little Hosmer Pond would return to its normal lazy self with a few floaters not yet claimed by the various raptors eyeing the feast, but dead fish were not unusual in a shallow pond where there was little respite from the hot sun. Pete was careful not to overuse the dynamite option in lieu of live bait. He did not want to give Duke Turner, the game warden and county forester, the opportunity to catch him in the act as would be required for prosecution.

Elise and Clovis's son Emile had a small camp on the west shore of Lake Willoughby not far from the Canadian border. It was the last camp on a singlelane dirt road. An abandoned logging road, overgrown with blackberry bushes, extended beyond the camp down to Blueberry Cove where the Keewaydn Kanoe Kamp lands began.

When Emile first bought the camp, the last section of the access road had been corduroyed with twelve-foot cedar logs. In the woods on the high side of the road for as long as anyone could remember, there had been a four-acre beaver pond that kept the road a muddy swale when not frozen solid. A small trout stream ran from the beaver dam's outflow, down through the woods, under the corduroyed road through a partially collapsed culvert, and meandered on down through the woods below the road, debouching into a cove near the camp's boathouse. Under the mossy overhangs of the stream's bed lurked a silvery school of brook trout, which his children would catch for breakfast and enjoy with a heap of scrambled eggs.

The beaver pond was the reason for the perpetually sodden road. The corduroy kept the few passing vehicles from sinking into the mire, but often tires would simply spin on the wet lateral logs, going nowhere. Emile decided finally that the beaver pond had to go. It had drowned four acres of valuable hardwoods and made a mire of at least twenty acres below it. In those days, no permits were required to alter a waterway. No selectmen deliberated. No consultants opined. No public hearings were warned and convened. One simply consulted one's neighbors and began work.

Emile enlisted his children to help. Mike and Bill slogged up through the mire with their father to tear apart the dam with a three-pronged hay-fork, a potato hook, and a rusty brush hook. They did enough damage in several hours of work to increase the outflow considerably and returned home satisfied that the pond would drain quickly. They planned to return the next day to complete the destruction, catching a half-dozen "brookies" on the way home in the now roiling stream.

After breakfast the next day, the trio returned to find the dam fully repaired by the beavers. The outflow was back down to a trickle and the waterline back at its prior level.

Surprised and disheartened, they did no further damage to the dam, but returned home to take advantage of the hot sun and go for a swim.

Later that afternoon, Emile decided on frog's legs for dinner, so Mike, Claire, and Bill were dispatched back to the beaver pond with two fishing nets and a creel. The net handles were extended by attaching them to four-foot whistlewood shoots with baling twine.

Mike, unbeknownst to his sister and brother, had secured an M-80 from an acquaintance who dealt in cross-border enterprises like hooch, fireworks, and scoot pictures when he could find them. The M-80 was a cherry bomb producing nothing more than a very loud noise, a puff of smoke, temporary hearing loss and huge welts, if not thrown promptly after being lit.

The M-80 simplified immensely the harvest of frogs. They filled half a five-gallon bucket in only the time it took to gather them. As a bonus, the charge yielded three large "German browns" as well. The three sat on the shore of the pond on a fallen birch tree and spent the next half hour performing slimy amputations with dull pocket knives. They had clear instructions from their mother to bring back only the legs and to bury the remainders. The final harvest, rinsed in the stream, would fill a large pie plate.

"That was quick," noted their mother with no hint of skepticism in her voice.

"Sunny, lot's a frogs out." Mike responded looking straight at her.

In an often repeated ritual, they watched with fascination as their mother emptied the large pile of web-footed legs into a hot cast-iron skillet with melted butter, salt, pepper and garlic. As they hit the hot iron, the legs came alive again, contracting and stretching actively for the first few seconds until they were seared and finally cooked through.

"Good catch," their father opined, looking up with butter glistening on his stubbly chin. "I've asked Pete to come up tomorrow to take a look at the beaver dam," he added.

The kids, especially Mike, were thrilled. Kids liked Pete. He used dirty words, swore heartily, and generally treated kids as adults when Elise was not there to stop him.

Pete showed up in his truck the next day at about seven. The family was up and about except for Emile's wife, Cynthia, who was sleeping in. Claire was making toast and Emile was scrambling eggs and frying up the three browns "caught" the day before.

After breakfast, Emile, Pete, and the kids left Cynthia to sleep, heading off along the corduroyed road to where the brook flowed underneath it. They turned into the woods, following the brook up to the spillway of the dam.

"Goddam, that's a helluva dam ya got here," said Pete in his rich baritone, surveying the breadth of the dam. "You could pull that bastard apart all day and the beavers would have it fixed by dusk. There must be four or five families in here. Did ya count the mounds?"

"No, but it seems to be a good four acres of water," offered Emile.

"Only one thing for it," said Pete.

"Dynamite," Emile guessed.

"TNT to you, boy," fired back Pete.

Pete led them back to camp, making it clear to all, including Emile, that he would be in charge from here on. Back at camp he spun on Claire, then only nine, and said sternly to her, "You ready for a big bang, sister? This here's dangerous shit. Ya don't mess with it. Ya hear?" Claire's small freckled face nodded earnestly. He went to his truck, opened the passenger door, and took out a fifth of Seagram's Crown Royal.

"This calls for the good stuff," he said casually to Mike. Mike nodded earnestly, thrilled to be included in such a momentous decision as to which whiskey was necessary for the detonation of a beaver dam.

Pete gathered up his gear. He carried an army surplus steel ammo box containing the small plunger, a lantern battery, and a small waxed box of dynamite caps in one hand, and an armload of coiled wire in the other. He signaled to the two boys to grab a large wooden box stenciled in blue on all sides with the words, "Caution, dynamite. Keep away from flame, heat, or moisture."

Thrilled to be entrusted with the job of carrying the explosives, each grabbed a rope-handled end of the box and hefted the load between them. Pete winked at Emile and said, "You two young pricks better be careful of that load. One shiver'n' we'll be collectin' yer parts outta these woods like blackberries. Hold 'er steady now."

The boys stiffened and clutched the rope handles, trying to keep the load of dynamite sticks level. Together the five headed up the sodden path. "Keep that stuff up high between ya's, gets wet it's useless," ordered Pete. They hefted the box higher. At the culvert they again turned up into the woods, following the stream up to the dam. The sun was high in the sky.

"It take me few hours to set dem charges," declared Pete, swilling from the sculpted bottle with its dark blue velvet bag and gold string tie. He passed it to Emile who took a modest nip to be cordial. Then Pete passed it to Bill saying, "You'll be needin' some, too, but don' git greedy, save some for dat li'l brudder and sister." He roared with laughter. Emile looked at his son and frowned, indicating that he should decline.

Pete set to work immediately, wading into the smaller pond of water fed by the spillway just below the four-foot dam. He placed charges along the dam, adding caps, and connecting the small wires. A beaver traversed the backwater, disappearing after a few minutes with a slap of his tail.

After an hour and a number of tugs on the Seagram's bottle, Pete ordered everyone back to camp, saying he needed more time to figure out exactly how the dam would go when it blew. Emile looked nervous for the first time and gathered his kids up for the return to camp. He sent them on ahead and then consulted with Pete about what to expect.

"Explosion infernale!" laughed Pete, "suivie d'un déluge magnifique! Make de 'hole lac a foot 'r two deeper." He roared again with laughter. As the kids retreated out of earshot, they heard something about "staying on high ground near the camp and away from the shoreline."

Emile met them back at camp twenty minutes later with a worried look on his face. He talked with his wife until her face, too, took on a worried look. The kids were enthralled.

The sun began to lower into the western sky and the family could hear Pete singing at the top of his lungs several hundred yards back in the woods.

"Si mon moîne voulait danser,

Un pipe du plâtre ils ont fumé. Deedle um dee.

Demi-tour à droit, demi-tour à gauche,

Les femmes sont chaudes. Da deedle um dee."

The singing stopped and was followed by a several minutes of dead silence. Then a loud roar from the woods,

"Prêt à exploser....

"Five, four, trois, deux, un...." And again silence.

Then came a staggering roar, followed immediately by three more deafening blasts.

From high on the bluff where the small camp overlooked the lake, the family quickly looked inland to where the beaver pond was. The sky above the woods filled with debris from the dam. It hovered for a moment in the sky as if time had stopped and then began to rain slowly back to earth. Their mouths hung open, both from the sheer magnitude of the deafening blasts in rapid succession and from the dark cloud of debris raining down everywhere.

A thundering shout of "Sacré bleu et tabarnak!" followed the lingering decay of the blasts, the ringing in their ears and the reverberant echoes off Mount Pisgah and Mount Hor. They then heard a series of hoots and hollers from back in the woods.

Emile shook his head ruefully. "I knew when he pulled out the bottle...," his voice trailed off.

Suddenly they became aware of a rushing sound that swelled steadily to a roar.

"Uh-oh," Emile said.

Just then they saw a roiling wall of water five feet high, carrying trees and uprooting others, leaving dead logs and debris in its wake. The four acres of water about six feet deep roughly followed the former streambed down through the woods towards the cove and the boathouse. Emile described it later as the sound of a hurricane hitting shore.

The great mass of water came fast and subsided quickly. The damage was done in fifteen minutes. The first onslaught of brown, peat-stained pond water lifted the white clapboard boathouse off its stone foundation, leaving it bobbing at an odd angle half underwater in the cove.

Emile decided it was safe enough to leave high ground and go back and check on Pete. He told Cynthia and the kids to stay on the camp porch and wait for his return.

Emile found Pete sitting on a fallen birch log grasping an empty Seagram's bottle in one hand and picking diligently at his right nostril with the other. "Helluva blast, eh?" he observed casually.

The pond was now less than half an acre surrounded by mud flats, a few flapping trout, and land-locked frogs. There were no beavers in sight.

Ruefully Emile suggested that they walk downstream and see what damage had been done. Pete signaled his agreement by hurling the empty bottle into the mud and they set off to follow the new waterway down to the lake.

Pete expressed dubious and somewhat guilty surprise to Emile at the extensive damage done to the former roadbed. There was no trace of any road. There was only a muddy chasm where the culvert and corduroyed bridge had been. The swath cut by the onrush of water had left a gap in the road about sixty feet across. There was no longer any way out from the camp except by boat or on foot.

Pete reeled back to camp humming loudly to himself. He avoided Cynthia, who was doing a poor job at concealing her anger at being stranded by Pete's endeavor. Emile, not comfortable with his wife's simmering anger, set out on foot for Mr. Billing's to call the town clerk in Westmore to ask him to send over the road commissioner to negotiate a repair to the road. Emile knew he would have to bear the cost of the repair as the road was not a town road but a private right of way.

Mr. Billing's camp was about a mile back up the road and, like the camps owned by most local folk, was never locked. He had the only telephone on the West Shore Road. Next to it sat a small saucer to remind campers who might avail themselves of the phone to leave something to defray the costs. Almost all calls from Westmore were long distance.

Bill and Michael were commissioned to swim out and try to recover the powerboat from the boathouse bobbing in the cove and secure the boathouse with a mushroom anchor in the cove until it could be hauled out and set back up on its loose stone foundation, little of which remained. The dented and patched Grumman canoe was afloat, but full of water and adrift in the cove along with tons of woody debris, dead fish and frogs, a number of cedar logs that had once formed the road, fern fronds, leaves, chunks of moss, a wooden tent platform nobody recognized, and the empty rope-handled wooden crate neatly stenciled "Caution, dynamite. Keep away from flame, heat, and moisture."

Pete sat down in a rocker on the porch and dozed off snoring. Emile returned with a commitment from the Westmore road commissioner to come over next day to assess the damage and give an estimate for a new culvert, the yards of crushed rock and gravel, and the hours of bulldozer time that would be needed to rebuild the road.

Mike and Bill eventually freed the lapstrake motorboat from the half-sunken boathouse and hauled it up on the rock shore. They then swam out again and rescued the drifting canoe, after which they took turns picking leeches off one another. The lake had no leeches but the pond had been alive with them, so they were now everywhere in the cove, making swimming less appealing. Claire sat with her mother watching the proceedings while Pete still snored on the porch, occasionally mumbling something in French.

That evening as the sun set, a lone beaver swam across the cove and out into the lake.

In the morning, Pete was gone. He had apparently made it across the muddy swath that had once been a road and through the subsided brook, using his comealong and a sturdy pine tree to pull the truck across the gap.

Emile and his family, however, were left with their '54 Ford wagon on the wrong side of the brook and had to wait four days for a new road to be built. They got food supplies across the lake by boat and, when all was said and done, rather enjoyed being stranded.

By fall the beavers had fully restored the dam. The brookies returned to the stream. The browns returned to the pond. The leeches disappeared from the cove. The road commissioner and Emile managed with the bulldozer and log chains to haul the white clapboard boathouse onto eight new cinderblock pylons, and the new gravel road was high enough above the surrounding quagmire to present few problems. Life at camp returned to normal.

The Ferlands' Pet Pigs

CÉCILE AND THÉRÈSE FERLAND had just returned from taking their mother, Laurette, on her annual pilgrimage to St. Joseph's Oratory in Montreal. After eleven years of escorting their mother to the basilica looming over Côte des Neiges, the mystery of countless miracle healings wrought by the intercession of Brother André to Saint Joseph on behalf of petitioners from all over North America had long since faded for the two sisters. But the resplendent city of Montreal, with its endless shops and boulangeries filled with exotic pastries made the trip a continuing source of pleasure for the two sisters. The annual pilgrimage included a brief shopping foray for the girls on Boul. Ste. Catherine and lunch at Ruby Foo's Chinese restaurant on Avenue Décarie in Notre-Dame-de-Grâce or "NDG" as the locals called the neighborhood.

Though it embarrassed them acutely, the sisters would watch distractedly as their mother climbed the 283 carpeted stone steps from the parking lot to the basilica high up Mount Royal on her swollen knees. With breaks, the whole ascent took about two hours and most of the time she was lost in a crowd of other pilgrims making the same painful ascent. Her age and periodic "spells" made Cécile and Thérèse uncomfortable leaving her alone to go off and browse through the bins of devotional trinkets offered in the gift shop.

Over the years, Thérèse remained intrigued by what she called the "crutch room," where the crutches, wheelchairs, and prostheses of healed pilgrims hung by the hundreds from the walls and ceiling. Thousands of devotional candles filled the shadowy room with a paraffin haze and one could often hear the distant strains of an organ in the basilica above. Cécile thought the room was "creepy" and preferred to remain outdoors.

Laurette's mumbled petitions, either to Brother André, who founded the Oratory, or to St. Joseph, its patron saint, remained a secret all her long life, although both Cécile and Thérèse suspected that it had to do with the palsy that had wracked their Tante Lucienne's frail body from early in middle age and the congenital baldness that had embarrassed her as a young girl and ruled out a propitious marriage.

Each year their mother's ascent made a deeper incursion into their fun time. On this visit, she arrived at the summit well into the lunch hour and, with the help of her daughters, stood up stiffly, regaining her composure. She dabbed at her craggy face with a tissue and promptly descended to the parking lot in an elevator to go have lunch at Ruby Foo's.

Having learned only to "drive tractor," Laurette repaid her daughters' indulgence in making the trip by letting them choose, and buying for each, some needed addition to their modest wardrobes, one year a sweater, another year a skirt, a purse, or a particularly well-fashioned blouse. For her daughters, it was the fun part of the trip, along with the endless array of unrecognizable, sugary meat dishes, alien seafood, and exotic vegetables at Ruby Foo's lunchtime buffet.

After lunch they went straight to Boul. Ste. Catherine, where they paused to look in the window of the sprawling Centre de cuir with its cheap mannequins scantily clad with blue and red-dyed leather mini-skirts, faux buckskins, and rhinestone-festooned motorcycle jackets. Thérèse moved on to the window of a small pet shop next door. It was filled with open-topped pens. One contained three double-toed, angora tiger kittens nestled in fresh wood chips. Another held an over-coiffed, café au lait toy poodle eager to escape. The pen on the far right housed what looked like a black piglet.

Cécile and Thérèse knew pigs. Their father, Laurent, after failing to extract enough milk from his dwindling herd of Guernseys and Jerseys to make his bank payments, had negotiated a six-month truce with Adrian Morris, the president of the Union Savings Bank and Trust Company in Morrisville who had a well-known soft spot for farmers, borrowed a hundred dollars from his brother, and went into pig farming with a renewed sense of purpose. He made enough in his first year to pay Maurice back in full and catch up on all but two of his delinquent bank payments. The key, he soon learned, was to sell litter runts locally as piglets, while he raised the choicer ones to market weight, slaughtering and selling them as finished cuts nicely wrapped with hand-lettered labeling to people in Stowe as "farm-raised pork." The term "organic" was several decades away in Vermont, although the Ferland Farm was, of necessity, organic.

The "pig" in the window did not conform to Cécile and Thérèse's image of a piglet. It was immaculate. Its skin was a dark charcoal gray rather than pinkish and it had few, if any, bristles, but sported a sparse, cosmopolitan down. Its snout was shorter than that of a Yorkshire piglet and its rounded abdomen explained the "pot-belly" on its name card. It was without doubt a pig, though the girls had never imagined pigs as household pets.

Thérèse entered the store and inquired in French of the clerk the price of the pig in the window. The clerk answered as he distractedly dumped an overdose of tropical fish food into a tank of neon tetras. She came back out and gasped, "Eighty-five dollars Canadian for that piglet. That's more than Dad would get for a litter of ten and the sow."

"If Dad got that for his pigs," observed Cécile. "We could spend the night in town and shop again tomorrow."

Laurette was tired from her knee-walking ascent and was looking forward to the ride home when she could snooze as a passenger in their rust-blistered but comfortable Ford Galaxy. Cécile sensed her fatigue and the three returned to where they had parked on a side street off the boulevard.

The piglet and its extraordinary price emerged several times in conversation during the ride home. The border crossing at Rock Island was largely perfunctory unless some recent criminal activity had officials on alert. Locals, whose town straddled the border, walked and drove back and forth with a simple nod to the customs officer on duty.

In summer, breakfast at the Ferland Farm was a half hour earlier than in winter, as summer work required every waking moment of the more plentiful daylight. Laurette, in her frayed cotton bathrobe, was at the four-burner cook stove at 4:30 a.m. A pale light suffused the Worcester Range to the east, and flames blinked through the cracks in the cast-iron firebox, warming the chill early morning air in the kitchen. Water boiled in the tin kettle and Laurent huddled over a plate of scrambled eggs and a piece of toasted homemade bread with rhubarb and strawberry jam, his right hand wrapped around a handleless mug of unpasteurized milk, black coffee, and a hefty dollop of sugar.

Cécile entered the room still rubbing the sleep from her eyes. It was her day to help Laurent bring in the first cutting. Her job was to drive the baler hitched to the Farmall C along the neatly raked rows of hay as soon as the dew was off while he stacked the 70-pound bales on the trailing hay wagon. The harvest required father and daughter to keep moving at the same pace.

Except for two remaining Guernseys that provided milk for the family, the "girls" had been sold to buy pigs, but Laurent continued to hay his fields and sell the harvest, first to the horsey set in Stowe, and the remainder, for substantially less, to local farmers who had come up short for the winter.

"Pe-père, you should a' seen this $85 black piglet we saw in Montréal," Cécile yawned.

"Ettie-fie doller, das a lot 'fer a cochon," answered Laurent sipping his coffee.

"Who buy dat in Montréal? No place ta farm dere."

"It was in a pet shop on Ste. Catherine. People want them for pets. They're cute. They're house-trained, too," chimed in Thérèse.

"You s'pose dem Stowe folks pay dat for a color piglet?" asked Laurent warming his hands around the ironstone coffee mug.

"Maybe, Pe-père. They do in Montréal."

"What color dat piglet be?

"Black."

"Ettie-fie doller?" "Yup."

Laurent shook his head in disbelief. "Dem pibbles in Stowe pay crazy for anyt'ing."

"They like your pork," Laurette offered.

"Dey do." Laurent confirmed, nodding his head.

The haying went without a hitch. The regal white thunderheads forming aloft in the blue sky withheld their heavy raindrops until the last bale was off the 28 acres north of the barn and the tractor and baler were stowed in the sagging pole barn.

The back door to the weathered farmhouse opened into the kitchen. A red-and-white-checked oilcloth-covered oak table and eight ladder-back oak chairs filled half of the room and the Glenwood cook stove with overhead warming bins and a copper-lined hot-water reservoir dominated the other half. A castiron sink atop a waist-high, pale green pine cabinet occupied the back wall. A window over the sink looked out over the bustling hen house, the unused milking shed, and a rhubarb-rimmed manure pile left over from the dairying days. Worn linoleum covered most of the pumpkin pine floor. Laurent's light blue rocker sat near the front door, and an unpainted pine box near the stove held a good supply of finely split biscuit wood.

The room was redolent with the rich smell of a venison-and-root-vegetable stew simmering in the Dutch oven on the far right of the stove. Just before bringing the stew to the table and setting it on a trivet, Laurette would sift a cup of white flour into it, stirring it steadily to thicken the broth into rich brown gravy. When ladled out, this would puddle on the white ironstone plates warmed at the edge of the stove and each family member would then help himself to two boiled potatoes, mashing them down into the gravy.

"Ettie-fie doller eh? Tabernak! Das a lotta dollars for a pig, non?"

"Everyone seems to want them. They make great house pets, like a hound dog, and the clerk said they were very clean. She said they learn tricks. They are house-trained and smart, too."

"I know dat. So be da fella what sells 'em for dat prise," said Laurent, a forkful of venison in mid-air. "You s'pose dem pibbles in Stowe pay dat for a black piglet?"

"I wouldn't be surprised," chimed in Thérèse, silent up to this point. "I can stop by Mountain Pets on my way home from work Saturday. They carry everything. If black pot-belly piglets are pets, they'll have 'em. I'll find out."

Baling the new-cut hay in the south meadow was on hold for at least a week. The storm that succeeded the last haying had persisted and steady rains soaked the hay. Anxious to try out his rebuilt mower, though, Laurent had cut the wet hay. It would have to be tedded again and left to dry a day or two before being baled.

That night at dinner, Cécile announced excitedly that Mountain Pets had sold three such pigs and were trying in vain to get more. What's more they had said that the pet stores in Waterbury and Burlington were looking for stock as well and that the demand was so great that breeders of the little pigs could not keep pace. Mountain Pets charged $110 for each pig and would pay up to $60 apiece wholesale for decent stock. With that, she tossed on the table a $2 pamphlet entitled "Vietnamese Pot-bellied Pigs as Pets."

This announcement was followed by silence as each family member individually scanned the pamphlet. It meant little to Laurette for whom the wasteful ways of skiers were a matter of legend. Her friend Lucille got $8 from people in Stowe for the three-layer wedding cakes she baked and decorated herself, while the few well-heeled people in Morrisville who commissioned one would never pay more than $5. After all, the ingredients amounted to less than fifty cents.

Cécile was already imagining a shopping spree on Boul. Ste. Catherine, spending the night at the elegant Reine Elizabeth with dinner at the Beaver Club.

In a similar reverie, Thérèse was dickering with Pete Demars for his '61 Chevy Biscayne, having long yearned for the freedom and élan of having her own car.

With two sows currently suckling 13 piglets, Laurent had already reached a conclusion about the enterprise and was reviewing the math on a note pad. He would have black piglets in Stowe as soon as they reached eight pounds.

Laurette stood at the sink washing up from dinner. There were no dinner scraps to add to the blue enamel slop bucket under the sink for which the pigs waited anxiously when Laurent went to the barn. Cécile dried the ironstone dishes and tarnished nickel silver utensils, putting both away in the cabinet beside the stove.

Thérèse sat at the table thumbing through a *Look* magazine from last fall. Laurent, his heavy eyebrows overhanging his closed eyes, rocked quietly in his chair by the door, overwhelmed by the pleasure of a good meal and the fatigue of a hard day's work.

Friday brought back the sun and by daybreak, Laurent had hitched the tedder to the tractor and was tossing hay into new windrows to be dried by the sun. He was done by eleven.

Thérèse had left early for her job in the cafeteria at the Mountain Company in Stowe and Cécile and Laurette had gone to Morrisville to Patch's Market to get some flour and canning supplies and to run errands on Portland Street. Laurent needed bar and chain oil for his saw from

Graves' Hardware. Cécile needed alum from Peck's Pharmacy for her canker sores. Laurette would get a darning needle from Gillen's when she picked up the black fabric dye Laurent ordered for the piglets.

They returned home a little after two to find Laurent ready and waiting. The equipment for dyeing the pigs was set up in the old milkhouse, now emptied of all the unused items tossed in there for storage. The large scalding vat was set up outside with a small fire beneath it warming the water inside. Laurent kept checking the temperature with a dairy thermometer. There was a boar-bristle paintbrush nearby.

"You got dat dye stuff?" Laurent asked even before greeting his wife and daughter.

"Yeh, it's here," answered Laurette. "Fifteen packets."

"Eh bien, tanks. Ya help yer Pe-père, Cécile?

"Sure," answered Cécile, curious.

Laurent rechecked the water temperature and asked Cécile to read and explain the directions on the packets of dye.

"Add packet to four gallons of hot water, immerse fabric for three minutes swirling constantly for even coloring and then hang until dry. Repeat if necessary."

Laurent Ferland's English was confined to the few hundred words needed to trade for goods in town, consume food, complain about weather, and express his affection for his family and animals.

"You figger doze tings, I fetch da piglets."

Laurent took a large laundry basket lined with a tattered quilt and disappeared into the barn. Cécile built up the fire under the rusty cauldron until steam began to form above the water and bubbles formed on the side. Doing a quick mental calculation she tore off the corners of four packets and added them to the now roiling water. She grabbed a nearby piece of kindling and stirred the cauldron until the swirling color was evenly distributed and the water had turned to inky black. With the same stick she pushed the fire from under the cauldron, spread it about and stomped it out.

Laurent returned from the barn with four pink piglets jostling one another in the quilt-lined basket. He set the basket down and said, "Cool down a bit, eh?"

"Cool down a lot Pe-père. We don't want to scald the piggies, but it does need to be somewhat hot. I'll get a wash tub of cool water and some rags to dry them."

With that, she left Laurent to guard the boisterous piglets, pushing them back down into the basket as they scrambled over one another to look out. Soon they were all tangled up in the quilt and one another. With his index finger, Laurent tested the temperature of the dye.

Cécile returned lugging a washtub half full of cool water with two threadbare towels hanging over her arm. They compromised on the temperature, Cécile concerned that the piglets might squeal in pain and rile the sow within earshot in the barn, Laurent advocating for enough heat for the dye to set.

Laurent plucked a piglet from the tangled quilt and plunged it squealing into the hot dye. He was careful to keep the piglet's bleating head out while swirling him around upright. After less than a minute, the dye had done its work and the still squealing piglet was handed off to Cécile to pat dry. Laurette hung fresh laundry from the clothesline nearby and watched the proceedings warily.

Cécile took the small paintbrush, swirled it around in the dye and began to daub color onto the cheeks, chin, and forehead of the forgiving and now curious piglet. This produced a mottled look similar to what Cécile had seen in the store and the pamphlet that Thérèse brought home.

"Not too bad, eh, Pe-père?" she said, holding the curious animal up to her father.

"Alors, dat looks like in dat paper what Thérèse brings home," averred Laurent.

They dunked and swirled the remaining dozen piglets, having to reheat the dye only once. The colored piglets were left free to romp on the grass in the yard as the dye dried and set in the warm sun. Cécile paused for a minute to admire their handiwork and then put away the rags and smaller things while Laurent overturned the cauldron, leaving a large patch of black dirt in the middle of the farmyard.

The piglets were returned to their color-blind mothers who had seized on the brief sabbatical to enjoy deep slumbers and didn't even notice the return of offspring to their sore teats. Laurent made no effort to return the right offspring to the right sow. He grinned as he left the sows, imagining in a spontaneous reverie Laurette's surprise had Elda, the local midwife, handed her a colored newborn instead of the pink bundle that was Cécile, their firstborn.

The dyeing of the piglets affected neither their health nor their growth. Within two weeks they reached market weight. Thérèse, recalling how the careful packaging had enhanced sales of her father's pork, paraphrased the basic tenets of care and feeding from the pamphlet onto some fancy lavender stationery given her by her Tante Lucienne, rolling and neatly tying each instruction with a pink ribbon. These would accompany the piglets to market.

Saturday on her way to work, Thérèse called on the owner of Mountain Pets in Stowe and negotiated an order for five piglets. Long-distance phone calls to Burlington, Montpelier, and Waterbury completed the sale of all thirteen piglets at a net figure of $700. That Sunday another sow gave birth to six more marketable piglets. Deliveries were completed early in the week and orders were in hand for another dozen pets as soon as Laurent's five breeder sows could produce them.

Dinner conversation that evening was rife with suggestions for spending the new income. Thérèse's initial sale of thirteen equaled a month's regular farm income. If production kept pace and the demand for the trendy pets held, the family enterprise might easily double its annual income.

The market continued to grow well into the first snows of winter, maintaining a more or less steady flow of hand-colored piglets into the pet market. After Christmas, however, retail activity slowed to a crawl and there were fears that either the local market was saturated or that enthusiasm for the fad was waning. "It's jes' winter," opined Laurette, whose skepticism for the product had suddenly vanished with her purchase from Montgomery Ward's catalog of an electric mangle. "Peoples hole up in da winner. Dey start buyin' again springs come."

Laurent nodded solemnly from his rocker at his wife's wisdom.

The first call came from Jim Mertz, the owner of Mountain Pets. He had gotten a call from the Baroness von Trapp up on the hill at Cor Unum saying that her little Fritz seemed to be a bit larger than her friend Hilda's pig, which never weighed much over 55 pounds. Fritz was nearing 140 pounds and his little hooves were beginning to make deep marks in the soft pine floor in the lobby and his behavior in the dining room, over which he had thus far been given free rein, was deteriorating.

Cécile took the call and, recalling advice imparted by her favorite high school teacher, simply listened, offering to "look into the matter" with Laurent and get back to Mr. Mertz.

Cécile raised the issue of Fritz's weight at dinner. The topic raised no eyebrows.

"Tabernak! das nuttin', dat pig be five hunner' in springs," observed Laurent munching a mouthful of pickled beets. "Good val-yous, better dan dem li'l fellas in dat booklet you bringin' home."

"But Pe-père, they're pets," interrupted Thérèse. "They're supposed to be cuddly and do tricks."

"Dey do tricks ahright. Dey get big so, dey can shoots dem and make jambon and baconnes. Still be good deals, like two fer one, pets den baconnes."

"Pe-père!" sighed Thérèse, "People in Stowe don't eat their pets like in Quebec."

"Why not dat?" inquired Laurent, this time with his mouth full of mashed potato.

The conversation wound to a halt as Laurette set on the table four unmatched saucers and the remains of an upside-down cake made the previous day.

The calls became more frequent, first from pet store owners, then from their confused or irate patrons. Store owners, anxious to appease and retain their testy customers, referred them directly to the "breeder" in Mud City for further information regarding their weight gain and perhaps some suggestions about dietary modification.

Hilda Baccari's piglet, Esther, had topped 170 pounds and showed no sign of moderation. Esther had long since lost patience for the tricks Hilda had taught her at 25 pounds, such as standing on her hind legs to reach up for a bonbon. Now she would simply stand on her hind legs, set her forefeet on Hilda's breast, knock her over, and help herself to the entire box of bonbons.

The bonbons led to a passion for cream and sugar and she learned quickly where to find both. She was now tall enough to reach the Tupperware creamer and sugar bowl on the dining room table. Esther's highly articulate snout would ease them both onto the floor, stir them about until they reached the right consistency, and then, frantic with pleasure, lap it all up. She soon came to expect this treat twice daily and grew cranky if the ingredients were not where she expected them to be.

Lloyd and Martha Squier's pet, Ruby, held the lead for weight gain, eating her way rapidly towards 200 pounds seven months after her purchase at twelve pounds. The key to this extraordinary weight gain was the diversity of pet food available to her. She inhaled dry dog food, and savored wet cat food and the accompanying bowl of cream. She also appreciated the nutmeats that Pélé, the African gray parrot, pushed onto the den floor for her, and the scrumptious sunflower seeds that were plentiful on the bird-feeding platform on the deck. This surfeit of protein propelled her weight to new heights each month and the exhaustion of digesting all this rich protein would see her snoring on the wicker love seat on the front porch, the feet of which began to splay ominously outward.

Ruby's life was not without exercise, however, which toned her up nicely even in the face of her extraordinary weight gain. Her best friend Muzzy, a rather dumb golden retriever, loved to chase cars, but only five or six a day passed by the porch on Blush Hill Road. The two, sleeping soundly on the front porch, could hear the cars coming down the road on the gravel. Their ears would perk up and their eyes would light up. They would look at each other and scramble to their feet. Ruby had learned this game from Muzzy, whose owners had never been able to break her of her habit of chasing cars. At first Ruby could keep up with Muzzy on the gravel road, but as her rich and ample diet increasingly layered her in lard, her pace slowed and she would quit about 200 yards down the road panting and waiting for Muzzy to return so they could amble back to the front porch together and flop down to rest up for the next pursuit.

Late in September, the cushioned wicker love seat collapsed under Ruby, making it considerably more accessible as a resting place for her inordinate weight, which by now severely handicapped her in the merry chases with Muzzy.

Joe Fortin's pig, Amber, just grew up mean and had little patience for the manners Joe and Mabel had worked hard to instill in her. The first sign of her bad temper came a few days after her arrival in the Fortin household when she stole the baby bottle out of Alice Fortin's cradle. Losing patience with the Slo-flo nipple, Amber bit it off, improving the milk flow considerably. The habit of stealing milk from the baby was so hard to break that Joe simply bought Amber her own calf-feeding bottle and kept it full and available. If Joe was not assiduous in refilling it, however, she always had recourse to the smaller one in the cradle.

With no other household pets to steal food from, her keen and agile snout became adept at finding new treats in the kitchen behind the warped cabinet doors whose latches no longer made contact. She also attacked the occasional baked goods cooling on the low windowsill when her owners retired to the living room to watch the evening news, or whatever else she could find that was more flavorful than the drab Blue Seal mash provided by her owners. She soon developed an urgent taste for Sugar Pops cereal, leftover casseroles, and also for red Kool-aid mix, much of which remained on her jowls in her frenzy of consumption. This gave her a tarted-up look that did not appeal to her Methodist owners and betrayed another assault on the lower kitchen cabinets.

When she was 450 pounds, the Fortins unceremoniously released Amber inside Lenny's Pet Shop in Waterbury where they had bought her. Her ravenous appetite made short work of the packaged pet food stacked on the floor. She was finally subdued by two men with ropes as she gulped water from a 50-gallon aquarium full of cheap goldfish, conveniently placed on a low stand to entice juvenile buyers.

Word spread rapidly among pet owners of the renegade strain. In all, about seventy of Laurent's dyed pigs made it to market and the indignant owners' stories continued to reverberate in the three retail pet stores that had sold them.

A number of pigs, disgruntled with the paltry diets outlined in Thérèse's instructions, simply left their owners in disgust. If more and better snacks could not be rooted out of cupboards, countertops, teenage bedrooms, den couches, and pantries, the Yorkshires simply moved out in search of better pickings.

Several "seasonals" with down-country accents reported heatedly to local officials, who struggled earnestly to look appalled and stifle their amusement, sighting immense pigs snuffling through trash on Mondays when driveways along Mountain Road sprouted fresh garbage for the weekly municipal pickup.

The swine insurgency continued in Stowe into the fall until sporting locals inaugurated a stealthy hunt and began removing the increasingly feral pigs to freezers on sagging front porches.

One buyer did not seek recourse. Jake Leriche lived south of Stowe on Route 100 and "drove dump" for the Stowe Street Department. Jake had bought the dyed piglet for his wife Annette who was afraid of dogs and allergic to cats. They adored their "Ti-chou" and were disappointed that her weight eventually made it impossible for her to sleep on the bed as she had when she was little. Jake retrieved an apparently new twin mattress from a roadside "free" pile on Mountain Road in Stowe, tossed it in his truck, and installed it at the foot of the bed they shared. Annette made it up nicely with a contour sheet and an old quilt she found at a neighbor's lawn sale. Ti-chou felt comfortable close to her doting owners. Ti-chou's weight burgeoned to 550 pounds after three years at table with the Leriche family. She eventually exfoliated the black dye in blotches and resumed the healthy pink color of a Yorkshire sow. She remained a spinster and member of the family until her demise nine years later. One night, as her owners slept soundly in the bed next to her, she trembled slightly and her gentle snoring simply ceased.

The "swine scandal" was viewed as such mostly in Stowe, whose wealthier citizens were among the few who could afford to spend that much on a pet. Locals in Morrisville relished the brouhaha and read with delight the indignant weekly updates and outraged letters in the *Stowe Reporter*. Morrisville's own *News and Citizen*, under its editor-publisher-owner and occasional reporter, Clyde Limoge, reported the enterprise with objectivity and subdued relish.

Laurent suffered no economic ill effects from his initiative. Buyers in Stowe of "farm-grown" pork seemed to make no connection with the recently burst bubble in the market for pet pigs.

Rumors persisted for several years in Stowe of an immense pig, said to be close to a thousand pounds, spotted periodically rummaging through trash behind some ski lodge or in an open garage, assaulting and emptying pole-mounted birdfeeders, or lumbering across the Toll House practice slope in the summer.

Doc's
Come-along

THE MUD CITY LOOP ROAD meanders deep into the Sterling valley and back out to Morristown Corners. Morris Orvis and Doc live along the north branch of the dirt road in a slumping L-shaped farmhouse, the sills of which are skirted with mushroom-dappled hay bales. Two well-muscled Belgians graze about the surrounding fields, and a John Deere B tractor rusts near the shed. A larger Allis Chalmers, with traces of its original orange paint and evidence of recent use, is parked by the side door. A homemade wood splitter extends off the tractor's three-point hitch and is linked by hydraulic hoses to the circulatory system of the tractor. Morris's woodpiles are legend to those few who drive by on the Loop Road.

One hundred ninety acres remain of the original Orvis farm. Morris's fields are the last open land hikers cross when they ascend Sterling Mountain. The two-story white farmhouse sits 50 feet back from the Loop Road. The roof line sags near the chimney. The shed and summer kitchen extending off to the right have lost their paint to the harsh weather. The shed is crammed with well-dried wood. There is enough room left for a chest freezer dappled with rust, drawing its power from an extension cord running into the house through a living-room window.

Morris and Doc live without benefit of the growing number of social services available to them. Doc is a drinker, but Morris doesn't drink because he has "the sugar." Together, they support Doc's consumption of alcohol, Morris's "sugar med'cine" and have enough left over to buy canned foods. They sell cordwood to log truck owners who buy the wood from them and haul it to the paper plant in New Hampshire, selling it there for a hefty profit. Twenty cords a month yields $400 and pays for life's necessities and the taxes. Doc also sells firewood to those who don't dicker and are experienced enough to know that wood comes wet and green and needs to be cured a year before burning.

They have no immediate neighbors, even as the Sterling Valley succumbs to Stowe's outward push of kitschy ski chalets and unheatable glass aquaria that pop up here and there along the dirt roads that used to link vanished hill farms, sugar works, cedar oil mills, and lumber camps.

Doc is not a doctor but earned his moniker as a kid. His father was in France "fightin' krauts" and his mother was tolerating the sexual attentions of their mortgage holder at the Lamoille County Savings Bank who had found her "saucy" as she pled for forbearance on their $28-a-month payment. Back at home her son Royce Denton heard screams coming from his neighbor's house and ran over to find Bessie Pixley lying on her kitchen floor in a pool of blood-stained water, beginning a birth process with which, at seventeen, she was as unfamiliar as Royce. He asked over her screams what to do as he stared at the small head emerging from Bessie. "Anything!" she screamed. "Just save my baby." Royce gently grabbed the head and pulled. At each pull, Bessie screamed louder and finally Royce just pulled the new Pixley boy out and Bessie fainted from the pain.

Royce knew enough to cut the cord and did so with his jackknife. He washed the baby off with a towel, and wrapped it in some more towels that were drying near the woodstove. He saw blood continuing to trickle from Bessie. Neither family had a phone, so Royce ran out with the baby, started a pickup truck in the yard, and drove to town to get Doc Goddard. Bessie was dead when they returned, but the baby thrived and Royce became known at the age of twelve as "Doc."

As a young man, he appeared to have few prospects. But in time he found he had an uncanny ability to diagnose and repair heavy equipment like tractors, skidders, splitters, and anything involving hydraulics. He learned to weld from a neighbor and became a master welder, but the sustained, low-level inebriation that began in his late twenties gradually took its toll, not on his skills, but on his sense of industry and purpose. Over time, he declined more and more outside work, choosing instead to focus his waning industry and vision on the maintenance of his own equipment. This consisted mainly of the 28-horse Allis Chalmers tractor with its tangle of hydraulic hoses linking the front bucket, the splitter, the leaky pump and reservoir. A burst hydraulic hose under pressure had rendered his lower left forearm useless; he could still grip objects with his left hand but he couldn't move them.

Mounted on the tractor's power take-off is a drum cylinder whose belt drives a 30-inch frame saw that Morris keeps razor sharp with a bevy of flat files. Doc has already lost an index finger and half a thumb to it.

Morris and Doc have lived in Sterling Valley for as long as anyone can remember. Morris, shy and uncomfortable in the company of strangers, is generous to a fault with his waning coterie of ageing friends. Neither Morris nor Doc claims any relatives, although Morris is said to have a deaf sister in Quebec who lives in a convent there, though she did not take religious vows.

As a child and later as a young man Morris worked in a lumber camp near Coplin Plantation on the shores of Flagstaff Lake in Maine. He started in the camp kitchens peeling potatoes and then carrying food tins to the lumbermen in the woods for their 30-minute lunch break. Over lunch, he heard stories of men crushed under falling trees or collapsing log piles, drowned as log piles awaiting the river runs cascaded into icy lakes and rivers, maimed when pinched saws whipsawed their operators and took off a leg or shredded an arm. Later on, he became a sawyer, working one end of a two-man saw until the first Oregon 72D and Homelite XL 12 chainsaws appeared in Maine in the early '60s. Those first power saws were little more than heavy outboard motors with chains instead of propellers. They took more strength than the old hand saws, which required patience and teamwork. The handsaw's slower cuts made far more predictable "fells." The speed with which a chainsaw operator could go through a 30" trunk meant less care taken in the fell, and more accidents. A two-man saw that got pinched in a fell just hung there limp while a fast-moving chain pinched in a fell sent the operator reeling as the saw bucked back.

Morris never got lumbering out of his blood. At 74, with failing eyesight and poor circulation in his legs, the cutting, splitting, and stacking of firewood is all that is left to him. Doc keeps their three chainsaws, the tractor, and the splitter running, and he helps with the cutting and splitting, though he draws the line at stacking. "Mule's work," he calls it.

Morris' freestanding woodpiles take three shapes: the conventional linear pile with its garrison-stacked end-supports, an elegant tepee-shaped pile that enables one to stack a large amount of wood in a small space and has the added effect of protecting the wood from rain, and, finally, commercial cord piles, eight by four by four. This last style makes manifest the honesty of the purveyor, enabling buyers to see and measure, as one did in the old days, the exact amount of wood being bought for earnest money.

Near the stacks sits a five-foot-high pile of badly rusted twoby twelve-foot galvanized tin roofing sheets scavenged from barns and sheds whose owners had replaced them or whose outbuildings had collapsed. These sheets protect the many woodpiles from rain and are weighed down by chunks of unsplittable wood—crotches, stump-ends, and the like. Near the house is a pile of maple burls that Morris sets apart for a woodworker in Eden who turns them into bowls for craft shops in Stowe and Woodstock.

The field across the road had been bought by a fellow from down-country who dreamed of having a Christmas tree farm. Doc had no truck with the fellow. He had gotten off to a bad start by dickering over the price for some green firewood for his house back in New Jersey.

"Tried to jew me down on a quarter cord, b'lieve that? Maybe on twenny cord, but a quarter cord?" he'd muttered, pulling hard on a pint of liquor he kept in the hip pocket of his brown coveralls mottled with chain oil and hydraulic fluid stains.

The summer after the Jersey man arrived, a flatbed truck with several hundred small bagged and balled balsams and Scotch pine showed up. Two men unloaded the trees in the meadow and left. Three days later, two high school boys drove up in a '62 Chevy truck with some spades and shovels and a few bags of fertilizer. With lime, they marked out a bunch of lines parallel to the Loop Road and began digging holes the size of basketballs along the rows.

"Goddammed unnatural," muttered Doc to Morris as he surveyed the industrious boys dropping trees into the freshly dug holes, tamping back the earth and ringing the drip-lines with fertilizer. "Looks like a goddam' vaudeville house with them trees all in a line like 'at. You know how hard the Languerands worked to clear that goddam' field of trees and rocks, and that was afore tractors. Did it by hand with that blood-red ox they kep' and a stoneboat I welded up for 'em."

Doc went inside while Morris watched as the lines of trees continued farther and farther back from the road. By the weekend the trees were all in the ground and three acres of tillable land was planted in balsams and Scotch pine for later sale in New Jersey.

"Goldang'd criminal if y'ask me," muttered Doc, checking the level in his upheld flask.

The following spring the trees were thriving. One or two had browned out, but the rest would make a fine selection to be sold in a couple of years on the streets of Chatham, Union City, and Summit. The neat rows of trees, however, were like a canker sore to Doc who saw only a field that a generation of Languerands had struggled to clear.

Late in the fall, after a two-pint day of ornery work cutting pulp, Doc decided to restore the field. He drove his '51 Dodge Power Wagon to the town sheds, filled a couple of empty sap buckets with chloride and returned home under cover of darkness. After Morris was in for the night, he made a pot of coffee, poured a cup into a Mason jar, added four tablespoons of sugar, and filled the rest with whiskey. He told Morris he was going to disconnect the saw from the tractor power take-off and ready the tractor for splitting in the morning.

Morris sat in his pale blue, badly stained recliner rubbing his painful shins and nodded assent. Doc headed into the night with his Mason jar of stimulants, grabbed the buckets from the Dodge, and crossed the road. Starting at the south end of the field, he went from tree to tree ringing the three-foot trees with a liberal dose of road salt. It took a little under two hours in the dark to complete the task.

For the next few days, Doc watched anxiously for rain clouds, taking an inordinate interest in the WDEV weather reports that emanated from the brown Bakelite Philco in the kitchen. Doc and Morris always listened together to "The Trading Post" to see what the neighbors were selling, although they themselves never traded there. Neither one understood how it worked but both enjoyed listening to the descriptions of Jersey cows, milking equipment, tractors, and used appliances. When the weather report came on, Doc would bend over and listen closely to the radio near the slate sink.

Six days later, Doc was relieved to wake up to a torrent of rain outside, gray and overcast, heavy with fog. Doc looked out the window towards the trees and shook his head up and down. "Ain't workin' in that shit," he muttered to Morris, who was reading the headlines of a *News and Citizen* from late spring. The "sugar" had affected his eyesight and made it hard to read the small print in the articles.

The chloride did its work. Within days, the trees browned out and within weeks they were all a pale cinnamon red. A month later the fall rains had washed the dead needles away and nothing remained but rows of evergreen skeletons. At Thanksgiving, Jackman came up from New Jersey. He stayed with friends in Stowe, and brought them over to see his Christmas tree plantation.

Still uncomfortable with Doc over his anger and unwillingness to give him a discount on wood for his fireplace, he knocked on the badly weathered door. Doc looked out the window, saw his down-country neighbor, spat a dark wad into a Mason jar and walked into the kitchen ignoring the knock. Morris struggled out of his lounger and hobbled to the door.

"All my Christmas trees seem to have died. Any idea why?"

Morris shrugged honestly and stepped outside, lest Jackman ask to come in.

"Nope. I see'd it happen, but figured it must be the soil or no water. It's hardpan clay and the water jes' runs off it down ta the brook." "Seems strange not a one made it."

"Yup, happens 'at way sometimes."

Jackman nodded and left, anxious to get back to his car where he explained to his curious friends, who stayed in the car on seeing Morris, what had happened.

As Jackman departed, Morris offered to brushhog the dead trees and Jackman accepted, not knowing what it meant. On his own, Morris had periodically brushhogged only the perimeter of the field where popple shoots and chokecherries threatened to encroach. The next day, there was no trace of Jackman's enterprise.

When Doc moved in with Morris some 35 years earlier the network of back roads that wove together the outer districts of the villages were simply scraped and graded cow and buggy paths, widened and kept open by a steady flow of traffic. There was no advance engineering, no substrate of drainage gravel or crushed stone, just widened dirt paths rolled in winter with large horse-drawn wooden rollers to pack the deep snow. Snow removal was unimaginable. Nowadays, big butterfly snowplows with scarifier blades and side deflectors came roaring through in the middle of the night guided only by pasture fencing and hardwood stakes in the snow, making short work of a two-foot snowfall. In many respects the rigors of winter proved easier than the miseries of mud season.

April was true to its reputation and it rained all but four days that month. The outlying roads became impassable and those who still had workhorses or even riding horses pressed them into service to fetch supplies and otherwise get around. A late spring snowfall of several inches only added to the morass of mud and snow. The road in front of Doc and Morris's was like soup. In the daylight, the treacherous mud looked firm, but the springs in the meadow above the shed kept the clay road soupy to a depth of several feet. A rock ledge from the mountain prevented drainage.

It was dusk and Doc and Morris were in for the evening. Morris was in his favorite chair, reading an old *News and Citizen* and rubbing his left leg to encourage blood flow and assuage the dull, constant ache with the other. The one bulb hanging from an open socket spread its glare through the windows to the environs of the house outside. Doc was opening a can of Spam with a key and another of beans with a dull knife. This usually was the extent of their evening meal unless Pete brought by a load of perch or a small northern pike, or Reba Batty sent out a macaroni casserole with the mailman, who would then return her dish the following day. Doc nipped occasionally from his flask.

A cock and five hens roosted inside on the back of a couch in front of the window. Cracks in the couch's black leather ran everywhere and several holes revealed the horsehair stuffing inside.

Enraged at a marauding raccoon, Doc had moved "the girls" indoors after every effort to stem the nightly slaughter of his shrinking flock of laying hens had failed. They seemed to enjoy the indoors. Egg production rose significantly, although Doc now had to look around the house for eggs as "the girls" were constantly finding new and more out-of-the-way places to lay them.

Morris's tiger cat ignored the hens as they were larger. No one lacked for food. Leftovers and indolent mice made evening meals peaceable for all. Morris's cat usually managed her "business" outdoors while the five hens and their one cock were incontinent. As anyone who has chickens knows, however, waiting until their shit is dried makes for an easy clean-up.

Doc kept a metal spatula on a hook near the door for this purpose to differentiate it from the one in the drawer he used to cook eggs.

Doc spotted car headlights about 500 yards up the road and muttered, "What ta hell?" Morris looked up from his paper.

"Goldang fools to be out on a night like 'iss. Lost or drunk. I ain' diggin' em out," continued Doc.

"Whassat?" muttered Morris, looking up from a story about a fire last fall.

"Some goldang eedjits out walk'n their car in the mud."

Doc went into the kitchen to check on the Spam and beans frying on the woodstove.

The slow-moving car wound its way down the hill and sank to a halt in the mire in front of the house.

From his chair, Morris looked out the window and then back to his paper. Doc hollered from the kitchen, "They stuck yet?"

Morris responded without looking up, "Yep."

"Serve's 'em right, goddam' eedjits. They'll be a knockin' at the door, jess wait."

"Allus do," muttered Morris.

The car sat for about 25 minutes with the interior light on and four people moving around inside. Efforts to open any of the doors on the pale blue '58 Ford station wagon proved useless as the mud was well over the bottom of the doors. Finally one of the occupants rolled down a window and crawled out headfirst, falling sidewise into the mud. He managed to get to his feet and tried to assess the situation in the dark.

The car sat just on the edge of the light oozing from Morris and Doc's living room, which was just enough to reveal that the occupants would not be pushing the car to drier ground 30 feet ahead. The mud-covered scout, who was not the driver, leaned back into the open window and said, "We're stuck in the mud."

"We need a shovel," volunteered a perky female voice in the car. "Maybe those people who live there would lend us one."

The scout, whose name was Lewis, turned around and looked at the farmhouse, looking as if he had been invited to sleep in a cemetery.

"You ask 'em," he said. "They're bound to be nice to a girl."

"I'm sure they're nice people," responded the perky female voice. "Just poor."

"Poor or not, someone has to go ask to borrow a shovel so we can get out of here. I have to be back in Nyack by 7 a.m. to go to work. Tomorrow is Monday."

"Phil, you go, you're big. They won't mess with you," said the scout.

The perky voice responded, "You guys are being silly. I'll go."

Phil said, "I'll go," and clambered out the window feet first.

Landing on his feet, he slogged through the mud towards the house, slowing as he approached Morris and Doc's. Instead of going toward the door, he detoured toward a living-room window and looked in.

"Now they'se peerin' in," observed Morris, seeing the face in the window.

"Leaf peepers, house peepers, what ta hell's next?" muttered Doc."

Phil returned to the car.

"Jesus!" he panted. "There's chickens sitting on the couch and an old man sitting in a chair reading a paper. The chickens are just sitting on the couch looking at him. It's too weird. I'm not going in there."

"I'll go," said the mud-covered scout. He headed up to the farmhouse. He knocked on the door.

Morris rose stiffly from his blue chair and limped to the door.

"Help ya?" he asked.

"We're stuck out front. Can we borrow a shovel for a few minutes?"

"Yep," responded Morris, "There's shovels in the shed. Help yerself. See that ya put 'em back. By th' way, yer' gonna need 'em for mor'n a few minutes. Yer axles is buried."

"Thanks, we'll bring them back," said Lewis, grateful that the old man wasn't crazy and could talk, even though the rural dialect and his desire to get back to the car caused him to miss Morris's observation about the submerged axles.

In the dim light from the living room, Lewis groped around inside the shed until he noticed several shovels leaning in a corner. He grabbed them all, including two snow shovels, and scurried back to the car.

Using a round-head shovel, he removed the mud from one of the rear doors until he could force the door open with the help of the girl Jen, who pushed from inside. The remaining occupants emerged from the car and Lewis handed them each a shovel.

"Let's dig this out and get on the road," said Lewis, whose earlier daring had earned him a leadership role.

After twenty minutes of digging, there was no visible progress, largely because the constant flow of springwater kept refreshing the aqueous mud. Phil made the least progress, and complained the entire time that snow shovels were useless for shoveling mud.

Doc and Morris settled into their supper of Spam, beans, and baked potatoes. From his days working the lumber camps, Morris had learned to bake five pounds of potatoes at once and keep them in the icebox for rounding out the occasional meal. He sat in his chair with his white ironstone plate in his lap and Doc perched on the edge of the couch that he shared with the curious hens, nipping occasionally from his pint.

"How's 'em city boys doin', you s'pose, with their exacavatin' project?" Doc muttered.

"Dunno," answered Morris through a mouthful of cold baked potato and ketchup. "I'll go an' see after I finish my supper."

"Do as you please. I ain' goin' out there. They'll wan' our help an' it's gonna take Kyle's dozer to getch'em eedjits out."

"S'pose so," responded Doc, chewing on a mouthful of Spam.

There came another knock on the door. Morris set his plate down on the floor and rose painfully to his feet. The cat ambled over to lick up the grease and ketchup.

"How's it goin'?" said Morris to Lewis who was again at the door.

"We keep digging, but the station wagon seems to keep sinking in. Is there a wrecker service that could pull us out?" asked Lewis plaintively.

"In Morrisville or Stowe mebbe," answered Morris, "but they ain' comin' out this way, 'specially this time a' night, for love ner money."

"Could you pull us out with your tractor? We could pay you?" asked Lewis glancing sideways at the old rusting Allis Chalmers near the shed.

"S' Doc's rig and she ain' much in the way of traction, even with her ring chains on. Twenny-eight horse, don' cha know," answered Morris.

"What can we do?" asked Lewis plaintively.

"Start cher goddam trip over and stay on the paved roads," observed Doc from the kitchen, where he was wiping the grease out of the black iron frying pan with an old *News and Citizen*.

"Late at night to go callin' anyone with 'nough power to getcha outta that mud," observed Morris.

"How much money ya got on ya?" called Doc from the kitchen.

"I'd have to check with the others," allowed Lewis nervously.

"Better check if you wanna get home," said Doc, emerging from the kitchen.

Lewis flinched at Doc's appearance and at the hip flask he was swinging in his hand.

"I'll check with the others," he quavered, turning and running down to the car.

"There's two of them and I think they plan to rob us," said Lewis to the others standing by the mired vehicle. "They want to know how much money we have. I think we better tell them. There's a big gun in the living room and the skinny one seems violent."

Back up at the house, Lewis announced that they had a total of twenty-eight dollars among them.

"Bet it all I can't pull you out singlehanded?" challenged Doc.

"Don't see how you could," muttered Lewis.

"Put cher money where your mouth is," challenged Doc.

OK," said Lewis, defeated, "you can have all our money if you can get us out by yourself."

Doc took a long pull on the pint, drew on a pair of oil-stained coveralls hanging on a nail by the door and brushed past Lewis, disappearing into the shed.

After a lot of noisy rummaging and cursing, he emerged from the shed dragging a very heavy tool characterized by a large cast-iron ratchet and frame spooled with heavy cable. After dropping this by the car, he returned to fetch three 28foot logging chains that together weighed more than Doc's slight frame.

His approach to the car caused a tremor and slight retreat among the mudspattered travelers, who withdrew to higher ground.

"Need any help?" twittered Jen.

"Lie down in front of the car so there's some traction," muttered Doc, causing further retreat of the vehicle's occupants.

Doc grabbed a round-headed shovel leaning against the car and, with the false energy of inebriation, dug a small tunnel under the front of the car. He grabbed one end of a log chain, lay down in the wet mud and, reaching into the burrow he had dug, looped the log chain around the wagon's front axle. He pulled it taut and clambered back to his feet covered with mud. He clamped the grapple hook at the other end onto a second chain and to this he connected the third chain. Now about 50 feet from the front of the station wagon, he let the taut log chain onto the ground.

He strode angrily back to the car, cursing audibly and incomprehensibly in the French he had learned from loggers in his childhood. He grabbed the heavy cast-iron come-along and dragged its considerable weight to the end of the last chain. Releasing the ratchet lock, he unspooled the cable for another twenty feet and let the mechanism drop to the ground.

He went back to the shed and returned with a large section of cut truck tire. He looped the loose cable from the come-along around a large sugar maple by the side of the road, pulled the cable tight, and then tucked the broken tire in around the cable to protect the old tree from scarring by the cable.

The four people in the car stood whispering to one another in the shadows and watching as Doc moved rapidly from chore to chore swearing a blue streak.

Finally, he looped the other end of the 3/8" steel cable's hook to the grapple hook on the last of the three log chains. This made a continuous line from the axle to the 40-inch maple.

Doc then unscrewed the cap from a new pint, took a long pull, picked up the come-along, relocked the ratchet catch and began to pump the short steel handle until the whole line of chains and cable lifted from the mud and became taut.

"He thinks he's gonna pull it out by hand, the old drunk. He probably doesn't weigh 120 and he's gonna haul a 4,000-pound car out of a mudhole. I'd like to drink what he's been drinking," observed Phil from behind Jen.

Doc stopped pumping the ratchet handle and left the come-along hanging in mid-air. He went back to the shed and emerged with a four-foot section of steel pipe. He returned to the come-along, slipped one end of the pipe over the ratchet handle for further leverage and began pumping again, this time more slowly and clearly with more effort.

He paced himself and interspersed every ten or so strokes with another pull from his flask. The chain began to spin slowly in place as it tightened ever more and, to the sudden shock of the car's occupants huddled nearby, the sound of shifting mud came from beneath the car. The front began to lift slightly and a great sucking sound emerged from below the car as Doc pumped the large section of pipe slowly back and forth.

With eerie and lubricious sounds of suctioning mud, the car moved inch by inch towards higher ground until the front half was clear of the mud. Doc did not even seem winded by the steady back and forth of the ratchet lever on the come-along suspended in mid-air.

When the mud-covered car was on a firm section of road about thirty feet forward of where it had been, Doc yelled, "Out the goddam way! I'm releasing the tension and you could get killed." The kids ran up towards the light of the house and huddled together.

Inside the hens pecking at the beans left on Doc's plate made an odd pinging sound.

Doc pulled the lever halfway through its arc and then released the ratchet lock. He then let the lever swing back and the cable unwound quickly for a few feet and the now slack log chain fell to the ground.

Doc unwrapped the cable loop from around the maple, letting the protective tire strip fall to the ground, gathered up his log chains, and lugged the whole mess back into the shed, where he dropped it unceremoniously into a pile on the dirt floor.

The kids fumbled with their wallets extracting what cash they could find. Jen was emptying coins from her change purse into her hand when Doc emerged from the shed.

"You win, Mister. Here's all our money," volunteered Phil, who had mustered all the pluck that had failed him before in the now certain knowledge that they were either going to be killed outright or would have to spend the night in the mired car.

"If your goddam headlights are outta my failing eyesight in three minutes, you can keep yer goddam' flatland money and just owe this old bastard an endless debt of gratitude for the rest of yer life. Now put yer money away and beat it, quick-like afore I change my mind and push you singlehanded back into the mud," said Doc, with the delivery of a Calvinist deacon.

He then disappeared into the house and slammed the door.

"They out?" asked Morris without looking up.

"No thanks to you," answered Doc, flopping down next to the hens on the couch.

"They pay ya?" asked Morris.

"Wan't worth it," answered Doc.

Duke's Mudwasps

JEAN AND DUKE KITONIS's place was high on the hill just across the road from Jack's. It had been there as long as anyone could remember. Saul Douglas's grandfather had built the house sometime during the Civil War and not much had been done to it by man since then. Nature, however, had done a great deal to it, which is why Duke had undertaken to build a new home about seven years ago, 32 feet to the south of the old one, adding to the new structure as their limited resources would allow.

The cellar floor of the "ranch," as Duke liked to refer to the new place, was tamped earth, and the perimeter walls were scrounged cinderblock laid up dry and slathered with "Block Bond." The ground floor was framed atop the cellar wall and covered with 5/8" plywood that was beginning to buckle from the four harsh winters with no covering but an old blue tarp shredding in the sun and dotting the already littered yard with thin blue ribbons. To Duke's great pleasure the cellar hole, however, remained quite dry year round, an auspicious sign for the their future home.

The old place, the "homestead" as Jean called it, bore no residual signs of paint and Duke's plan was to tear it down when the new place was done and sell the weathered exterior to city folks to put in their living rooms. Jean had heard there was a factory in Wolcott that made weathered wood with some kind of process, but heard it didn't look as good as the real stuff siding their home.

The state, at one point, had prevailed on Duke and Jean to weatherize their home to help them lower fuel costs. The work and materials were free to "qualified" homeowners which Jean figured meant "welfare kin." The engineer who came to the house calculated that if Duke burned six cords of wood heating the house now, it would only take three cords after the insulation was installed, so they cheerfully accepted the state's offer, especially as Duke was running rapidly out of unguarded woodlots where he could scavenge free firewood.

The truck arrived on Thursday morning at eight as arranged. Three young men eyed the house curiously and then mounted ladders to drill 4-inch holes in the soffits and under the eaves and in between the stud work into which they would blow the expanded mica insulation that resembled breakfast cereal. A large truck that looked like a canister vac with a cab sat filled with the stuff next to the house.

When the holes were all drilled, one man, wearing a mask, climbed the ladder again and inserted a wide hose connected to the truck into a hole and signaled to his partner in the truck to turn on the blower. A loud whirring sound came from the truck and the limp hose stiffened somewhat as the insulation coursed through into the cavity between the studs. This continued for some time, to the surprise of the hose operator. The cavity between walls would usually fill up in three minutes or less and it had been closer to ten minutes. This sometimes happened when studs were 24" on center, but few houses were made that poorly, even a century ago. He eased a lead weight on a string through the hole, feeding out twine until it came to rest on the bottom. He then marked the spot on the string, raised it back up and noted the distance to the insulation's level. The hole in the siding was just under the roof soffit and the weight had stopped well below ground level. He climbed down the ladder, signaling to his partner in the truck that something was amiss. Duke, curious about everything, was underfoot and asking a string of questions that went unanswered.

"We got to take a look inside," said the ladder man, who was clearly the crew boss.

"Foller me," answered Duke,

"Jean, you decent?" asked Duke as he entered the kitchen with the crew boss trailing.

"Is there a cellar?" asked the crew boss looking confusedly at the intersection of the wall and the floor.

"Yup," replied Duke, "the stairs is over here." He lifted up a trapdoor in the pine floor where some rickety stairs with no railing descended into the dark. The basement exhaled a deep wave of dank humidity and rotting vegetables.

"Root cellar," declared Jean who had joined them in her housecoat. "We put 'em down 'ere and then always seem to forget about 'em."

"It's generic," added Duke, "We was both born with terrible mem'ries."

Duke, eager and grinning from ear to ear, handed the crew boss a battered aluminum flashlight with a bright beam and the crew boss picked his way carefully down the creaking stairs into the cellar. He came back up minutes later and asked Duke when he thought the house was built.

"Round about the Civil Wars," Duke responded proudly. The crew boss had never seen "balloon construction" where the studs run the full height of the house. The insulation they had blown in lay knee-deep on the cellar floor.

"We'll have to come back and try something else," announced the crew boss.

Duke looked despondent, not at the thought of having to scrounge the extra wood, but at the thought that the canister truck, with its neatly coiled hoses and earnest helpers, might not return.

Jean and Duke watched the truck disappear down the driveway and went back inside to finish the coffee in the blue enamel pot bubbling on the woodstove.

Feeling let down, Duke poured a healthy dose of tonic into his coffee and offered some to Jean, but she declined with a nod of her head. "Tonic" was blackberry brandy in a pint glass bottle that fit neatly into the owner's hip pocket, long a favorite of Duke's. The bright colored labels on Smith's flavored brandies looked more like labels from fruit preserves than brandies. Duke had tried all but the nut-flavored ones and, for the last two decades, had settled on blackberry, which was far and away his favorite. Duke's mother and grandmother had drunk "fruit tonics" for various ailments but disdained liquor for the nasty behavior it brought out in their men. The state store in Waterbury kept a stash of small brown paper bags they got from Greaves' Dairy in Morrisville so that ladies who consumed "tonic" would not have to suffer the ignominy of toting bags marked with the scarlet letter logo of the Vermont State Liquor Commission.

Duke turned his attention to the John Deere B rusting in the yard and his efforts to design a homemade snowplow for it. The plow was two halves of a 55-gallon drum cut evenly in two and welded together on the edge, all braced with some re-rod welded onto the back to stiffen it. Duke's dilemma had been how to raise and lower the plow from the driver's seat without any hydraulics.

Luke Higbee, his neighbor and sometimes friend, had solved the problem. They installed a long piece of three-inch steel pipe just in front of the driver's seat extending over the front of the tractor to a chain welded to the top of the plow. In the back two tractor weights totaling 100 pounds counterbalanced the weight of the plow. The driver could manipulate the plow up and down by hand while plowing. Although it looked odd, the equipoise contraption worked well enough.

After a couple more shots of tonic, this time without the benefit of coffee as he was outdoors, Duke gave up and set about another chore. Flitting from chore to chore for most of the day and finding in each a reason to proceed to the next, he again fortified himself with tonic, lay down on the sofa and took a loud nap.

When he awoke Jean had gone to the store. He took a wake-up dose of tonic and lay there staring at a lake of mold on the plaster-and-lath ceiling. Much of the plaster had long since fallen away, exposing the lath above, but some plaster remained and had become home to a brownish mold that made the ceiling look oddly like the topographical maps Jean's brother always had rolled up in his truck. He was the county forester and forest fire warden for Lamoille County.

Duke was interrupted in this reverie by a familiar buzzing. It was not the buzzing he heard in his ears on waking after too much tonic. It was not the buzzing that his friend Luke complained of hearing 24 hours a day in his left ear and called "tin-oi-tis." It was the all too familiar buzz of mud wasps again taking up residence in his home. Duke not only hated them but was terrified of them as his father had been. They were both "'lergic" to stings of the various bees, wasps, yellow jackets, and hornets that lurked around the homestead. Duke vividly remembered his father after a bee sting, his swollen face, the trip to the Copley Hospital, and the terror of bees and other flying stingers that his father had transferred to him.

"It's generic," he often said when regaling someone with the tale of his fatal allergy. "'Herited it from Dad."

When Jean returned, Duke was in a swivet, racing around armed with a flashlight, a can of Raid, a flyspray handpump filled with some oily yellowish fluid, and his 12-gauge pump-action shotgun.

"Where the hell's 'em birdshot loads? Where'd I put them bastards?"

Jean, used to Duke's frenetic behavior, assumed bees. Pouring herself some coffee, she asked calmly, "Find another nest?" while putting a gallon of milk and a large brick of Velveeta in the fridge.

"Hell, no. Goldang mudwasps, huge nest in the attic, they'se everwhere. Armin' myself to get rid of 'em right now. D'jou git more tonic?"

"In the glovebox, help yourself. You gonna do it yourself this time 'stead of getting' some help? You get bit, I ain' takin' ya to the hospital. You drive yerself."

Duke froze as he took in Jean's words. Getting bitten was like dying. Going to the hospital was like going to hell. He set everything down on the old chrome and Formica kitchen table and ran out the door yelling, "Find me some bird shot."

"Just a minute," yelled Jack Daulton from inside his restored farmhouse diagonally across the dirt road, "I'll be right there. Please stop hammering on the door."

"Deadly mudwasps in th'attic, need j'er help. Need j'er help ta git rid of 'em!"

"What are mudwasps and why are they dangerous?" said Jack calmly and somewhat suspiciously, catching the familiar fruity smell on his neighbor's breath.

"Deadly," insisted Duke. "One bite from 'em bastards'll kill you dead. My pa barely survived an attack of 'em."

"What exactly do you need me to do?" asked Jack.

"Jes' what I tell you. I'n gonna shoot the nest and you run up 'n empty a can a Raid on 'em. They won't bite then. You'll be safe. If 'n I get bit, I swell up like a dead pig and go blind 'n all and Jean won' take me ta th'hospiddle."

"And if I get bit?"

"Y'aint 'lergic, is ya?"

"Only to ragweed."

"C'mon. Let's git afore it gits any darker."

Jack pulled on a green L.L. Bean anorak, looked at himself skeptically in the hall mirror, and followed his neighbor up the hill.

Duke ran ahead yelling, "He's gonna help me, Jean. He said as he'd help me. Yup, yup."

They entered the kitchen where Jean sat smoking and carving chunks off the Velveeta brick that sat in its blue and silver foil on the dinette table. Next to it stood a quart of Old Fitzgerald beer about half gone and a *TV Guide* from last year.

"Good luck," she said calmly without looking up from her *TV Guide*.

Since Jean and Duke didn't have a TV set, Jean got her viewing pleasure by reading out-dated *TV Guides* she got from her friend Marcia. The many articles outlined plots and sketched characters in the shows. It was not as good as watching, but made for an adequate "viewing" experience. Duke had brought a TV back from the dump last year and told her he would "get 'er runnin' roit," but the vast array of wires, tubes, and strange parts exceeded his knowledge of car repair and after several arcing shocks, he took the set out back and added it to the large pile of things "fer later fixin'."

Duke had set the homemade ladder up against the trapdoor into the attic of the house. It was in the hall ceiling between their two bedrooms. The house footprint was about 1,200 square feet and contained only two bedrooms and the living-eating space, half of which was taken up by the woodstove that also heated the house. There were no interior "facil-ties." Although Duke had acquired from Lyle's dump all the used porcelain to convert the second bedroom into the bathroom he had promised Jean when she moved in as his bride, he had not yet found shelter for the car and tractor parts in there so he could begin work on the project. The outhouse was a short walk from the house.

"Foller me," Duke said, heading warily up the ladder trying to grip the 2" by 4" verticals and carrying the Raid, the sprayer, and his shotgun. When Duke disappeared into the dark, Jack followed with his L.L. Bean flashlight.

"Careful where ya step," said Duke. "Ya got's ta step only on the rafters, the lath won' hold ya. You'll go through the ceilin'."

Jack picked his way deftly across the hand-hewn rafters that formed the attic floor. There was no insulation between them or between the roof rafters, he noted with surprise, having overinsulated his own house to save on heat. Duke lay prone across two rafters, pushing a charge of bird shot into the barrel of the 12gauge pump.

"Git down here like me," he said. "Don't want to rile 'em critters. Wait till I load this up and I'll tell ya the plan."

Jack shined the light around the attic, which was empty except for an ancient mattress eviscerated by mice.

"What exactly are we after again?" asked Jack.

"Gimme yer light. See over there what looks like a big splash of hardened mud with holes in it? That's the houses them bastards build, just like mud huts 'em Pygmies live in Aferca, biggest 'un I ever see'd. Hear 'em buzzin' around. People say they don' bite when iss dark, but that ain' true. I been bit sittin' in the shitter 'n the middle the noight 'n got bit where the sun don' shine. Gotta s'prise 'em bastards. Here, wan' some tonic?"

"No thanks. What exactly is the plan again?"

"I'ne gonna shoot the nest from here with a bird load 'n you jump up, runs over and empty that there can on 'em. They'll all drop dead and it'll be over."

"Is that overkill?"

"Wassat?" responded Duke.

"I mean isn't shooting that nest with a shotgun a bit much?"

"I done it afore. Gotsta shock 'em bastards. 'Sides, iss only birdshot. Ready?"

"I think so," responded Jack with evident unease.

"Here goes."

A roar from the 12-gauge pierced the night and the corner sheathing and shingles of the attic blew clean away leaving only the corner beam. The starlit sky was evident through the hole.

"Oh, shit!" roared Duke, "she gave me the wrong shells. Run, run quick; they's all pissed off now!"

Jack saw the shattered mud nest against the night sky still clinging to a piece of lath. He leaped forward, took one step with his finger on the button of the Raid can and disappeared through the floor.

"Oh, shit!" roared Duke again. "Ya's sposed to step on the cross beams. Now look what cha done."

Jack landed on the Formica kitchen table where Jean sat emptying the quart of Old Fitzgerald beer and perusing the *TV Guide*. She looked up nonplussed and asked Jack if he was OK.

Jack scrambled off the table and dropped into the other unmatched chair, still clinging to the can of Raid.

"He get 'em wasps?" asked Jean casually.

"I don't know," answered Jack, as a still-agitated Duke descended the ladder and took a long pull on the pint in his pocket.

"Shit !" repeated Duke for the third time. "Ya mussa gave me a slug or goose loads; blew a hole in the side of the house."

"Not surprised," said Jean without looking up from her *TV Guide*. "D'jou git 'em?"

"Nope," replied Duke, "haffa try again."

"Blow the other half of the wall out and we'll be movin' into yer celler hole faster than we 'spected," noted Jean, taking a sip from her plastic tumblerful of flat beer.

"No need to be sharp wi' me," pouted Duke, staring at his empty flask.

"Need any more help?" asked Jack, dusting himself off and noting the large smear of yellow cheese on his new pants?"

"Mebbe later," said Duke. "Don' settle in."

"I'd settle in if I was ur'n," opined Jean. "One more like 'at and the house may come down on us all. S'pose the roof 'll stay till mornin', Duke?"

Duke just shook his head in disgust.

While making coffee the next day, Jack heard a thunderous crash. He looked up the hill and saw Jean carrying a toaster oven and percolator towards the cellar hole. Duke sat astride his John Deere and looked with pride at the collapsed homestead. A log chain ran from the roof beam to the three-point hitch and the house had settled down on to the ground like a collapsing parallelogram.

Several hours later the state insulation installers returned and stared at the rubble. There was no sign of Duke or Jean, who slept peacefully in their cellar hole.

Darcy and Father LeFarge

ACCORDING TO HIS lifelong friend, Père Renaud, who was with him at his bedside when he died, Father LeFarge's last words were, "I have never forgotten the face of any woman, young or old, who smiled at me."

"It could have been worse," noted Père Renaud wryly to a friend at the gathering at the bishop's residence after Father LeFarge's funeral. "He could have said, 'My God, my God, why hast thou forsaken me?"

Father LeFarge was well known for making his bishops uncomfortable. In his earlier years, he had been a fond student of South American liberation theology, a doctrine that posed a deep political and ethical dilemma for Rome. After a Calvados or two, he would expound to his good friend on the impossibility of reconciling the ethical spectrum and the socio-economic one—"camel through the eye of the needle" and all that.

His steadfast unwillingness to brush aside spiritual exigencies in order to absolve the wealthy of their various peccadilloes to the pecuniary betterment of the church had exasperated many patient bishops. One bishop, particularly irritated, had gone so far as to hold up Christ as an example of what happens to someone unwilling to "make accommodations."

Father LeFarge noted, with respect, the bishop's pastoral right to declare God's word as he saw fit and asked only that, as a man of God, he be allowed the same courtesy. As a result, he was frequently reassigned, going to a new parish until, inevitably, a complaint arose and the bishop would reluctantly send him to another parish, making up some diplomatic excuse about "in the service of our Lord."

To his friends' suggestion of a possible middle ground, LeFarge would bellow, "Absurd. It has nothing to do with church doctrine; it is about Thomas à Kempis's *The Imitation of Christ*. I simply ask myself, 'What would Christ do?'"

In his heartfelt remarks in remembrance of his good but recalcitrant friend at the funeral service, Père Renaud gracefully sidestepped some of the thornier moments of his friend's pastoral career, but the obsequies were still peppered with allusions, subtle though they were, eliciting broad smiles among the fraternity of priests present, even from the bishop.

In the 1950s, when more complaints came, the bishop felt on firm ground transferring Father LeFarge from the tiny—36 Catholics—but still devout parish of Websterville to Stowe, a ski resort where it could safely be assumed that only widows and transients might attend Mass, seek absolution, or request sacraments, and that only sporadically. The newly arrived von Trapps had their own chapel and their own spiritual advisor, and would probably only attend Father LeFarge's Christmas and Easter high Masses.

In 1950, Stowe was hardly the den of iniquity some locals felt it was becoming, but neither was it a destination for spiritual pilgrims, perhaps excepting the von Trapps. The immigrant aristocracy had just begun to acquire failing hill farms from the banks and to establish themselves as the ruling class over the locals. Stowe was still a dry town and liquor had to be discreetly taxied from Waterbury ten miles away.

Around that time, a woman of a certain age named Darcy Kurten settled in Stowe. Darcy had consumed a legendary number of husbands and in the process had managed to amass enough money to sustain herself, making her ongoing affairs a matter of sensual pleasure rather than economic necessity. She was said in certain Stowe circles to have "hinges on her heels," arousing insecurity in some of the plainer women in the community and indeed proving a source of transient pleasure to some of their husbands and sons.

She lived alone in a modest studio apartment above the Powder Keg, making the après-ski rounds at dusk. Her age and a life of skiing moguls in Stowe, Mt. Tremblant, Chamonix, and Aspen had made her somewhat "unsteady on her pins" and a candidate for knee surgery. But she resisted, as one of her past husbands had been an orthopedic surgeon and she had seen the results of his work firsthand while posing as his nurse.

Darcy was beginning to show her age. The steady inhalation of Chesterfield cigarettes had produced wrinkles about her chin and along her jawline. There were spidery blue capillaries and darker varicose veins behind her knees and on her once-venerated calves. The long blond hair that had turned heads on ski trails as it blew out behind her was beginning to show streaks of white. Her onceresplendent breasts now showed stretch marks in her saucy décolletage. None of these signs of age, however, seemed to attenuate the attention she received from men of all ages. They were drawn to her evident and insouciant enthusiasm for sports of the flesh as well as her uncanny ability to display tender empathy for issues their own spouses or partners might miss or ignore.

Darcy had been raised a Catholic by her father, her mother having left for greener social and economic pastures when Darcy was six. Like all lapsed Catholics, she sequestered the faith deep inside her for later use, remembering the *Our Father*, the *Hail Mary*, and the contingent *Act of Contrition*, which allows absolution from one's sins in the absence of a priest and proper confession while dying. Darcy practiced it periodically to ensure its place in her memory should she need it. These three artifacts of her faith were deeply rooted within her, even as she had abandoned the practice of the faith that had provided her with her first sexual experience at the age of nine.

Darcy felt age closing in on her, in her knees and in the recently diagnosed chronic obstructive pulmonary dysfunction Dr. Ryan had explained to her. Not one to hedge her bets, she had begun to recalculate somewhat the putative steps to salvation. She was not ready for a real renunciation of the sensual joys that had brought her much pleasure over the years and many enduring, if fleeting, friendships. She still corresponded by letter and phone with many of her lovers and several of them made restorative pilgrimages to visit her.

When her good friend Emil Gruening, a local ski instructor, died prematurely of cancer, Darcy went to the funeral. It was the first time since her first marriage at nineteen that she had been inside a Catholic church.

The new priest in town, Father LeFarge, had broken architectural tradition as it related to New England churches and built a very modern and austere church reminiscent more of a Mediterranean chapel than a typical New England brick and mortar Catholic church. The few French Canadian parishioners who attended were horrified at the disappearance of their familiar plaster statues of Mary and Joseph, and the gaudy, faux baroque reredos behind the altar. The new church, which made the *Journal of Ecclesiastical Architecture* in Rome, had a black marble floor, dark-stained cherry pews and, most troubling of all, a Greek altar that faced the congregation. The Stations of the Cross were modern block prints of Christ's travail to the cross instead of the gilded plaster intaglios cast en masse for most new church construction. This departure from tradition gave the faithful the most to mutter about. These mutterings naturally reached the bishop who, in this case, supported categorically his iconoclastic pastor, especially since considerable diocesan funds had already been expended to build the architectural anomaly.

The matter died down in time as the faithful got used to the modernity and some even expressed pride when photographers set up their equipment to photograph what had become a celebrated example of modern church architecture.

Being inside the church for the funeral of her good friend gave Darcy an overwhelming sense of tranquility and peace. The cool shiny black floor with its luminous veins of white and the minimalist interior imbued her with a sense of security and calm that she got neither from her small apartment nor from the après-ski bars in which she spent so much time. It recalled for her the serenity she felt when she accompanied Emil skiing the trail sweeps near dusk, when the mountain emptied of people. With the sun low and the chill of night coming on, the mountain returned to itself.

During the service, she barely heard the encomiums of Emil. They were not about the sybarite she knew and loved. Emil was selfish and self-indulgent, and he took his pleasure where he found it. His funeral was in the Catholic Church only because it was assumed by his colleagues that, coming from Austria, he must be Catholic, an assumption no doubt reinforced by the presence in town of his fellow Austrian and Catholic, the Baroness von Trapp.

Darcy caught snippets of the Latin Mass she had found so mysterious and beautiful as a child. She remembered her father pointing out to her the Kyrie Eleison, part of the Latin Mass that is in fact in Greek. Her favorite part of the Mass, however, when she learned what it meant as a little girl, was the *Agnus Dei*—"Lamb of God who takes away the sins of the world, give us peace." This saying came back to her like the smile of her young father, and she felt tears welling up and discreetly dabbed at her face. She missed the astonished looks of the few who saw her weeping and, as usual, it was not for the reasons they thought.

After the church emptied and Emil's raucous colleagues and ex-girl-friends trudged off in a light rain to the nearby cemetery for the interment, Darcy stayed on in the cool church to enjoy the comfort she felt. An altar boy shuffled about extinguishing candles, returning the cruets of wine and water to the sacristy, and repositioning the stark altar furniture for the next service.

That evening over the customary Calvados, Father LeFarge was hold-ing forth to his friend Père Renaud: "The role of the father-confessor is to lead his flock not where they wish to go, but where they must go to achieve salvation." After digesting this brief homily, Père Renaud responded, "Yes, but there are tricks of the pastoral trade that make their journey to the same place easier."

"Another evasion," replied Father LeFarge. "Christ did not have an easy road and why should we?" It was an endless dialogue between the two close friends, marinated in the French Calvados of which Père Renaud seemed to have an endless supply.

The Sunday following Emil's funeral, Father LeFarge noted Darcy's presence at the ten o'clock Mass. Afterwards, there was a hesitant knock on his door. "May I come in?" she asked, with an ambivalent smile.

"Of course, please do," Father LeFarge responded. He ushered her into his living room and motioned with his open hand to the overstuffed chair in which his friend usually sat. His other hand held a book. Darcy set-tled comfortably into the chair and pulled the hem of her skirt discreetly down over knees.

"What brings you here today? I saw you at Mass."

"I'm not sure," began Darcy, sounding, however, quite confident. The Roman collar did not distract Darcy from the fact that she was talking to a sentient male and she was undaunted.

"You probably see me as a loose woman, because I am unmarried and have many male friends and—let's say it—lovers. I am not ashamed of the life I've led. There is as much love and goodness in my life as there is in the many marriages you have performed as a man of God. I might add that my first sexual experience was with a priest. I did not, as you may assume, seduce him. I was nine. Nor am I here to seduce you," she made clear. "I am here to ask your spiritual advice."

Somewhat nonplussed, Father LeFarge set his book on the coffee table that separated them. It was a treatise by the French Catholic philosopher Teilhard de Chardin.

He looked up at Darcy and to her surprise said, "We could become good friends."

She knew instinctively that this was not a louche remark, but a sincere one.

"What are you looking for?" continued Father LeFarge.

"The peace and sense of safety that I knew from my father as a child, that I feel after lovemaking with a man who cares about me, and that I have felt in your church today."

"What were the circumstances of the abuse you mentioned?" asked Father LeFarge.

"Quite pathetic really. The priest was so terrified of what he proposed that, in retrospect even at nine, I had all the power. I did what he asked and he fled. It was all rather silly really. I was more embarrassed for him than I was angry."

"Did you tell anyone?

"You."

"Do you believe in God?" said Father LeFarge, consciously changing the uncomfortable subject.

"I think so," answered Darcy, settling comfortably into the chair and showing a bit more leg, "though there are so many different faces to your God."

"Is this perhaps about going to heaven?" asked Father LeFarge incongruously.

"No, more about being in it now," Darcy responded.

"How exactly can I help you?" continued Father LeFarge. "Do you wish to study the faith and begin taking sacraments?"

"I would appreciate you being my friend and advising me from time to time."

"Are you willing to make changes in how you live?"

"It depends. What changes?" Darcy asked. "Are you prepared to follow the life of Christ?"

"I would need to know more about him, I guess."

Father LeFarge got up and went to his bookshelf. He took down a small red leather-bound book and handed it to Darcy.

"Read this and come for coffee after Mass next Sunday."

Darcy thanked Father LeFarge with a gracious smile. She held out her hand which Father LeFarge took, but did not shake. She took the book and left the rectory. She stopped at Lackey's to pick up a Sunday paper and a pack of Chesterfields.

"Was that you at Mass today?" teased an acquaintance also picking up his Sunday paper.

"Surprised to see you there," retorted Darcy. "I didn't think your wife let you get up that early."

"Don't go getting religion on me now," her friend whispered to her.

"If I do, it won't affect our friendship," Darcy said aloud.

She took her paper, pocketed her cigarettes, and left.

That evening Father LeFarge was telling Père Renaud about the encounter. The two often shared a light Sunday supper of cold pickerel pâté, fresh bread, small pickles, and a thick, homemade vegetable soup that Mrs. Carignan left off every Sunday as part of her devotions. Père Renaud was vastly fond of her pâté, calling it the "miracle of the loaves and fishes." He brought his trusty Calvados to round off both the meal and the conversation.

"People will talk, you know," warned Père Renaud. "You are surely aware of her reputation."

"Did Christ consult the social register when he befriended Mary Magdalene?" said Father LeFarge.

"I expect not," sighed Père Renaud, who had largely given up hope of winning arguments with his friend. "Nevertheless, they will talk."

"Let them," retorted Father LeFarge.

Darcy made regular appearances at late Mass on Sunday and sat confidently near the front of the church despite a tradition that those most confident of their salvation sat in front while sinners and penitents sat in the back near the holy water font. She dressed demurely and greeted acquaintances confidently, those with and without the benefit of her intimacies. Occasionally, a pillbox hat-topped matron would swivel her head like a barn owl away from Darcy's greeting to her and her husband, while the husband just stared at his shoes.

The Sunday afternoon sessions between Father LeFarge and Darcy continued for several months. She explained to her new friend that her enthusiasm for living had taught her more than what she had learned vicariously in books and she confessed to not having finished *The Imitation of Christ* that Father LeFarge had lent her.

Over time, religion figured less and less in their long chats. Father LeFarge's usual lapsarian pronouncements and abrupt judgments gradually gave way to a sincere interest in the ebb and flow of the sensual life she had led and the extraordinary intimacy she felt for her many friends and acquaintances.

Darcy's pulmonary affliction took an abrupt turn for the worse. She began toting behind her a green steel oxygen tank on a cart connected to her nostrils by clear plastic tubing. Oxygen deprivation took a toll on her dark, wind-burned olive skin. She seemed to Father LeFarge to be aging week to week as the two met and talked now about their own lives and occasionally about religion and the spirit.

Père Renaud came earlier and earlier each Sunday evening until by chance, or perhaps by choice, he had the opportunity to meet Darcy. His parish was in nearby Hyde Park and only rarely was he able to attend his friend's Masses, so he knew only what he had heard from his friend or villagers about Darcy.

Given her reputation, he was surprised at how old she looked, but his kind demeanor betrayed nothing. He greeted her warmly, saying, "My friend's friend is my friend as well."

Darcy stayed on and shared their traditional Sunday meal and left the rectory around 8:30.

Talk had, of course, developed in Stowe about the friendship between Father LeFarge and Darcy. The vulgar assumption was that it was more than pastoral. Word reached the bishop, who knew his charge well enough to know that the chances of Father LeFarge becoming inappropriately involved were slightly less than the pope's doing so. The bishop defended Father LeFarge and expressed confidence in his good judgment and his good intentions, knowing full well there were few parishes left to which he could be assigned. The slough of gossip persisted, however.

Father LeFarge was captivated by Darcy's intimacy with life itself, her proximity to human frailty and emotional sustenance. He had spent the better part of his childhood and adult life ablaze in the world of ideas, ethics, and aesthetics— the mathematics of existence—all described and measured in texts, all vicariously rendered but never lived.

In their time together, he was in fact becoming Darcy's student. Her warm Dionysian parables of life's rushing rills, placid tarns, and hopeless quagmires captured his imagination. Unlike his rigorous and moral Sunday homilies, her stories passed no judgments; their purpose was the telling and the resultant joy or sadness. He would interrupt occasionally, but only to ask for clarification or to pose a question.

Darcy's health declined fast. The rapid progress of her disease surprised both her and her doctor, leaving her less and less able to converse. The words that so enthralled Father LeFarge exhausted her, but she appreciated the pleasure he took in them. He would wait patiently through her increasingly frequent pauses as she gathered enough breath to continue.

As a young girl, Darcy had been baptized and had her First Communion with her father at her side, and had been confirmed in the church as a "soldier of Christ." Father LeFarge assured his new friend that he would be with her until the end.

As Darcy lay drowning in her own fluids, a nun in a black and white habit administered an anodyne dose of morphine that relieved her fear and considerable pain. Father LeFarge heard her last whispered opiate confession, which was little more than a brief expression of gratitude for his friendship. He gave his friend her last communion.

Preparing for the last sacrament, Father LeFarge opened the small black leather pouch with the cruciform embossing that he carried when attending the dying. He removed the two vials of oil from the leather rings that held them in place, and the small black leather book containing the ritual words of the last sacrament. Touching his index finger to the first small vial, he inverted it and made the sign of the cross on Darcy's forehead near her thin hair, now almost entirely white. He intoned the Latin words that were so much like mysterious music to her as a little girl. She died early that evening with her friend at her side reciting his breviary and holding her hand.

He left the hospital hurriedly after thanking the nuns for their care and went straight home. Père Renaud was waiting for him in the living room and had already poured himself a Calvados.

"I am sorry," he offered, putting his arm on his friend's shoulder. "She was a good friend."

Father LeFarge broke down, collapsing in his rumpled cassock into his

accustomed chair, saying only, "I have known so little of life."

His friend tendered him a small glass of Calvados, which Father LeFarge took gratefully. There was a long silence in the room while the two friends sat in quiet introspection.

The funeral service was the following Saturday and Père Renaud offered to assist his friend in the funeral Mass. A very small crowd of mostly men and a few women trickled in just before eleven, clustering in the pews nearest the door.

Father LeFarge conducted the ritual Mass for the Dead in his black chasuble and stole while Père Renaud assisted with a white surplice over his black cassock. When the moment for the eulogy arrived, Father LeFarge approached the lectern unsteadily, coughed softly and addressed the small assembly, who looked up cautiously, wondering what the stern Father LeFarge would concoct to say about their lusty friend.

He started to read the parable of Jesus meeting the woman at the well but his voice trailed off quickly into silence. Père Renaud looked up nervously to see what had overtaken his friend. He was close enough to see the tears flowing down his cheeks. The assembly waited while he fumbled for a handkerchief several vestments down and made a pretense of blowing his nose. He cleared his throat and looked up at those clustered in the rear of the nave.

"Darcy was a friend to all of us here," he started cautiously. "The ways of her friendship differed for some of us," he continued ambiguously, "but she was our friend," he persisted, seeming to address someone other than those assembled, perhaps only himself.

He turned swiftly around and resumed the Mass, ending shortly with the ritual "Ite, missa est." One or two people familiar with the Catholic service responded under their breath, "Deo gratias."

The church emptied and the two clerics retired to the rectory for a toast to Father LeFarge's departed friend.

Father LeFarge finished out his pastoral career in Stowe, whose residents speculated until well after his death about his close friendship with Darcy.

Edgar's Mother's Chimney

⌣⌒⌒⌒

THE FLATS ROAD, lined in parts with regal old sugar maples, meanders east, turning almost immediately to dirt after diverging from its sibling, the Centerville Road. In fall, the road is a joy to travel, rivaling the town's few paved roads for comfort, whereas in the spring, surface melt and rising groundwater combine to brew a rich morass of mud into which vehicles routinely settle only to be hauled out with a neighbor's tractor or occasionally with Egnor's grunting dozer. Various dirt tracks head off into the woods, leading to abandoned farms, renegade trails to the top of Sanders Mountain, teenage trysting spots, sugaring operations, or active logging sites.

Few houses line the road, but of those that do, the Levarne Farm is the grande dame. Many of the large wood-frame houses in and around the town were built by Si Jewett and his boys in the latter half of the nineteenth century. Si offered few design options, so most of the homes are the same, varying only in scale and color. The main entrance is in the center, and either four or eight symmetrical windows flank it depending on the buyer's financial standing and family size.

Charlie, the Levarne patriarch, was a respected mason in town. He could raise a fireplace and chimney in a matter of weeks, and, unlike other masons, would be on site daily as long as every sixth or seventh load of bricks hauled up to his current elevation by his assistant Whitey contained a frosty Old Fitzgerald from the mortar-spattered blue cooler.

Like a woman of a certain age, the Levarne homestead was settling a bit into its foundation. The sills, flexible now with dry rot, allowed the house to conform to the seasonal movements of the landscape on which it sat rather than the builder's level that had fixed their position more than a century earlier. This gravitational compliance and seasonal frost heaving caused the roof line, on occasion, to trace the rolling horizon in the distance with uncanny precision.

The house had been recently painted, but the painter had wasted no time scraping or masking the windows. The job looked as though it had been done in hours rather than days, leaving the elderly lady resplendent in white, but flocked all over with curling paint and a psoriasis of discoloring dry rot beneath the new coat. The edges of the window panes were slathered in a translucent white. The painted-over bright blue trim was only slightly less blue. The whole affair reminded one of an ancient aunt in her dotage whose makeup applications became less accurate as her acuity faded until she looked more like a febrile clown than the family matron.

A wooden-headed carpenter's maul hung from baling twine by the front door. This was used in the summer to shut it, as the jamb no longer conformed to the door and a blow was required to get a tight fit on leaving or entering, especially in wet weather. As in most Vermont homes, the front doors were hammered shut in the winter and sealed with canvas framed in lath. Everyone entered and exited through the summer kitchen ell and woodshed in the back. The house was skirted with square bales of mulch hay to provide additional insulation. It seemed like work to remove them in the summer, so they were left year-round to abate the dry rot consuming the sills.

Vermont at this time was enduring an influx of *Whole Earth Catalog* missionaries and hippies. Sturdy tribes of Birkenstocked Amazons lived in tepees during the summer, wannabe healers and shamans fresh from Darien offered chakra point alignments to local farmers. Pasty-faced Rastas who worked earnestly on their gardens of pot and vegetables picked self-consciously at their gnarled dreads.

One newcomer, Luke Densmore, was determined to find a worthy trade among the natives and, to that end, apprenticed himself immediately to Charlie. Much to the astonishment of Charlie and Whitey, Luke announced his mastery of the trade the first morning and celebrated by smoking a pungent hand-rolled cigarette. Luke thanked Charlie and left that afternoon to begin his career in earnest.

Shaking his head, Charlie climbed back up his ladder with a beer and trowel in his back pocket, his hod in his left hand, calling for a load of bricks and mortar from Whitey. They chatted on and off through the afternoon about the speed with which Luke had mastered the trade.

Charlie was known to welcome apprentices foisted on him by a neighboring parent or former customer at their wits' end with their son's lack of enterprise. Some of these apprentices went on to become heavy drinkers or accomplished stonemasons, often both. Charlie understood the risk of creating a large supply of masons, but his reputation for showing up clearly differentiated him from the competition.

The one exception, however, occurred when Edgar Stanton bought a slumping farmhouse and fourteen acres of land from Ned Stewart. The house had a fitting for a woodstove but no fireplace and no furnace, so Edgar sought the services of a stonemason.

Though Edgar was new in town, he considered himself a veteran Vermonter, having gone to Camp Abenaki for two summers when he was twelve and thirteen. He knew the wily ways of countryfolk and would have no wool pulled over his eyes. Egnor was his first bidder for a new driveway and misread the line traced on the plat map so the driveway meandered past the house up to a marshy spot farther up the hill. Edgar calmed down when Egnor's wife relented and reduced the cost of the excess roadwork.

In his rural zeal, Edgar informed his neighbors that, like them, he would be heating with wood. With that purpose in mind he chose a large and burly hardwood on his property, fired up his new bijou chainsaw, reduced it to a pile of firewood so neat as to make it evident to all passersby that he was a newcomer. Few Vermonters had the spare time to align their logs so that none protruded from the pile.

Edgar's nearest neighbor, Duke Kitonis, was a curious type. Duke and his wife, Jean, watched warily from their hilltop home as Edgar negotiated with natives about the restoration of his farmhouse. Duke occasionally helped Edgar with imponderables like skunk removal, culvert location and differentiating between sugar maples, swamp maples, and poplars, all of which Edgar tapped energetically in March.

Duke heard the crash as the ancient hardwood dropped 180 degrees from where the chainsaw directions told Edgar the tree should have fallen. Edgar immediately set to limbing, bucking up and splitting the wood, and then spent the next few days piling it in a perfectly aligned pile directly under the drip line of his new home's roof.

That Saturday morning when Duke meandered by in his unmufflered pickup on the way to the dump, he shouted to Edgar, "Oil's a lot cheaper," as Edgar pointed at the pile of green, wet wood with pride.

"How's that?" retorted Edgar in his New Jersey accent.

Duke slowed to a crawl. "Oil's 'bout 22 cents a gallon and that tree's worth about two thousand on the stump," answered Duke.

"You're trying to put one over on me again," smiled Edgar, somewhat annoyed that his new woodpile was so little appreciated.

"Morris and Doc's wood'd be a lot cheaper," answered Duke.

"Wood's wood," said Edgar, annoyed.

"Yah," said Duke, "But that's black walnut. 'Em logs'd be worth 'bout twenny bucks each if 'n you could git 'em back on the stump where they came from. I meant ta tell ya about that tree. Folks had their eye on that fer decades. I'se scared when I hear'd the crash that you might a dropped it."

"What do I do now?" asked Edgar.

"Burn it if it ever dries out. You can't make shotgun stocks, pianers, and gitars out of a twenty-inch chunk," he said, letting in his clutch.

Edgar knew that his country house would be incomplete without a fireplace. The cracked flue tile and cinderblock chimney that had only a thimble connection for a woodstove when he bought the place would never work for a fireplace so, as in everything Edgar needed done, he posted a bid request in the Hyde Park General Store for a fireplace and new chimney.

Locals responded poorly to his down-country "biddin' process." In fact they did not respond at all except to write suggestive or catchy remarks on the posted request. Locals responded only to bids posted by the selectmen for civic work like roadside mowing, snow removal, cemetery mowing, culvert replacement, and roadkill pickup.

But Luke Densmore, Charlie's sometime apprentice, bid on Edgar's masonry job. Luke had no frame of reference or experience for costing the job so he simply bid his next three months' rent and the cost of a new guitar amp. Edgar had no frame of reference either, so he accepted the bid and Luke showed up the next day with a transistor radio. This should have been a bad sign to Edgar, but they settled on the price and Luke started work that day.

Luke had spent the last of the "new start" stipend his father had given him at Graves' Hardware in Morrisville on a bewildering array of tools and supplies listed in Audel's *Book of Stonemasonry* that he pilfered from the Hyde Park Library and was using as a text. He asked Edgar where he thought the fireplace should go. Edgar indicated the north end of the living room, centered in the middle.

Luke smoked what looked like a flattened cigarette, took some cursory but craftsman-like measurements, fired up Edgar's new yellow McCullough chainsaw and drove a plunge cut into the north wall. The saw chewed through the stud wall like lightning, hurling new pink fiberglass insulation about the lawn. The wavy line progressed down the side of the exterior wall. Suddenly, Luke let out a howl, let go of the saw, and fell back onto the ground. The saw hanging from the wall dropped back to idle, hanging there like a new appliance wired directly to the house's electrical system.

Luke's release of the chainsaw interrupted the house current's path through him into the moist ground, no longer posing any threat of igniting the gas in the chainsaw and causing an explosion, unless of course someone touched it again. Edgar had gone to town, so Luke was left alone to try and decipher the unlabelled breaker box. This challenge called for another of his pungent cigarettes, inspiring him to turn off all the circuit breakers. This proved a success allowing him to finish the more or less rectangular cut through the wall.

Soon he had exposed a fireplace-size hole into the living room. Although the edges were a bit ragged with hanging bits of Romex cable, tufts of pink insulation and shiny foil, the hole, he determined, should work fine. He noticed with some concern that the chainsaw teeth had caught in the new wall-to-wall carpet pile and made a rather nasty run the length of the living room shag.

Luke then laid some bricks out on the lawn in a rectangle approximating the outer measurement of a chimney hearth. No matter how he tried, though, he could not get the bricks to sit level on the lawn. He determined that the ground would somehow have to be leveled first, which he proceeded to do with his new shovel. He then mortared and laid up three initial courses of brick on the lawn. On the sixth course he noticed that he was a bit farther from the house than he thought and that the bricks were no longer level, as one side of the new chimney seemed to be listing a bit away from the house.

Another flat cigarette and the first day's work was done so he left for home to solve today's small problems in the clearer light of tomorrow.

Edgar returned to see the carnage and the meandering courses of brick layed directly on the lawn and immediately resumed his ugly flatlander demeanor. As there was no phone in Luke's yurt, Edgar waited for him to show up the next day, rehearsing in his mind the invective he would use to exact retribution and dismiss him in a volley of abuse.

That evening after a few more of his cigarettes, Luke decided to become a reggae bass player instead of a mason and offered his new cement mixer in trade for a used Fender bass guitar.

Edgar lay in wait for Luke for two days and then began asking around town for him, but no one knew where he lived, nor had they seen him since he had taken up his new avocation.

Cold weather was setting in and Edgar's small kerosene heater made little headway against the fourby five-foot hole in his living room wall though it was now covered with canvas and duct tape.

He phoned Charlie, who was finishing a job for a "rich person." Charlie said he would be done in another week and would come over to "eyeball" Edgar's job.

True to his word, the following week, the job was scoped and a price of $3,800 was agreed upon—$3,200 more than Luke's quote for the same work. There would be some additional work to repair the hole. This was subcontracted to Whitey's father, a retired carpenter, and was over and above Charlie's bid. Some rewiring also would be needed, but Whitey's father was a jack-of-all-trades and agreed to splice the ragged wires back together with some wire nuts.

Edgar vowed to recover the additional costs from Luke, who now lived with five other Rastafarian musicians in a tiny apartment in Glover where they practiced the native music and religion of Jamaica while dabbling in hydroponic growing techniques.

Work began in earnest on Thursday and the new chimney began to rise against new cedar clapboards. Charlie's work and word were true. He showed up day after day and the work progressed except for Saturday afternoons when Charlie visited his brother down at the VA Hospital in White River and Sunday, a day of rest to be enjoyed with Thelma fishing for bullpout in the Lamoille River.

Just before the first light frost, Charlie laid the capstone on the chimney to keep rain out of the flue, repointed a few mortar joints that looked ragged and climbed down the mortar-covered ladder to assess his work with Whitey. With the stubby pencil in his hatband, he wrote on a single piece of white note paper, "due and owing to Charles Levarne, stone mason the sum of $3,800." This he handed to Edgar who promptly wrote and handed over a check for $2,500. "I'll get the rest to you next week when I get to the bank," said Edgar.

When flustered, Charlie stammered. "Th th th th... at wasn't the deal," stuttered Charlie.

"Don't worry. You'll get your money," said Edgar, annoyed at the slight against his creditworthiness.

Thelma was Charlie's business manager. She had little to do as she simply denied credit out of hand and had a rigorous system of payments devised to avoid the situation in which Charlie now found himself—one third down to start, one third half way, and one third before the capstone. Charlie was not fond of confrontation and so adhered to his wife's arrangements or referred those seeking credit directly to her. Discussions with Thelma about credit were brief.

Thelma began her collection proceedings against Edgar immediately, starting on the four-party line when it was open, and then putting threatening notes in Edgar's mailbox. This was technically a federal offense, but the prohibition, like building codes and other "gov'ment stuff" was often ignored.

Edgar generated a proliferation of excuses, never saying he wouldn't pay, but postponing the date indefinitely. This was new to Thelma whose rare bad credit encounters often produced "can' git blood outta a stone."

The Stanton deficit lingered on the Levarne books through winter and on into spring when out of the blue Edgar called and asked pointedly to talk to Charlie when Thelma answered. Thelma handed the phone to Charlie with her hand over the receiver, admonishing him to collect the money. She paced as Charlie uttered some noncommittal grunts. Her face lit up, however, when he said, "Bring Thelma the check and then we'll talk."

The next day when Charlie came home buzzed a bit more than usual from "wetting his whistle," and spackled with more than the usual daubs of mortar, a smiling Thelma greeted him waving Edgar's check. Charlie smiled and crawled out of his coveralls and into the jeans that hung by the woodpile.

He laid out for Thelma the deal he struck with Edgar. Edgar's elderly mother was moving up to spend her waning years near her son. Her only request was a warm fireplace to sit by in the cold winter months. This city-folk reverie amused Charlie and Thelma immensely. Vermonters knew full well that a fireplace could suck the heat out of a house faster than peeling back the roof. The lion's share of Charlie's work was building or repairing flues for heating stoves or old Sam Daniels furnaces in the cellar.

Edgar had bought and was restoring the place next door, a nondescript raised ranch called a "Wonder Home." These heavily advertised box affairs from the '50s were delivered on two flatbeds and set up in a couple of days by an experienced crew. Edgar's sat next to the road in a clearing just wide enough for a driveway and an unattached and severely listing one-car garage.

The front door facing the road was positioned between a picture window and a small bathroom window. The single-story house was painted light green. Very little chimney elevation would be required to clear the roofline and induce the draw necessary to suck heat, smoke, and flue gasses out, putting a severe strain on the undersized gas furnace in the crawl space underneath.

Charlie and Whitey finished the work in less than a week. Thelma posted herself at the site periodically, demanding checks from Edgar as the flue rose skyward. She had secured all but the final check for $800 and Charlie was about to set in the decorative chimney pot Edgar had bought from a mail order catalog clearance sale. Charlie warned Edgar that it would retard the draft, but Edgar, infatuated with the gnome shape, insisted.

Thelma's voice was livid in Charlie's head as he climbed down the ladder. He already sensed a stammer developing in his windpipe as he contemplated asking Edgar for the final payment before mounting the chimney pot. The confrontation went like this.

"I don't pay for unfinished work."

"And I d-d-d-d-d... on't finish work for people who don't pay."

Charlie let the chimney pot fall to the ground, climbed down, loaded his truck with his tools and left—alone, as Whitey, knowing the end of a job could be managed by one, had taken the opportunity to go to Rutland with his girlfriend.

When he got home, Thelma was perched in her lawn chair drawing fiercely on a Chesterfield. She saw his sheepish look and said, "Where's the check?"

"He'll pay."

"Goddamit."

"I know."

They both went inside and no more was said that night. Thelma's collection efforts began again, to no avail. She embarked on a campaign to impugn Edgar's credit throughout town. This worked well. Edgar was now required by any and all sellers of goods or craftsmen to tender cash in advance for goods and services. His checks were greeted like used toilet paper. Thanks to Thelma's woebegone presentation of the facts, his glib, flatlander tongue and empty promises now fell on deaf ears.

All this, however, did not help Thelma and Charlie collect the final payment; it may in fact have steeled Edgar's resolve to avoid payment. Charlie took this and other of life's injustices with aplomb and a six pack of Old Fitz. Thelma, though, was a mistress of grudge, composting slights and debts into a rich ferment of revenge.

In August, the ranch near Edgar's farmhouse was ready to receive its elderly occupant, who had never ventured outside New Jersey except to visit the Liberty Bell in nearby Philadelphia as a young girl on a school trip. Even her honeymoon with Edgar's father took her no farther than a fancy hotel and the boardwalk in Atlantic City.

Her modest widow's possessions preceded her into the refurbished home, distributed clumsily about the house by her dutiful son. She stayed in the guest room in Edgar's house until he finished readying her new abode. The day for her move came. Edgar got up early, went over and turned up the heat, as she abhorred the cold and was happiest at an ambient temperature above 85 degrees. Edgar had long since given up trying to burn his infamous black walnut as it remained perpetually moist under the drip line of his roof. Swallowing his pride, he paid Morris and Doc fourteen dollars a cord cash for dry, split wood for his own fireplace. As a direct result of Thelma's offensive, Doc knew to "see the color of his money" before any delivery was made. Edgar brought over some dry logs for his mother's new fireplace.

He crumpled up some yellowed sheets from the *News and Citizen*, topped them off with some kindling he bought at the general store to the great joy of the store's owner, who had never sold a single bundle of kindling to a local. Three logs, a match, and soon he had a nice crackling fire burning on the still-white firebrick hearth.

He then went into the bedroom to make up his mother's single bed with the childhood quilt she had brought with her. To his great pleasure, the rich smell of burning wood soon pervaded the house.

To his surprise, however, the pleasant scent soon thickened into the acrid smell of smoke. As he tried to tuck the small child's quilt in under the mattress, his eyes began to tear up so he could barely see. Sensing trouble he rushed into the living room where he was met with a thick wall of blue smoke behind which he could see the flames licking up and outward into the living room instead of up the flue.

He rushed into the kitchen, filled a mop bucket with water, the thick smoke following in his wake. He rushed blind into the smoke-filled living room, hurling the bucket of water towards the fireplace. He heard a loud hiss indicating he'd hit his mark, and then rushed around opening windows. After twenty minutes of waving a wet Rya rug in the front door, the smoke gradually dispersed, leaving only the sting in his nostrils, a faint smell in the house, and an indoor temperature of 42, less than half the required target.

Furious, he dialed the Levarne homestead. Thelma answered, surprised to hear Edgar, and even more surprised to hear him casting aspersions on Charlie's work.

She listened impassively as Edgar railed on about the flue not drawing correctly and lawyers and smoke damage and health consequences and other threats. After a bit she replaced the receiver.

Thelma never interrupted Charlie on the job. When he arrived home at 5:30, Thelma was in her spindly lawn chair drawing on a cigarette instead of fussing over dinner. He knew something was up.

"Edgar called today carrying on about how the fireplace you built him don't draw good," Thelma said calmly.

"Why should it? It ain't paid for yet," answered Charlie, heading to the fridge in the woodshed and withdrawing an Old Fitz. Thelma nodded and resumed smoking her Chesterfield King.

After dinner the phone rang. Charlie never answered the phone unless Thelma was not at home, preferring to let her deal with the exigencies of the outside world. "It's for you," said Thelma calmly. "It's him."

"Yup," said Charlie, holding the receiver at a distance.

"But you ain't paid for it. Eight hundred dollars cash in hand and I will see about fixing it for your mother."

"Then tomorrow will have to do. I ain't takin' your check. Call me when you have the cash and I will see what went wrong. Might be sumpin' stuck in 'ere, like a grouse. Just 'cause you see light up there, don't mean the smoke shelf ain't blocked. Call when you have the cash."

Charlie hung up and took a deep sip of his beer. Thelma, satisfied with Charlie's end of the dialogue, resumed smoking.

About twenty minutes later, Edgar's truck careened into Charlie's driveway. Edgar emerged leaving the door ajar and stuck a wad of bills out to Charlie.

"Thought you had to go to the bank tomorrow," observed Charlie calmly.

"I found some cash in the house. You don't trust me?" Edgar said looking hurt.

Charlie nodded his head horizontally so as not to disturb his ciphering as he counted the bills and then handed them to Thelma for a recount.

When Thelma nodded to Charlie that the money was all there, Charlie grabbed a "roadie" and headed up the Flats Road towards Edgar's place. Edgar followed in his truck.

Charlie pulled into the short driveway leaving no room for Edgar who parked on the road. He grabbed a broken brick out of the back of his truck, set his short ladder up against the single-story chimney and climbed up to the top. He then dislodged the chimney pot from its mortar setting, set it next to him on the roof and peered down into the flue. He took the brick in his left hand and dropped it into the void. There was a loud shattering sound as if he had broken a window. He replaced the chimney pot, wedging it down into the set mortar, climbed down the ladder and left with Edgar yelling at him all the while about "making good on his word."

Worried that Charlie had somehow broken something else, he went in to examine the fireplace. There was broken window glass all over the hearth. Edgar scratched his head and peered up the flue, but could see nothing. Grabbing the flashlight in his glove compartment and a broom and dustpan in the kitchen, he swept up the glass and then lay down on the hearth to try and understand where the glass came from. About half way up the flue, there was a rim of broken glass around the very edge of the flue where Charlie had mortared a large pane of glass directly into the flue.

Edgar lay there as the whole ploy became clear. After some deliberation, he rebuilt the fire and lit it, all the while shaking his head. The fire drew immediately and soon the lingering smell of smoke was gone from the house.

Thelma, who did not generally encourage Charlie's taste for Old Fitz, had one waiting for him when his truck pulled into the dirt driveway next to their homestead.

Perched in their bent aluminum lawn chairs with some of the blue and white nylon webbing strips hanging loose underneath, Charlie and Thelma sat enjoying the view of the Lamoille valley and the occasional car or truck that meandered up the road and tooted a greeting.

Anne's Biddies

IT'S THE SECOND Sunday of Advent and Anne Stone braces for Christmas. Anne has been a nurse at Copley Hospital for 48 of her 69 years. As a young woman, she trained at the Jeanne Mance School of Nursing in Burlington and then served next door as a candy-striper at the Bishop DeGoesbriand Hospital in the late '50s when the twin towns of Winooski and Burlington shared three hospitals. She returned home in 1959 and began nursing at Copley Hospital for eighty-five cents an hour when it was still a four-story wood firetrap enmeshed in countless fire escapes.

Most of the time, Anne loves her work. She has opinions about many of the "advances" in health care, but she keeps them to herself. Anne's life as a nurse is made harder because she knows many of her patients and their life stories. She has been nursing in Morrisville for half a century and can often predict an inhabitant's admission to the week, if not the day. Anne knows sickness is a continuum that eventually ends up in an admission. The crisis that leads to hospitalization can be acute, like a farm accident or a stroke; or chronic, like emphysema, diabetes, or anemia but she knows from experience that there are few real accidents in life and that most illness has a long backstory—if you know the person and their story, you can usually predict their arrival at the hospital door.

Weather, daylight, and economics all play parts in the ebb and flow of hospital admissions. Anne chuckles to herself as she dutifully fills out the many data surveys and reports that are a routine part of her life as a charge nurse. The questions so often miss the larger points that affect admissions, the intangibles in people's lives that have nothing to do with vital signs, quality metrics, patient surveys, and the like. Anne can predict the ebb and flow often by the time of year and the surge of gossip that may engulf someone in the community.

"Did you hear? Peavine's back on the sauce."
"That bunch on Tiny's neck's gettin' bigger."
Anne can tell you within a week or two when he will show up at the front desk. Peavine reels in, always during the day, and collapses on the floor. He is then rushed to emergency where he is diagnosed with acute alcoholism, "weaned and cleaned," rehydrated, put to bed for a night, and then discharged to his 93-year old mother who again commits him to a life of sobriety. Whereupon they disappear in a taxi together with Peavine staring at his shoes and his mother staring straight ahead.

There is Glenna Farr, a distant cousin. For 14 years, Glenna has had "the sugar." She has managed it, more or less, with diet and insulin. Exercise was never an option. Glenna grew up on a farm where one's cunning was applied to find easier ways to accomplish hard work, not harder ways or ways to extend the work. Exercise was and remained counterintuitive, but then again so did eating foods like green vegetables, whole wheat toast without butter, and sugarless cereals with skim milk.

For years, Glenna has taken her annual turn hosting the ladies of the "Uplift Club" for their monthly meeting. Although the meeting has a set agenda in which members share ways to enhance their economic position in the community by learning crafts and skills such as crocheting, raising hens and selling eggs, custom baking, quilting, or crafting such things as tongue depressor lamp shades or milk-filter doll gowns, a meeting's true success was adjudged by the quality and nature of the goodies served during the "fellowship hour" that followed. These became the principal topic of conversation and certainly held sway in later gossip about how the meeting went.

When her turn came, Glenna would carefully plan what to serve, poring through cookbooks in the Morrisville Library to uncover novel delicacies that would enthrall her friends, dominate conversation, and leave an enduring and positive impression on her guests. Unfortunately, every recipe involved large quantities of sugar, flour, butter, and other rich ingredients that were denied her. As she combined the forbidden ingredients, slid them into the oven, and then inhaled the beguiling aroma, she firmly resolved to abstain for the sake of her health.

The stress of preparing for the meeting, the scrutiny by other ladies of her shabby furniture and lackluster china, the question of how her efforts would be judged, all overwhelmed her prior commitment to abstinence and, like her fellow members, she tucked into the lemon meringues that had held their teardrop shapes so well and the exotic macaroons, which proved to be a big hit.

The next day, Glenna would be admitted to the emergency room in a diabetic relapse. Anne would have advised ER staff of her impending admission and procedures would be followed such that Glenna could leave the following day after a night of close monitoring of her blood sugar.

Christmas was the most difficult time of year at the hospital. It seemed to staff as if half the town's personal stories came to some sort of head and the stoicism of small town life somehow unraveled. The arrival of bitter cold days with little or no sunlight, forced holiday largesse that only those with a decent job could afford, and the often painful intimacy of jovial relatives descending on them all pushed some folks over their limits. Anne saw it coming and she would recall her father's often repeated "red in the morning, sailor, take warning" weather forecast.

There would be a bloom of dormant alcoholics who usually managed to keep their lives under some degree of control, but in the waning light of December would toss caution to the wind and imbibe until either a vehicle, a relative, or their pastor intervened and they would end up in the hospital, as the nearest jail was 22 miles away in Waterbury.

The chronically ill who had to maintain some form of dietary, pharmaceutical, or bed-rest regimen would suddenly throw over the traces and do precisely as they pleased.

Those townspeople and farmers who had never managed to maintain their place in the town's fragile economy might have accidents. A broken leg or arm, a sprain or dislocation was a swift ticket to a bed and gentle care, surcease for a few days from the hardscrabble monotony of trying to survive.

Anne's favorites, however, were her "biddies," elderly, frail women, many of whom lived alone or in back rooms where their families tried to care for them— grandmothers, widowed aunts or mothers patiently counting out their days. Few men in town seemed to endure deep into old age. Especially poignant for Anne was the number of "children" in their seventies living on assistance and caring for ailing mothers or aunts in their nineties. Anne saw the exhaustion in the aged, craggy faces of these children and knew the harsh toll it took on them to be caring for an even older mother, at an age when they themselves might expect to be cared for.

Her biddies begin arriving after Thanksgiving, some slumped in wheelchairs, others shuffling slowly in bed slippers, most escorted by embarrassed relatives. Reasons for their admissions were varied, some real, some fabricated. It was the only time of year when Anne played her respected hand with the hospital administration.

In an unspoken détente, Anne would be given almost total control over available beds during Christmas. Her prescient knowledge of admissions trends enabled her to parse out beds to her biddies while ensuring adequate capacity for the few real crises like ski and car accidents, premature births, and coronaries.

Among all the fragile holiday visitors, Anne's favorite is Elise Desrochers, who every year arrives just a day or two before Christmas and usually leaves on Christmas afternoon. She shuffles in slowly on the arm of her daughter who worked for 34 years at Gillen's Department Store as a clerk in the fabric department before it closed down. Over the eight years she has been coming, Mme. Desrochers' complaints have ranged from "hip pains" to "female troubles." She is 96 and, although great attention is paid to her symptoms, they are nondescript enough to require only "observation and a few days of bed rest." Installed in her hospital bed with her lace nightcap framing an angelic smile, she looks to Anne wraithlike, weightless. She hardly makes a bump under the fresh-pressed hospital sheets.

Ginnie Bettis always arrives in a wheelchair with her red holiday nightie and a stained cotton coat. She is pushed by her 74-year-old son Arthur who has cared for her since he was 34 when she became disabled with a mild form of muscular dystrophy. Ginnie always arrives triumphantly, usually on the twenty-first, and is greeted warmly by the nursing staff. This year she brings peanut butter chocolate balls for the staff. These were given to her by her friend Molly Mudgett, but Ginnie is allergic to peanuts and never has the heart to tell Molly, as it is all Molly knows how to make.

Yvette Courchaine is an altogether different quantity, and generally means trouble. A large, imperious woman of French and Indian descent, she is usually wheeled in in her rolling throne by a hard-drinking neighbor, Ti-Jean Ferland. TiJean is only a few years younger and inhabits a badly tilted trailer next to Yvette's. A few years back when asked by the Overseer of the Poor if he wanted his rented trailer leveled, he answered only that "he purfurs it how it be," and "wants for exercise to keep from porkin' up like Yvette là-bas." Ti-Jean looks after Yvette when it doesn't interfere with his drinking and brings her into the hospital each year for her "tune-up."

There are four or five others who usually arrive about the same time. Each year one or two do not show up and others arrive to take their place, but Anne knows why and who beforehand. No one counts the days or initiates "discharge planning," since the people who bring them in will show up after Christmas to fetch them home.

Anne knows these women and their lives well. She knows it is her privilege to make room for them in December at Copley.

At Christmas, women who have lived this long should sleep in warm beds with clean sheets, have young attendants ask if they are comfortable, serve them hot meals, or help them to the bathroom if need be. It is a time for ladies who have reached this age to peruse a *Ladies' Home Journal* or just lie back and revel in the smell of freshly laundered sheets and daydream of what might have been.

CPSIA information can be obtained at www.ICGtesting.com
Printed in the USA
LVOW06s1551301115

464703LV00007B/839/P